Not Because It's Easy

Not Because It's Easy

A Novel By
George C. Schellenger

Copyright 2013 by George C. Schellenger

All rights reserved. No part of this book may be reproduced, stored, or transmitted by any means—whether auditory, graphic, mechanical, or electronic—without written permission of both publisher and author, except in the case of brief excerpts used in critical articles and reviews. Unauthorized reproduction of any part of this work is illegal and is punishable by law.

Paperback: 978-1-300-78514-9
Hardcover: 978-0-557-51055-9

First Trade Edition

To my Dad for teaching me how to get the job done.

To my Mom for pushing me to always take the spiritual approach.

You each provided me a solid foundation for a lifetime of adventure.

In memory of Neil Armstrong, first man on the Moon, and to all the others who followed and will follow.

Introduction

I can tell you of rocket ships, both large and small. Of night launches to space and of engine tests in the middle of office complexes, of flying machines without wings in the desert. I can also personally share what it's like to fly without wings, and I can relate to being submerged beneath crystal-clear waters at night completely surrounded by sharks.

I could share stories of my life, and you probably wouldn't believe me. And that's fine. I understand. So I will share with you the following, the stories of friends and enemies I may or may not have known for the past thirty years. It will be up to you to separate fact from fiction.

The one thing you must realize, above all else: any goal is possible if you can properly plan it, even going to the Moon. You must realize this.

But I'm already getting ahead of myself, as I'm known to do. So let's simply start at the very beginning…

If someone were to ask you, "What really matters?" What would you say? Your family? Your job? Your life? What compelling force makes you get up in the morning? Love, ambition, instinct?

Before you answer, consider the Moon. Its glow illuminates stories of romance and heartache. It tugs on Earth with an ambitious force and instinctively drives life.

The Moon is forever our evolutionary soul mate.

We look outside ourselves to see it – look inside to feel it. We hear the Moon as it brings on a rising tide but instinctively know its eternal silence in space.

Consider the Moon.

One day in December 1972, the Moon was not as desolate or silent as usual. A man was walking on its surface.

That man was Astronaut Gene Cernan. He'd lived on the Moon for a total of three days. Now, his mission to the lunar surface was over. So was America's Project Apollo. It was time for Commander Cernan to enter the Lunar Module so he could begin the journey home to his friends and family, to the life he knew. As he prepared to climb on board the LEM Challenger, the spacecraft that had brought him to the Moon, he knew he had to say what was in his heart. The people back on Earth, those still excited enough to watch, hung on his every word.

He contemplated the now familiar surroundings of the Moon and the valley of Taurus-Littrow, the lunar location he had worked for three days. Then he looked at the Earth, thinking about the trip back home. *The Earth, that beautiful dot of life in the sky. Everything he was or would be was represented by that shining sphere in the blackness of space.*

He caught his breath and spoke clearly back to Mission Control in Houston 240,000 miles away. "This is Gene, and I'm on the surface, and, as I take man's last step from the surface, back home for some time to come, but we believe not too long into the future, I'd like to just say what I believe history will record: that America's challenge of today has forged man's destiny of tomorrow, and, as we leave the Moon at Taurus-Littrow, we leave as we came, and, God willing as we shall return, with peace and hope for all Mankind. Godspeed the crew of Apollo 17."

Between 1969 and 1972, visitors from the planet Earth landed on the Moon six times, at a cost of twenty-four billion dollars. Twelve men left footprints forever on its surface. People died building the infrastructure to get there, countless other men and women were changed forever.

With Apollo 17, on December 14, 1972, manned lunar travel was over for the twentieth century. But as the new century began, the Moon was tired of waiting for humans to return…and so was one man.

Love, passion, and instinct were ready to take the next evolutionary step.

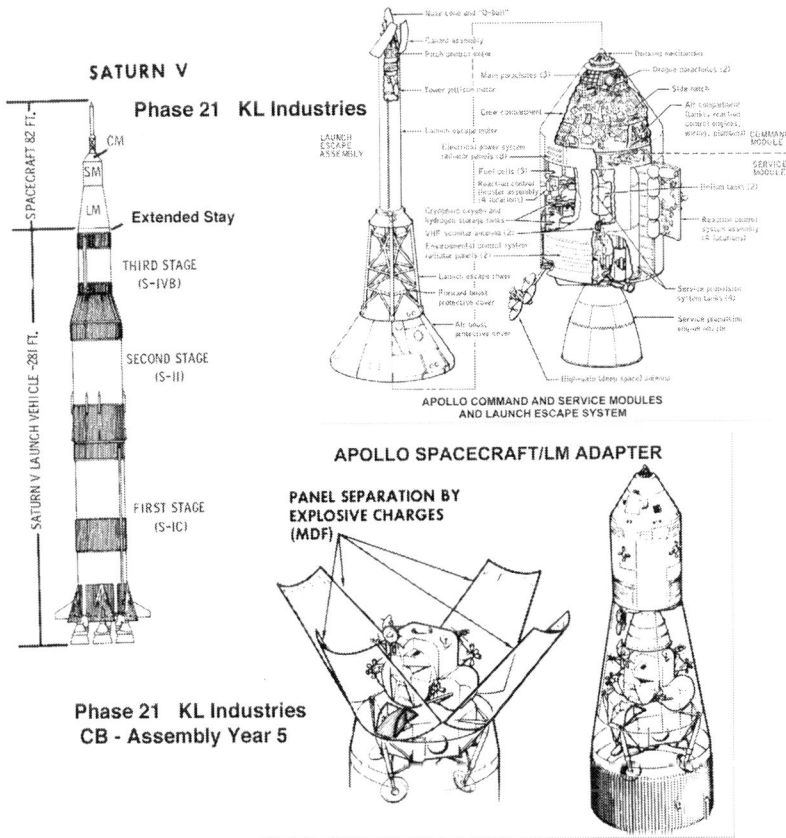

Not Because It's Easy

—STAGE ONE—

1

Everything Changes

Monday, October 21

Echo Air Force Base, Nevada: 1350 ET

A tarantula stood motionless on desert sand in the Nevada sun. A light layer of dust covered its furry, three-inch orange and black body, but perhaps one would have to get a little too close to notice.

Exactly how the creature got there was one of those chaotic things about nature. This arachnid had followed some basic primordial instinct. Perhaps hunting for food, perhaps hunting for a mate—either way chaos had led it astray, and in exactly ten minutes and five seconds chaos would see it torn apart.

The product of biological evolution was about to meet mechanical evolution.

The technician working just above the spider was too focused on his work to notice his eight-legged companion. The man wore sunglasses to protect his eyes from the sun's ultraviolet glare. His white uniform was also covered with a fine layer of dust, so was the rocket he was working on. Although "rocket" was a somewhat antiquated term for what was at its core.

It was silver, two meters tall, cone shaped, with a flat top and bottom. A small inconspicuous nozzle was at its base, secured by heavy wires. The entire device sat upright on a five-legged platform.

Somewhat tired of the sun, the tarantula quietly took a small step toward the platform to find relief in the shade.

Dean Conger wiped the sweat from his forehead and continued his work. As a technician with the perfect resume, Conger followed his own instincts. A graduate of MIT and first in his class, he found the best job at the best salary: a civilian building a better rocket for the United States Air Force.

He'd dreamed, of course, of going into space and being an astronaut, but for now that wasn't going to happen. He knew he'd go one day and kept a close eye on private space endeavors. The price was steep to be a tourist in space, but he wanted to see the curvature of the earth—he wanted the black sky and the overview effect. He had to have all that, which is exactly why he had a backup plan.

Nature, on the other hand, seemed indifferent to Dean, the rocket, and the spider. All brought together in time and space to Echo Air Force Base.

Echo Air Force Base, Nevada, didn't exist. The Air Force had a team of twenty tactical experts to make sure it didn't. All information about Echo was deeply compartmentalized, making Echo Air Force Base just that: an echo. A visit there was like a visit to a pleasantly arranged office park. The only difference was the base's massive runway. Even so, the runway would be extremely hard to detect from even the best spy satellite. The Air Force used a process called "thermal distortion" to hide the area from any electronic eyes in the sky. The best way to describe thermal distortion is like an electronic mirage, making the runway look like windswept sand.

Conger looked up at the enclosed, air-conditioned viewing stand nearby and caught a quick flash of safety glasses reflecting the sun. Those glasses belonged to General Greg Mitchell.

General Greg Mitchell ran Echo with all the fire and fury of his thirty-five years in the Air Force. Now, at the apex of his career, he was entrusted with the deadliest arsenal of weapons known to the world. Any decision he made could enhance or undermine the very core of national security. Decisions came easy for Mitchell. They had to. Echo was cut off from the world for stretches of three to six months at a time. It made it easier to keep the entire operation a secret. The general was a fair and friendly man, a diplomat, but he knew diplomatic moves had to be backed with decisive force. Sometimes, perhaps, with the force of a weapon. Mitchell was about six feet tall, well built, and worked to keep in shape by lifting and running. His hair was gray and thin, his tan face wrinkled by a life on the brink of war. Even so, the general knew age was an attitude. At sixty he could defeat most of his men in hand-to-hand combat.

On this sunny Monday afternoon, Mitchell sat in a small viewing stand looking at the effectiveness of his management skills. The rocket called XIA, for Experimental Instant Acceleration, sat twenty-five feet away from him on its special platform in the sand. On time and under budget, XIA was a prototype for what would be the deadliest delivery system ever built. Now it would be tested. Others may have been nervous. Others may have cracked under the pressure. Not Mitchell, he was in control over every aspect of the operation. He liked it that way. He didn't trust anyone except the men and women who worked for him. There was no one else to trust. He'd lost his wife to cancer ten years ago, and a plane crash in the War on Terror had taken his only son. Mitchell's life was Echo, his soldiers, and now this creation. He watched his chief technician make the final adjustments. XIA was minutes away from its first test flight at 1400. With a loud creaking sound, the door to the viewing stand swung open behind him.

Mitchell's top aid, Lieutenant David Shaw walked in followed by Senator Hugh Langston. Langston looked like a worn out CPA in early April. The stress went with his position. Langston was one of four members of Congress known as select compartment oversight members. Simply put, Langston was allowed to see into top-secret military "compartments" to watch spending for special projects. He'd received the title after his sixteenth year in the U.S. Senate. He was a career politician and former U.S. Army veteran with no political baggage. Langston had family money, a wife, and two children. There were rumors he'd run for president, but Langston loved power and didn't need the trappings of the White House to get it.

Shaw spoke first, "Sir, I'd like you to meet Senator Langston."

"Good afternoon, General Mitchell, it's good to finally meet you," Langston said, extending a hand, giving his trademark Washington, D.C., smile. The general gave Langston a firm handshake. "It's a pleasure to meet you as well, Senator. You're just in time. We're almost ready to begin the test to show you the extraordinary things proper funding can do."

Langston gestured to the rocket. "XIA?"

"That's all there is to it," Mitchell replied as he glanced again at the silver gumdrop. Mitchell nodded to Lieutenant Shaw, who acknowledged a hidden message and left. The general pointed to a seat. "Please, Senator."

"You've come a long way. I remember when we were just voting on this," Langston said as he sat down. "Needless to say, we're pleased this phase of the project is almost complete. When do you turn over the device?"

Langston was all business. Mitchell grinned. "Lima Company takes possession of XIA tomorrow at 0800. Most of the technicians, including Dean Conger out there, have been reassigned."

The senator looked through the glass at the technician working on the rocket. "What about you, General?"

"My retirement goes into effect next month. XIA was the big one for me."

Suddenly, an alarm sounded and a computer-generated voice bellowed, "Testing will commence in thirty seconds…twenty-nine, twenty-eight…" The computer continued the countdown. Conger walked away from the rocket and pulled off his sunglasses to put on protective glasses and a vest.

Mitchell handed Langston a vest and pair of thick glasses. "If you will, Senator, here's your safety equipment."

Ready for the test, Mitchell cleared his throat and said, "You know with this engine, future manned space flight would be pretty damn simple. We could get back to the Moon in a heartbeat. It's too bad this will only be applied to weapons technology. I'd like…"

Langston cut the general off. "With the war in the Pacific and the digital threat from the New Soviet Union, we need this weapon. We need to be ready for the worst. See space? I'd rather see the future, thank you very much."

The general looked at Langston sharply as the computer-generated voice continued the final countdown, "Three, two, one, ignition." The tarantula was vaporized even before the computer reached one, just as it was ready to take a step out of the shade.

Langston didn't see anything happen at first.

"Is it on?" he asked.

In a sudden, shocking move, the rocket shot straight up fifty feet into the air and stopped. Just stopped. Floating silently. XIA was so fast, it was scary. It was silent. No smoke, no exhaust. Just pure and simple motion. Instant acceleration.

Langston caught his breath. Mitchell just watched. The rocket plunged down twenty-five feet and stopped again to hover. Then, in a flash, the rocket moved toward the viewing stand. Langston started to jump to his feet but Mitchell firmly grabbed his arm. "Don't worry," the general assured the senator. XIA stopped five feet away from the protective window. It rotated slowly, almost mockingly, showing itself off. Langston broke into a sweat and swallowed. Then the rocket moved at incredible speed back to its platform. It hovered for a moment longer as if to make a point, and then landed precisely without a sound. The demonstration was exactly fourteen seconds long. The rocket looked like it had never even moved.

Senator Langston's mouth hung wide open. "Un-fucking-believable."

The general was satisfied. "Senator, you just witnessed true power. A reusable nuclear powered engine, with thrust control at our fingertips. Now you know why we call it 'instant acceleration.'"

Langston pulled out his handkerchief and wiped the sweat from his brow. "That's one hell of an achievement to retire on. Can it provide everything we were looking for?"

The general smiled intensely, "Everything you ordered. XIA can deliver tactical strikes in a heartbeat. It's very precise, to within an inch of the intended target. The operators even have a chance…"

A computer voice interrupted, "Alert, alert. This is not a drill. Radiation levels exceeded in sections B and C." Mitchell immediately got up from his seat and pulled out a small device from his pocket.

"Senator, this is section B. The rocket's nuclear engine must have been compromised during the test."

"What? How much have we been exposed?" Langston swallowed hard as his skin turned a slight gray. Mitchell was cool. "We were protected by this enclosure, but procedure calls for all nonessential personnel off the base. Please follow me."

The senator took a last look at the engine as he left the viewing stand. Mitchell also looked back at the rocket and slyly smiled. XIA would change everything about the future. The two men rapidly made their way to an adjacent building and entered the main hallway of the complex.

"Alert, alert. This is not a drill. Radiation levels exceeded in sections B and C. This is not a drill," the computer-generated voice shrilled.

General Mitchell pulled out a small communicator, and spoke into it. "Lieutenant Shaw?"

Shaw's voice beeped back over the device. "Yes, General?"

"Meet me in the lobby with the detector," Mitchell said. "Any idea on what happened?"

"We think it has something to do with a seal in the rocket but it should be easy to fix. It pulled twenty Gs in the last maneuver. The force may have turned a flexible gasket to jelly."

"Thanks, Lieutenant," Mitchell said.

The two men continued the walk to the main lobby. When they arrived, Lieutenant Shaw was already there. He carried a long yellow pole with electronic meters at one side. He waved it over the men. "Dean Conger is already in the infirmary. He was exposed," Shaw said, as he carefully examined the readout on the meters.

Langston swallowed hard.

"Exposure must have happened after the flight," Shaw told them. "You're fine, no indications," he said to the senator.

The senator let out his breath, "Thank God."

"But all nonessential personal must leave in case there's a bigger problem," Shaw added, looking squarely at Langston. "Your helicopter is waiting, Senator."

Langston looked at the lieutenant and then the general and knew from their expressions there was no other option. He extended a hand to Mitchell. "Well, General, I hope this problem won't affect delivery."

"Just a small hiccup," the general confidently replied. "We should be up and ready to test again by this time tomorrow. Just one small delay."

"I hope so," The senator said before he turned and walked outside to a waiting helicopter. Mitchell and Shaw made their way to a window to watch the senator's helicopter take off. Conger walked in from another room. Mitchell looked at him. "You don't look too bad."

"Alert, alert. This is not a drill. Radiation levels—" the computer started to shrill again.

"Sorry," Conger apologized as he turned off the computer warning with a remote control. "Everything checks out with XIA. All seven engines are ready. The test was flawless."

"Yes, good job, Dean." Mitchell said, watching the helicopter disappear over the horizon.

"Thank you, sir. I'll go make the final preparations for transit," the chief technician said as he hurried for a door. Mitchell walked over to a cooler and poured himself a cup of water.

Shaw looked at the general. "Do you think Langston believed the warning?"

"Are you kidding? Even the test scared the hell out of him. He bought it," Mitchell declared, taking a drink. "But just in case he didn't, we move tonight."

"Are you sure—" Shaw saw Mitchell's eyes and stopped.

"How many are with us?" the general said coldly.

"Everyone. They support you and the bigger project, Greg. They're ready to do whatever it takes."

"That may not be enough," the general said, taking another drink of the cool water.

***

Perigee Boneyard, New Mexico: 1512 ET

If you saw hundreds of planes sitting in the middle of the desert you may think it was a mirage. But why not put them there? The humidity is low and there's plenty of room. Perfect for long-term aircraft storage. Perigee Boneyard, New Mexico, was built on that principle. Hundreds of planes sat uniformly in the desert waiting for their chance to fly. It didn't really matter if it would take a year or a decade.

Among all these airplanes in the middle of the desert was something unusual: a woman standing on the sandy tarmac. Her long blond hair was pulled back to reveal a tan and silky face, clever nose, supple lips, and brown eyes. Even at first glance, it was easy to see she worked hard to keep in shape. Striking yes, but there was more to her than looks. You could feel her presence.

The soldier standing beside her found it hard to concentrate. He'd been in the desert now for three weeks and she was the first woman he'd seen since a very long September night in Albuquerque.

"Forgive me for asking, Miss Long, but these planes have been here two years. Nobody's wanted anything to do with them. Why now?"

Kathy moved closer to the soldier in a smart, catlike way. "I'd love to tell you, but I don't know. By the way, please call me Kathy. Damn, it's hot." She took off her jacket to reveal a silk, sleeveless shirt.

The soldier took in the view. As a farm boy from a small town, this much beauty was overwhelming. He swiftly got back to business. "Please sign here," he said, giving her an electronic pad.

Kathy glanced over the device and then signed with the tip of her finger. "Twenty planes. Good. My people will take them out. You can expect the move to begin as soon as possible, in fact, teams will be here in about an hour."

The soldier was surprised by her tone. "What? Why so soon?"

"As you said, these planes have been here two years. Well, it's time for them to fly again."

Kathy walked away, leaving the soldier standing alone among the airplanes. He looked at the paperwork once again and then to Kathy as she opened the door to her car.

He shook his head and headed back to his office.

***

Area 27 Army Base, California: 1530 ET

Area 27 Army Base is probably the second largest military base that doesn't exist. It's located just outside of Edwards Air Force Base in California. But instead of an office park with a large runway, like Echo, Area 27 is made up of ten large buildings, making it a perfect place to store big equipment.

The pilots who call Area 27 home, call it "Rotator Heaven." "Rotator," meaning helicopter. On this day, in one of the base's classrooms, a small group of men dressed in green flight gear sat uniformly in a small auditorium. A man dressed in an orange flight suit was in front of them. On the chalkboard were two words: "Real Stealth."

"So that's how the real stealth system works on these machines," the instructor said. "And that's why it makes them totally invisible to the eye as well. So right away, we're better than the stealth jet fighter. But gents, the VIS technology we're talking about came at a price: seven billion dollars." He paused to let the figure sink in.

Two pilots, Alan Grove and Sam Harris instantly looked at each other from across the room.

Grove gave a mock whistle. The instructor ignored the sound and finished his preflight lecture. "Let's keep this flight clean and simple. In this test, we'll use the Next-Gen Apache helicopters. Stick to your flight profiles and the timeline. Good luck."

***

At 1610 ET, the five Apache Attack helicopters were flying over the California desert.

They looked like average military helicopters and that was the beauty of this particular stealth technology. It called for the simple attachment of a black box under the rotor blade. Theoretically, any helicopter could be made invisible at the flick of a switch. Sam Harris loved to fly, and his Apache was performing well. His code name was "Apache Feather." His fellow pilots would tell you he could fly a helicopter as gently as a feather on a breeze.

Harris clicked on his radio. "Apache Feather to Black Cat," he said into the microphone. At the controls of his own helicopter, Alan Grove was known as "Black Cat" because he seemed to always bring his targets bad luck. He hoped today would be no different. Grove knew the time had come. He took a deep breath and said, "Go ahead, Apache Feather."

Harris knew once the word was given, his current life would be over and a new one would begin. "Black Cat, I'd like your approval to begin Operation Crystal."

Grove looked at the four other dull-green Apaches flying in formation. The team was ready, but not for what was about to happen. Harris must be sweating this out, Grove thought. "So am I," he muttered to himself

It was time.

"All aircraft standby. Tiger 27, are you ready?" Grove asked into the microphone.

Inside the radar room at Area 27, the instructor looked at the technicians. The lead tech made a final adjustment to a console and shook her head. "We're ready."

The instructor nodded and said into the microphone, "Black Cat, this is Tiger 27. Commence Operation Crystal at your discretion."

For Grove it was the moment of truth. All his training, his entire life for that matter, rode on what happened in the next sixty seconds. "Sometimes the course of someone's life is decided in seconds," he said to himself. Then Grove keyed the microphone, his voice clear, "Black Cat to all aircraft, engage VIS in order assigned and call it out. Begin on my call." Grove flicked a small red switch on the instrument panel. "This is Black Cat, VIS is on."

Harris was next. "Black Cat, Apache feather, VIS is on."

Instead of five helicopters, now there were only three. Grove and Harris's helicopters were invisible both to radar and to the eye.

Then came the other three Apaches.

"Black Cat, this is Class Act, VIS is on."

"Black Cat, this is No Retreat, VIS is on."

"Black Cat, this is Colombo, VIS is on."

In the radar room at Area 27, the helicopters blinked off the radar screen one by one. The portable stealth worked. The instructor looked at the radar and blinked. He knew the device well, in fact he helped engineer it, but he still had a hard time believing it. "Son of a bitch." He smiled.

"Sir, the choppers are clean. No return on radar," the chief radar technician reported. The instructor looked at the group of men and women around him. "Ladies and gents, war will never be the same. We can now make a machine invisible at the touch of a button."

The helicopter test area was supposed to be empty, but three teenagers had wandered in the area looking for a place to camp.

They'd decided to skip school for an adventure in the desert. The day had been fun and relaxing until they heard a loud noise. "What's that noise? A helicopter?" one of the boys asked nervously.

The young boys looked at the sky. "But where?" His friend replied. "It sounds so close." A strange whirlwind of sand was coming directly at them. Suddenly, three helicopters appeared out of nowhere two hundred feet directly overhead.

"Shit!" the tallest teen yelled, "Let's get the hell out of here." The helicopters quickly passed overhead as the three trespassers ran in the other direction.

Back at Area 27, cigars had already been passed out. The radar operator halted the celebration. "Sir, three bogeys are back on the scope."

"What?" the instructor asked. "Malfunction?"

"It appears so."

The technicians scrambled for their consoles.

Out in the desert, three helicopters were now visible again. And they were targets.

Grove took a look at his watch. Harris checked his watch as well. The helicopters they flew were still invisible.

Class Act was the first to try and report the malfunction with the equipment. "Black Cat, this is Class Act. For some reason, my VIS is off. Repeat VIS is off."

Colombo was also ready to report, but in seconds his helicopter's tail rotor was destroyed by gunfire from Grove's helicopter.

Class Act tried an evasive maneuver, but he was no match for the invisible enemy, an enemy who knew him all too well. His tail rotor was also disabled in seconds.

No Retreat had no choice but to retreat.

Back at Area 27, the instructor was holding his breath by the radio, waiting to hear what had happened. He watched in shock as two of the three radar reflections disappeared. Was the device working again? As he started to pick up the microphone, a panic-stricken voice came from the speaker. "Tiger 27, this is No Retreat. We are under attack! I repeat, we are under attack!" Seconds later, No Retreat's helicopter disappeared from radar. The instructor looked at the screen.

"This is Tiger 27. Come in, No Retreat, come in. Black Cat, report on the status of the mission. Black Cat, report on status immediately."

The speaker was quiet, the instructor confused. "Let's get a rescue team out there and find out what the fuck happened." He paused for a second. "And get me the Pentagon. Now!"

The three teenagers watched as the last of the helicopters landed on the desert sand. "We better get the hell out of here. This place will be crawling with cops in no time."

"I'm with you, let's go home."

In the comfort of his invisible Apache, Grove also watched the final helicopter autorotate to the desert floor. The pilots would be rescued in a matter of hours, and by that time, he and Harris would be long gone.

Grove switched his radio to a private channel. "That was too damn easy," he said, keying the microphone.

At the controls of his invisible Apache, Harris knew his life would never be the same. But he'd made his decision and had taken action. He keyed his microphone. "Make sure you keep your anti-collision meters in the green. We don't want to hit each other. And Grove, don't worry, it's about to get a lot harder. If this doesn't work, we're dead."

The two invisible helicopters turned to a new heading.

***

The National Archives, Washington, D.C.: 2000 ET

It was the strangest fire Washington, D.C., rescue workers had ever seen. Twelve units had been called out to fight the blaze at the National Archives Building. Only one area of the building had been damaged—an area containing medical records from the 1940s and 50s. It would take weeks to evaluate the damage. The firefighters shook their heads, trying to figure out exactly how the fire had started, and why the damage had been so concentrated.

***

Echo Air Force Base, Nevada: 2259 ET

The final chapter to what would become a very long day for U.S. Intelligence was written back at Echo Air Force Base. The lobby where Senator Langston had been standing only hours before with General Mitchell was quiet. Under a large "Thanks for not smoking" sign sat a rather large box. On top of the box was a timer, a timer counting backwards. The timer was easy to see because of its large indicator lights. It would have sent even the most seasoned bomb expert running for cover. Fourteen boxes just like it were spread all over the base, all with electronic timers counting backwards. Outside of Echo Air Force Base there was a hill where General Mitchell would sometimes eat his lunch. This location would have provided the best view as explosives leveled every building on site.

The two hundred people who had given the base life were already long gone. Echo became just that, an echo, on time and under budget.

***

Somewhere over Virginia: 2346 ET

A private jet gracefully breezed through the night sky at 465 knots on its way to Dulles International Airport in Virginia. The jet carried seven charter passengers willing to pay the extra price to avoid airline hassles. Captain Tony Velocci and co-pilot Justin Pasker were eager for the long day to be over. So far, things were looking good. They'd made it out of New York at a reasonable hour. All the passengers had shown up on time, for a change.

"Want some coffee?" Justin asked as he stretched in the right scat and yawned.

"Nah," Tony replied. "I've already had too much."

Justin twisted the metal buckle and removed his shoulder harness to reach around for the coffee urn.

Back in the passenger cabin a man in a black crumpled suit typed on his laptop. He was completing an important presentation and he wanted to have it done before the rubber of the wheels hit the runway. After two weeks of solid work, he would take the next day and drive to Annapolis to spend the day on his sailboat. The only thing that would prevent him from doing so was the report.

Hunter Algier took his work seriously and he didn't like things hanging over his head. Hunter had dark hair, blue eyes and a serious, yet youthful face. He was someone who could blend in very easily.

Charter flights provided a perfect way for Hunter to travel. They beat commercial airliners for speed and efficiency, and as a covert tactical aviation specialist for the National Security Agency, the less he was seen by large groups of people, the better.

The thirty-five-year-old agent had been on a dozen missions in five countries. Most of the time he was safe, mainly because no one knew to look for him and because of his keen ability to blend in. He liked to think of himself as slightly beyond anonymous. The best spies are boring, he liked to tell himself.

The trip home from Japan to Virginia by way of New York was taking its toll. Hunter closed his eyes and rubbed his face. "What a long day," he muttered.

"Mister, who are you talking to?" Hunter opened his eyes to see a pair of eyes under red hair looking at him from over the seat in front of him. The youngster reminded Hunter of his own desire for a family. But fate had intervened.

Hunter smiled, but beyond the seat, the child's mother was getting tired. "Turn around and sit still," she said.

The child disappeared behind the seat. He was probably a hospital patient being flown for medical treatments in the Washington, D.C., area, Hunter thought. The other passengers were either sleeping or reading. Hunter looked out the airplane's window into the blackness.

Back on the flight deck, Justin sipped the coffee and looked at the fuel gauge. "Hey, Tony, did you see that woman behind the counter in Teterboro?"

"I couldn't miss those—"

Suddenly, without warning, the plane was hit with what sounded like gunfire and the jet began to vibrate wildly. "Damn, Justin! That's hail!" Monster-sized hail pummeled the aircraft. The pilots looked outside in terrified amazement.

Back in the cabin, amid the noise, passengers were now trying to find the nearest window to see what was going on. Hunter yelled, "Everybody, fasten up!" He'd said it just in time. The cabin gyrated wildly as severe turbulence tossed the plane around like a grizzly cub playing with a Pacific Northwest salmon.

Without his seatbelt in place, the force threw Justin forward in his seat, spilling coffee everywhere. Then as the plane hit more turbulence, Justin's head hit the controls with a sick thud, knocking him out.

"Justin? Justin?" Tony said looking at his co-pilot. "Clear-air turbulence with fucking hail thrown in. You've just got to be kidding me." Tony watched the control panel light up. The number two engine was dying. Tony compensated swiftly. He reached for the radio. "Dulles Approach. This is zero-one-five-four Lima. I need to declare an emergency."

Hunter had never gotten airsick in his entire life, but now he was on the edge of losing the six-course meal he'd eaten only a few hours before in New York.

The door to the flight deck opened.

"Dr. McConnell, hey Dr. McConnell, I need your help," the captain yelled from the flight deck. A heavy-set man in his 40s got up carefully and made his way to the flight deck, leaning against seats to keep his balance in the turbulence.

"Damn, I'm glad you were on this flight. Justin hit his head pretty hard. What can you do for him?"

The plane shuttered again, but not as violently this time.

"It's a damn deep cut. I'll need to get him back in the cabin to take a look." The doctor turned around to the shocked passengers. "I'm going to need some help." Hunter was out of his seat in a heartbeat holding on to keep his balance.

Maneuvering in the small flight deck, Hunter and McConnell were able to pull Justin out of his seat and back into the main cabin. Hunter went back up to the flight deck and looked at the captain, who was on the radio to Dulles International Airport.

When the pilot was finished, Hunter said, "Sir, my name is Hunter Algier, I'm a multi-rated engine pilot with over three thousand hours and a lot of that turbo time. You look like you need some help."

"Sure, my name's Tony, grab a seat."

Hunter looked at the blood-soaked co-pilot's seat and sat down.

"I'll need you to work the radios and what's left of our radar. I've tried to explain to Dulles Approach what happened, and they're clearing a path for us," Tony said to Hunter. "Fucking clear-air hail came out of nowhere. Never seen that before."

"Me neither," Hunter said. He looked outside as the stars began to disappear. "Now it looks like we'll get our clouds."

The calm only lasted for a second. One by one the instruments on the flight deck began to die out. "Oh no," Tony gasped. "If the visibility gets any worse, we'll have to turn north to find an airport away from this cloud cover." A bolt of lightning shot past the window. Hunter knew exactly what to do. "Uh, Tony, I think I've got something we can use to get us home."

Hunter turned around and peered at the passengers. He picked the woman sitting closest to his seat, her son holding on to her for dear life. "Miss, I need my computer bag," Hunter pleaded. "My computer bag, it's under my seat."

The child looked at Hunter, then at his mom. "Don't leave me," the youngster whimpered. Hunter knew there wasn't a lot of time. The storm was growing worse and the plane was in the middle of it, with no radar and few working instruments.

"What's his name?" Hunter asked the child's mother.

"Alex," she whispered nervously.

"Alex," Hunter said calmly to the child. "Alex, your mom has got to help us. She'll only be gone for a second."

The child's cries subsided. Hunter nodded to the woman as she got up to get Hunter's bag. Just as the child started to cry again, the woman returned to her seat.

"Open it, please," Hunter said to the woman.

As she opened the bag, the boy started to cry loudly.

"Alex, Alex. I need your help," Hunter pleaded again. The child looked up again. "Give me the black box inside."

The child's cries stopped. The youngster reached into the case and pulled out a thin, flat device.

Hunter took it from the child with a smile, turned, and set it on the instrument panel.

"What is that?" Tony said, looking out of the corner of his eye.

"At best, salvation; at worst, an experiment." Working as fast as possible, Hunter punched some buttons on the side of the gadget. The top opened, and out popped a small screen. The screen slowly came to life. "Come on, baby," Hunter encouraged his machine.

Hunter pushed a button inside marked EXECUTE. The screen now read:
SYNTHETIC VISION CYCLING.
Tony watched in terrified fascination.

Synthetic Vision would now be put to the true test. Engineered by Hunter, the box represented years of research. Synthetic Vision used microencapsulated-infrared radar to see through clouds even at night.

"Next time it gets a faster driver," Hunter muttered, through clinched teeth, as he watched the program cycle. He quickly added almost silently, "If there is a next time."

While Hunter was waiting, he reached for the plane's radio microphone. Hunter read the plane's identifying code off the panel in the center of the cockpit and then said, "Washington Center, this is zero-one-five-four Lima."

"Zero-one-five-four Lima, Washington Center. Turn left zero-niner-zero, maintain eight thousand, expect I-L-S approach for left…"

"Ask them to help vector us through this storm," Tony interrupted while flicking a switch.

"Washington Center, is there any way I can turn twenty degrees left to get through this storm."

"Zero-one-five-four Lima, roger. How many instruments are working?"

"Washington Center, the radio and that's about it," Hunter said. But with the Synthetic Vision working, they could still make the most of the plane's crippled instruments. The entire device was its own sensor. Hunter designed it to be portable for use in emergencies exactly like this one.

It was Hunter's kind of luck when it came to testing equipment in the field. He always seemed to get a chance, no matter how screwy the circumstances. He'd taken this job with the government as a covert tactical aviation specialist because of the excellent pay and because it allowed him to keep up with the latest developments around the world. He'd just finished a difficult mission meeting officials in China, trying to determine if they were planning their own version of a national space plane—an aircraft that could make a flight from Beijing to New York in under two hours. The plane could be used in peace but also as a bomber. He found out some information, but his research was difficult because off the Pacific Conflict. The skirmishes and rhetoric between China, Taiwan, Unified Korea, and Japan had grown in intensity during the past two years.

It had been a difficult trip, and now hair and a crippled aircraft was bringing it all to a very interesting conclusion.

The woman behind him starred at the burned-out control panel with Hunter's tiny computer screen now apparently running everything. Hunter looked back to see her look of shock. He smiled. "It's not as bad as it looks." Her eyes glazed over. She looked like she was about to throw up. Hunter lost his smile and turned back to the control panel and saw the approaching runway lights on the Synthetic Vision scope.

Tony smiled at Hunter. "That's an amazing piece of machinery. Mr....?"

"Algier."

Watching through the device, Tony maneuvered through the clouds, the ground clearly visible, as if it was a bright day. Everything appeared to be going well until the final blast of turbulence hit the plane. The aircraft shuttered, the passengers screamed, and the Synthetic Vision fell on the floor of the flight deck before Hunter could catch it.

"So much for high-tech," Hunter conceded to Tony. "It's in your hands now, Tony." He turned to the passengers. "Make sure you're secure in your seats!"

Hunter watched as Tony concentrated on the landing. With the plane leaking fuel and with damage to the outside of the aircraft, they'd only get one chance.

The rescue crews on the ground watched as the plane made its approach. Tony crabbed the aircraft slightly to compensate for the wind. At the last moment, he straightened the flight path out and made a perfect landing.

The passengers applauded and a short time later the plane rolled to a stop.

"I'll get the door. Good job, Mr. Algier," Tony said as he extended his hand.

"Happy to help," Hunter said, already thinking about how to get away quickly. The last thing he needed was a reporter asking too many questions.

Everyone started to evacuate the aircraft as fast as they could. Hunter got up, grabbed what was left of the Synthetic Vision device, and patted Alex on the head. Alex's mother was crying with joy.

"Who are you? How can I repay you?" She asked.

"You already do pay me. I work for the government," Hunter said, wiping a tear from her face. "At least we're here on time." Hunter helped the woman from her seat.

Once she was out and the aircraft was empty, Hunter made his way back on board and to the emergency exit on the other side of the plane. He had to avoid the cameras lights and reporters. The passengers were led away from the plane to a waiting mob scene of TV cameras. Tony talked to the paramedics to make sure his co-pilot was okay. He looked at Justin, "You missed most of the fun."

Tony looked at the passengers and plane. Everyone had gotten out except for Hunter, who'd gone back in but not come out. Tony climbed back on board and went to the flight deck, but Hunter was gone. He looked back in the passenger cabin and noticed the emergency exit had been opened.

"Son of a bitch," Tony said. "Thank you, Mr. Algier," he said, looking at the exit.

A few minutes later, back on the flight deck, investigators surveyed the damaged controls. One of the men whistled and looked back at Tony, who was filling out an incident report. "It's a wonder you landed in one piece."

"No shit," Tony said as he looked at the control panel.

***

Hunter arrived at his home in Northern Virginia about twenty minutes later. At least living close to Dulles International Airport made traveling easy. He was grateful he didn't have to deal with the Washington, D.C., traffic gridlock. He walked inside and put his black computer bag on the floor. He was already over the emergency landing. He'd been through a few of them in his life. It wasn't the near disaster affecting his mood, something else was. For some reason he felt more lonely tonight than usual. Maybe it was the mother and her son on the plane and here he was, as usual, coming home to an empty house.

"Shit," he said.

He walked to the refrigerator and pulled out a pitcher of natural spring water. It seemed water was the only thing he could keep inside the refrigerator because he was on the road so much.

But tomorrow he'd have the day off. He could finish the China report early and still make it to Annapolis and the Chesapeake Bay. October was a good month for sailing and to just be in Annapolis.

He'd be alone of course. There was no one in his life, no one to replace the love he'd lost such a long time ago. It seemed his job was too demanding now for relationships anyway. But it hadn't always been that way. In another time and another place he'd have a big house with his own family. A time when he could put work out of his mind in exchange for flesh and blood to feed his soul and satisfy his heart.

He checked his voice mail and found twenty messages waiting. Deciding to tackle them in the morning, he hung up the phone and walked into his bedroom. He looked at the left side of the bed.

Even after seven years, he imagined his wife there, with her smile and textbook-funny lines to cheer him up. But she was in prison now, and it was his fault.

Hunter got undressed, put on some shorts, and got into bed. He fell asleep reading the latest issue of *Aviation Week and Space Technology*.

2

The Roswell Trinity

Tuesday, October 22

Dulles, Virginia: 0715 ET

Hunter's alarm clock woke him to the song "Spaceman" from Harry Nilsson. He felt tired but he also re-energized. He turned to the clock: 0715. He'd have to be in work in forty-five minutes.

Hunter lifted his head off the pillow and heard talking in the distance. It was the television. Why was it on? He got out of bed, grabbed his gun from a drawer, and quietly made his way downstairs to the living room. He quietly peaked around the corner to see his boss of ten years, Oscar Morrow.

Oscar looked at the gun and nodded. "Good to see you on your best defense Agent Algier, but you can put the gun away, unless, of course, you don't like the coffee I made."

Hunter nodded back and put the gun on the kitchen table. He knew Oscar's visit probably did not mean a good morning. Oscar Morrow, director of field operations for the National Security Agency, only went to an agent's home when something massive was afoot.

Hunter looked at Oscar and waited for the shoe to drop.

"As I said, I made you coffee. You'll need it. I was watching this interesting report," Oscar said, nodding at the television. "A story on Channel 4 about someone saving the lives of seven people on a charter flight and then disappearing into the night."

"Oh. Really?" Hunter said, pouring himself a cup of coffee.

Oscar walked up to Hunter to shake his hand. "I take it from the scene last night your Synthetic Vision worked."

"Yeah, except it fell on the floor of the flight deck about twenty seconds before landing. Scared the hell out of me. The pilot didn't know what to make of it. Of course his attention was focused on keeping everyone alive."

"Nothing like a little unscheduled field testing," Oscar said, pointing to the television. On the screen the aircraft sat in the middle of the runway, surrounded by television lights.

One of the passengers was being interviewed. It was the woman who'd had the young boy sitting with her. "And my boy was saved because of that man."

Hunter reached for the remote to turn off the set.

"What brings you out here so early? To congratulate me?"

Oscar took a long drink from a coffee mug. "We don't have a lot of time, so let's get to it. Have you ever heard of The Roswell Trinity?"

Hunter was suddenly wide-awake. "The Roswell Trinity," he whispered as he reached for a stool to sit down. "Everyone in National Security has. Three elements that make an army invincible: locomotion, invisibility, and perfect health. It involved secret research. Secret research on—" he stopped short and looked at his boss.

Oscar snorted, "On aliens?" He laughed again and took a sip of coffee. "Aliens. Damn. It's amazing how many intelligent people really believe that. Aliens."

Oscar let out a sigh. "But it's a great hoax isn't it?"

Hunter looked puzzled.

"Hunter, Roswell is actually a hoax inside of a hoax to protect the truth. After World War II, in the late 1940s, some of the people who'd built the atomic bomb moved to Roswell to work on a new project: The Roswell Trinity. As you said, three components to make any army invincible. Actually, it started as a backup plan in case we couldn't build an atomic bomb. It called for an army to be highly mobile, invisible, and healthy. An invincible army, the perfect deterrent to war.

"First, locomotion, the ability to move at incredible speeds anywhere on the planet, and if you could move without being seen, you'd even have more power. Fearsome power. That was the second part—stealth. And if you had perfect health even if you were injured on the battlefield, you could recover and fight again and again and again.

"So using the cover of a faked crashed alien spaceship." Oscar laughed again. "The military created the three components of The Roswell Trinity—locomotion, stealth, and health."

"Okay, Oscar. I follow, but why haven't they been used? There have been other conflicts."

"Only forty people knew about it, and I mean forty. We're talking compartmentalization and secrecy on a scale never since achieved. It was brutal secrecy. Twenty of the researchers died in a radiation accident. Seventeen were executed to protect national security. The thought was if we developed The Roswell Trinity to completion, the technology would leak to other governments and the deterrent would be gone.

"Three men were left to live, in a circle of fear. They constantly watched each other. But once we had the bomb, we had one-stop shopping for complete annihilation."

"Oscar, why is it an issue now?" Hunter asked as he moved from the kitchen to his couch.

"One of the men talked. It was inevitable. He talked to Senator Hugh Langston. So Langston decided, along with his oversight committee, to secretly rekindle The Roswell Trinity and finish it."

"So it's out there? Complete?"

Oscar nodded his head. "Listen to this scenario. Last night Echo Air Force Base in Nevada exploded into oblivion." Hunter's mouth dropped open.

Oscar continued. "The blast came hours after Senator Hugh Langston watched the test of a new rocket engine. He had to leave because of radioactive contamination. We believe that was faked. Today investigators are looking through the rubble of what was once Echo, but there's not much to see. All the buildings were flattened."

Hunter cleared his throat, "I went out there four weeks ago, back in September. Echo was testing a prototype nuclear rocket with the capacity to accelerate extremely fast. General Greg Mitchell called it XIA. An extremely powerful delivery device."

"Yes, see part one of Roswell."

Hunter nodded.

Oscar continued. "At Area 27 in California yesterday, two Apache helicopters disappeared during a training flight. Three other helicopters involved in the mission were shot down. It's been tough hiding it from the media. The test flight was called Operation Crystal."

Hunter nodded his head. "Operation Crystal. The pilots call it VIS for short. Instant invisibility. Portable stealth technology you can attach to an aircraft."

Hunter took a sip of the coffee, and then said, "Part two of Roswell."

Oscar knew Hunter did his research. "The disappearance happened moments after the test had started. Everything was fine at first. All five helicopters were invisible. Then three Apaches appeared again and were shot down. The other two Apaches never made radio contact again and simply vanished."

Oscar paused. "Then something else happened. Something that most people would think would be completely unrelated. A fire at the National Archives. There's one medical file in there not too many people know about called ZR5."

"ZR5? Come on," Hunter scoffed. "Oscar, ZR5 refers to secret health research. Research on the instant healing of flesh." When Hunter realized what he was about to say, his face turned white. "No fucking way."

Oscar shook his head. "The Roswell Trinity springs from the same source."

Hunter looked at his boss.

"Now you know why seventeen people were executed in 1949. But it was destined to leak. The ability to move in an instant, sneak behind enemy lines while invisible, and ZR5: instant healing. Someone harvested all three elements of The Roswell Trinity in a day."

"'Who?" Hunter asked. "Why?"

"I'll need the equipment in my office to give you more details. We'll continue the conversation there. I'll see you in my office conference room in about thirty minutes. We have very little time." Oscar looked at the television one last time. "Again, nice job with the landing, but it's time to get to work." Oscar took a final drink of coffee and headed for the door.

Only one thing was going through Hunter's mind: life will never be the same. This one was too big. He put his coffee down and rushed for the shower.

***

National Security Agency Field Office, Dulles, Virginia: 0755

Hunter Algier's office was in one of the most recognizable buildings anywhere in Northern Virginia. The sharp lines threw off the eye and may have turned some stomachs. The glass of the building was either green or black (depending on the time of day).

Less than two miles away from Dulles International Airport, the building went under the name The Virginia Center for Advanced Technology, but it was just a cover for the NSA. There were rumors about the building because of a legendary run-in between utility workers and military police and the fact that cell phone service always dropped out in the area, even in the footprint of several large towers.

Inside the building, Hunter's office was clean and neat with a large glass desk and black leather chair. On his desk sat gauges and dials from various aircraft and helicopters. The walls were covered with blueprints of some of the world's most sophisticated aircraft. He usually posted a new technical drawing of an aircraft on his wall every week to keep his learning curve sharp. The world had come a long way since the Wright brothers had made their famous flight in Kitty Hawk, North Carolina.

When he wasn't in the field, Hunter's work dealt with deciphering about twenty top-secret aviation papers a day. In those papers, he read about the weapons and aircraft various governments of the world were trying to build and fly.

He walked into his office and turned on one of his five high-speed computers. A computer voice said, "Good morning, Agent Algier. You have more than four hundred messages."

"It's going to be a long day," he said to himself as he looked at his watch. He only had three minutes before he had to meet with Oscar. He decided to try and read at least a few messages before he had to go.

A few minutes later, Hunter walked into the conference room as Oscar activated the secure communications line. It was a large conference room with seats for about twenty people. Oscar and Hunter were the only ones in the room.

Oscar nodded to Hunter. "It's just you and me and two people from the White House. Have a seat, Hunter."

Oscar dialed in a final code. "Secure line set. Speaker activated. Name and password?" The computer voice on the phone asked.

"Morrow, Oscar. Password: KLA, red, orange, blue, twenty-nine."

"Password accepted. Begin call," the computer voice said approvingly.

"Oscar Morrow and Agent Hunter Algier here."

"Good morning, gentlemen," a voice on the phone said. "I have one associate listening in on behalf of the president. Oscar, you may begin."

"Thank you. First, Hunter, this is for your eyes only." Oscar slid Hunter an envelope. "I'm giving Hunter the envelope."

Hunter opened the envelope. It contained a single piece of paper. On the paper was one sentence: *On Friday, October 25 at 5:00 p.m. Eastern Time a new world order begins. Prepare your citizens. Prepare your financial markets.*

The voice from the phone said, "It was found on the president's desk in the Oval Office yesterday. They have no idea how it got there. The White House Secret Service detail is annoyed to say the least."

Another voice on the phone interrupted, "We don't have a lot of time. It's already Tuesday. That means that whatever is coming is about eighty hours away. Let's get to it."

Oscar dimmed the lights of the conference room. "Hunter, this may not be easy for you," he said, hitting a switch. From a cube on the center of a table a 3-D image appeared.

The image of a man Hunter knew very well.

"Knox Long?" Hunter asked.

"That's right, Hunter, Commander Knox Long. He was one of twelve Americans to walk on the Moon. As you know, he's a billionaire. We think he's the one bringing The Roswell Trinity together."

"I've never met him, but I've researched his background. I've always considered this guy an American hero," Hunter said." What makes you think—"

"He's been very critical of the president," Oscar said, cutting Hunter off. "He's in a position to pull strings. And yesterday, while everything else was happening, an order came down to move twenty airplanes from Perigee Boneyard. The description of the woman who handled the transaction matches that of Knox's daughter, Kathy Long," Oscar said, pushing another button. The image of Knox Long changed into the image of a woman. Kathy Long. "This is our best lead."

Hunter looked at the image of the woman floating above the table. She was beautiful. "Oscar, I'm not sure I understand my role in this, other than the fact I've spent time studying the career of Knox Long."

"Exactly," Oscar said. "We've set it up. We want you to talk to Commander Long. You'll be going as a journalist from News Now on the Internet. It's a good cover, considering you've written twenty or more pieces for them."

Hunter wrote editorials on the development of new aviation technology for NNI. It was a quiet way to generate feedback from big corporations about potential breakthroughs in aviation. NNI was the biggest online news provider in the world. It had handily beaten CNN, FOX News, The Huffington Post, The Drudge Report and MSNBC in the Internet news wars. The reason? Journalists at News Now on the Internet could update information instantly, thanks to a special mobile publishing tool. The site was never out of date. It was like Twitter on steroids. The site also used an algorithm for fair and balanced reporting. Each reporter's story was graded as to how well they brought together details. With the grading system at NNI, readers had a scientific way to detect bias.

Oscar continued, "Our confidential tracking shows Knox loves News Now, and you already know he loves golf. So, using the cover of News Now, we set up an interview with him tomorrow at Pinehurst Country Club in North Carolina. Agent Phil Styles will pose as your digital photographer. The story you'll be doing centers on Project Apollo and the fact that it's been more than forty years since America left the Moon. First, see what kind of information you can get from him, then we'll see if we need to take more aggressive measures. Take your golf clubs. Commander Long likes to play golf with people to get to know them. You leave in two hours with Phil."

As Hunter listened, his mind was reeling.

Oscar turned off the projector and turned on the lights. "Hunter, I know you think Knox Long is a hero. He is. But we've watched him for a long time. He's dangerous and cocky. I want you there when he makes a mistake." Oscar paused and then added, "Stop by weapons requisition before you leave."

Hunter looked at Oscar with a grim face. "Oscar, you know I'll go. But, sir, I've got to ask, don't you have more tactical agents for this?"

Oscar just stared at him. Hunter had been with the agency for a long time. He'd been assigned many missions and had all the training for more aggressive work in the field. This was not the same. He looked at Oscar one more time and thought, *He's not telling me everything. But, in a way, it doesn't matter, I need something different. Knox Long is the last of his kind. One of the last men who walked on the moon.*

He knew he couldn't say what he was feeling, so he said what he usually did, "I understand Oscar."

Hunter quickly returned to his office to catch up on email and other paperwork. Everything had piled up during his trip to Japan. As Hunter went through his papers, he couldn't stop thinking about Knox Long. Here was a man he'd looked up to all his life. A man who'd actually walked on the Moon. A man who still flew sophisticated aircraft prototypes some test pilots wouldn't even think about flying. Hunter considered Knox a true patriot. After the voyage to the Moon in his spare time, the commander built a strong business renewing the metal industry with high-grade materials in the United States. Knox Long Industries always tested well with consumers and he'd become extremely rich.

Bring him down?

Then there was The Roswell Trinity. Oscar had given Hunter more information to read. *What would Knox want with an army?* Hunter pulled out the note that had been delivered to the president and looked at it again: *On Friday, October 25 at 5:00 p.m. Eastern Time, a new world order begins. Prepare your people. Prepare your financial markets.*

Hunter opened the closet to get his pre-packed overnight bag. He picked it up and started for the door. A strange feeling ambled along his spine, a feeling that he wouldn't be back here. He gave the aviation hardware and blueprints in his office a final glance, and then left. Hunter walked to his car, his mind filled with the mental images of how Astronaut Knox Long had changed his life. Hunter had always been fascinated by Project Apollo.

When Hunter was four, as a joke his dad's friend had given him a lump of coal and told him it was a Moon rock. Hunter carried it around for days. He remembered finding a book on Project Apollo that was part of a gas station promotion and looking at the pictures until the pages were dog-eared.

Arriving at his Land Cruiser, Hunter opened the hatchback and tossed in his overnight bag. His golf clubs were already in the back. As he reached in to make sure he had his new driver, he was hit on the back. The force knocked him down to the cement.

"Shit," Hunter said as he looked up. At first he couldn't see the face, the sun was right behind the attacker. But he recognized a smell—a perfume.

"You bastard! I've waited a long time for this." It was a woman's voice.

The voice of... Hunter held up a hand to block the sun. He could barely make out the face of...his ex-wife.

It was a face out of his dreams and nightmares. Hunter responded, "Angie, I thought you were still in prison."

Angie answered Hunter with a punch in the face. "How could you betray me?"

Hunter rubbed his face, "Angie—"

"You broke my heart," Angie whimpered. "I've been waiting for this moment for seven long years." She reached into her pocket and pulled out a gun.

Hunter looked into the barrel.

"Angie, if you kill me, you'll never get out of this complex alive."

"I'm not sure I want to live anymore, Hunter." She pulled back the trigger and aimed the gun. As Hunter started to close his eyes, two huge arms came out of nowhere and grabbed the gun as a shot fired harmlessly in the air.

"Jesus." Hunter fell to the ground in a complete release of tension.

Agent Phil Styles had arrived in the nick of time.

Angie looked at Hunter and began to cry. Phil Held her tight.

No one said anything until two armed security guards arrived on the scene.

"Hunter, are you all right?" Phil asked.

Hunter nodded his head and looked at Angie, her deep green eyes and fiery red hair.

He'd been deeply and passionately in love with her, and to a certain degree, he still was.

"We'll take it from here, Agent Styles." Phil released Angie to them.

"Arriving sooner would have been better," Phil said to the security men.

"Sorry about that. We saw her waiting on a closed circuit camera and got here as soon as we could," the taller of the security agents said.

"Ms. Black, we're taking you into custody."

Phil helped Hunter up from the ground. "Damn, Phil," Hunter said, watching the men take his ex-wife away. "For seven years I've thought about seeing her."

"I know, I know, but you knew she would be dangerous after what happened."

Phil had thick black hair. He stood six feet four inches to Hunter's five feet ten. At first glance, Phil looked like a linebacker. A person you'd always want on your side.

"She said I broke *her* heart," Hunter said angrily, feeling the newly formed bump on the back of his head. "Well, she broke mine. Let's get out of here."

Phil and Hunter got in the Land Cruiser and started the trip to Pinehurst, North Carolina.

An old wound had been ripped open deep inside of Hunter.

However, if given the proper time, all wounds do heal, and this time the healing would be permanent.

3

The Release for Reason

I-95 South, North Carolina: 1535 ET

For the most part, the trip to Pinehurst was quiet. Hunter used a secure wireless connection on his laptop to finish going through his email while Phil drove. They took I-95 South into North Carolina. From Fayetteville, they took secondary roads around Fort Bragg into the city of Southern Pines. As they neared Pinehurst, Hunter shut down his laptop and watched the tree-lined terrain of the Sandhills Nature Preserve pass by. Hunter was thinking about Knox Long, but he was also thinking about Angie. The attack by his ex-wife and flashback to the past depressed him.

It was finally Phil who spoke first. "You know, Hunter, my ex would have killed me." Phil's ex-partner was a football player.

"True," Hunter sighed. He'd been to dinner many times with Phil and his former partner.

Phil continued, "It's not your fault, Hunter. Seven years ago you had to turn her in. She was a great agent, and she knew what she was doing. If you hadn't stopped her, someone else would have, and you would have been an accessory to the crime of treason."

"Yeah," Hunter said. "That's what I keep telling myself."

He never wanted to turn her in…he had to. He was lucky they let him keep his job after the fiasco. It had been a long, tough battle. He just wasn't ready to have any contact with her. He wasn't sure if he ever would.

But Hunter was thinking about the other things the incident had brought up. Hunter hadn't made the best decisions in his life, and at times like this, he felt like he was still paying a price. The past never seemed to go away. Yes he worked hard, but was that it? What was he missing out on?

Now he was on the way to meet Knox Long, one of the few people he'd looked up to all his life. Someone he had respected, like Angie, someone else he may have to destroy. *Was destroy, even the right word?* Hunter thought. Hunter took a deep breath and looked out the window, he noticed his reflection. A bruise was already forming on his face from where Angie had hit him. He knew it would be only temporary. The bruise on his soul had been there for seven years. Somehow, Hunter knew that this time, both bruises would go away. The past was slipping away and a door to his future was opening.

Phil and Hunter arrived in Pinehurst and checked into a hotel near the club. After an early dinner, they headed back to their rooms. "See you tomorrow," Hunter said. "Get your rest, we have less than three days until the deadline. After the meeting tomorrow, anything could happen."

Phil looked at Hunter. "Don't worry, I always sleep well after a long drive." Phil stopped. "And, Hunter, sorry about what happened with Angie."

"You probably saved my life today," Hunter said. "Most days, I still try to wrap my head around that relationship start to finish." He had worked with Phil Styles on various assignments for more than a decade. Hunter knew he understood.

"Goodnight," Hunter said as he pulled out his key card to his hotel room.

***

Wednesday, October 23

Pinehurst, North Carolina: 0645 ET

Hunter woke up the next morning half-remembering a strange dream. He was floating under the ocean in crystal-clear water. In the distance, he could make out a shape—a long, dark shape. He felt like it was getting closer and yet the shape never changed, it just seemed to hover.

Quickly waking up, Hunter shook off the remnants of the dream and got up to make himself a cup of coffee with the miniature machine provided by the hotel. He drank deeply and turned on the TV to view the news. The War in the Pacific had taken another deadly turn. Four U.S. fighters had been shot down over Guam. The stock market would probably open 599 points down from the day before. Hunter remembered the days when the stock market was somewhat stable. Now these daily dips came at any time, and people just shook their heads. Most of the trading was computer controlled anyway. He took another sip of coffee and got in the shower. Cranking up the hot water, Hunter looked at his watch: 0650. He had ten more minutes to get ready.

Hunter got dressed and pulled on his rubber-spiked golf shoes. He took the right shoe and slid open the heel, revealing a maze of electronics. Reaching into his briefcase he pulled out a lithium-hydrogen battery. He tapped the battery twice and slid it into the heel of his shoe. He closed his shoe and picked up his bag of clubs, a set of Callaway RAZR XX Black Irons. He was proud of these clubs. He grabbed a jacket and a sweater out of his bag and headed for the lobby.

When he arrived, he found Phil waiting with a full set of photography gear.

"Good morning, Hunter," Phil said, speaking quietly. "Oscar set up the meeting with Knox at 0730 this morning, right?"

"Right," Hunter replied.

"How are you doing?"

"Good, Phil, fine. Did you see the latest news?"

"Yes, with everything going on in the Pacific, I'm surprised we're on this mission. And I read the dossier on Long. Typical businessman, angry at the president. But doesn't seem like a threat."

"I know." Hunter knew the dossier didn't mention The Roswell Trinity.

The two men loaded the Land Cruiser and started for the club. It was 0705. As they pulled into the driveway leading to Pinehurst Country Club, Hunter actually started to feel better. He loved golf and had always wanted to come here. The club was a spirited toast to the beauty of golf. The grass was dark, rich, and green and the colors of the flowers bright, even for October. The Carolina sky was already a beautiful blue with the rising sun.

Hunter found a parking space. They got out and walked by more gorgeous shrubbery and flowers on the way to the clubhouse.

As they entered the pro shop a young woman came up to them. "Hi, I'm Cindy. What can I do for you?" she asked.

"We're here to meet Knox Long," Hunter replied.

"You must be," she paused to look at some notes on the counter, "Hunter Algier and Phil Styles from News Now. I read your site every day. Commander Long is in the club grill waiting for you."

"Thank you," Hunter replied with a smile. The two agents headed for the grill.

***

Back in Virginia, Oscar Morrow was already hard at work reading a paper slot-faxed to him overnight. The slot-fax was a way of sending critical, top-secret documents without the possibility of interception.

As Oscar Morrow read the last line, his face became flushed. He punched the intercom to his assistant. "Mark, have the helicopters on standby to fly to Pinehurst." In the next instant, he was on the phone to the White House. "This is Oscar Morrow, please get me the president." Oscar listened for a reply then said, "Code DB3."

***

It took a few minutes to find the grill. Hunter finally saw Knox sitting by himself watching the latest news on CNN concerning the Pacific War.

There's something strange about meeting someone you've always looked up to, Hunter thought. In person, they may shatter your beliefs about them. Hunter took a deep breath and walked up to Knox Long.

The commander heard his footsteps. "Hello Hunter," Knox said, without looking up.

Hunter was thrown off by the unexpected greeting, but only for a second. "Mr. Long, it's a privilege to meet you," Hunter said, extending a hand.

Knox looked up. Hunter noticed the commander's ice-blue eyes. Looking in those eyes, Hunter knew the commander had spent time on the edge of life. Maybe a little too much time. The eyes seemed to look right into Hunter, examining the very essence of his soul. Hunter didn't flinch.

"Let's get one thing straight, Mr. Algier. I don't like journalists, even if they do work for a service like News Now. And no one who knows me calls me Mr. Long." Knox looked Hunter in the eyes, "Knox or Commander will be fine."

"Certainly, sir, Knox." Hunter said. "I'd like you to meet—"

"Phil Styles," Knox interrupted considering Phil. *So far so good with the cover*, Hunter thought.

"You'll need to wait outside, Phil. I'm not ready for the camera yet. I need to know what the hell Hunter is going to ask me."

Phil held in the anger and looked at Hunter. Hunter slightly waved his hand to let Phil know it was okay. "I'll be by the car," Phil said as he started to walk out.

Knox motioned for Hunter to take a seat at the table.

Hunter tentatively sat down as Knox took a long look at him. "What the hell were you doing when I was on the Moon? Still pissing in your pants? Or no, you probably weren't even born."

Hunter looked at the man he had admired for so long. Knox was the youngest astronaut to go to the moon, and now he was in his early 70s. He was five eleven, with a very full head of graying hair. He had a solid build and a rugged face. Hunter wasn't sure how to start the conversation.

Knox Long evaluated Hunter again without saying anything. The silence was awkward.

"What happened to your face?" Knox finally asked, looking at the bruise left by Angie.

Hunter said the first thing that came to his mind. "I had to kick a little ass to get this story," Hunter said. If the commander wanted gruff, he'd give him gruff. He was also hoping to break the tension.

Knox leaned back in his chair. "Good," Knox laughed and got up from his seat. "I like a journalist with a sense of humor, but I hate interviews in country club grills. Get your favorite golf club and meet me at the practice tee in five minutes. I'd like to see your swing."

My swing? Hunter thought to himself.

Hunter watched Knox walk out the door. The commander was like nothing he expected. Was it an act? A gut feeling told him nothing would be easy on this mission.

Hunter went to the pro shop to get a bag of balls and then went back to the Land Cruiser to get his clubs. Phil was waiting in the passenger seat and got out as soon as he saw Hunter.

"Nice guy," Phil said sarcastically.

Hunter reached for his golf bag in the back of the car. "The commander wants to hit a few balls at the practice tee. Meet us out there in about twenty minutes."

"No problem," Phil said. "Do you feel secure?"

"As much as I can, Phil. Do you remember that time we were chasing the nuclear warhead taken from the C-130 cargo transport aircraft in Argentina?"

"How could I forget," Phil said. "I've got the scars to prove it. What in the hell made you think of it?"

"Remember the hunches we had to play?" Hunter paused. "That's how I feel now. Everything about this assignment seems problematic at best. All I've got is my instinct. It tells me to spend time talking to Knox to see what I can learn. I'll be all right."

"Yeah, Hunter, you've lived this long. Your instinct is a great attribute. But remember, it didn't tell you to duck when Angie hit you over the head." Phil smiled, hoping Hunter would take it the right way.

Hunter grinned though the emotional pain. "Yeah, Phil, I know. I know." That's why Phil was his best friend—they held each other accountable.

Phil pointed to the side of Hunter's golf bag. "By the way…the gun is in the third pocket. Good luck."

Hunter looked at the third pocket of the bag. It could all be over in an instant. He wanted to say something else, but it would have to wait.

Hunter followed the signs to the practice tee. Despite the tension he was feeling, he found solace in the intensity of the October day. Everything at Pinehurst seemed to be overly vibrant, from the grass to the trees to the sky. The day's coolness gave Hunter fresh energy.

Knox saw Hunter walk up to the tee and looked at his bag. "I thought I told you to get your favorite club," Knox laughed. "I guess some people need fourteen clubs all the time. Doesn't matter. Tee up a few. Let me see your swing."

Hunter relaxed and put down the bag. He took out his three wood and put a range ball on a tee. He looked at the commander.

"Go for it," Knox said, ready to watch.

Hunter warmed up with a few practice swings. Then he took a swing for real. He hit the ball, hooking it into the woods. Knox rolled his eyes.

Hunter continued to hit balls. Some were good shots, but most were bad. Knox said nothing, only watching Hunter, carefully evaluating his swing. The commander didn't seem to care where the balls went.

Then in the middle of a backswing, Knox asked a question. "So you're a journalist, huh?"

Hunter finished the swing, sending the ball into a nearby pond. He watched as the splash subsided.

"I can see a lot by a person's full swing," Knox said. "Whether you're relaxed, how you're breathing, and if your soul is smooth. You have a pretty good swing. Not like most journalists I know. Most of them are simply too impatient, too hurried. Must be the new media. My guess is being a pilot has helped you out as well."

"Pilot?" Hunter asked. *This guy is good*, Hunter thought.

"You swing like a pilot. And being a pilot my entire life, I've known a lot of them." Knox paused. "You're also frustrated. I can see that too. Hit another one."

Knox watched quietly as Hunter hit the ball.

"You recently had a near miss," Knox said. "And a woman tried to beat you up. Actually, it seems she's been beating you up for years. Then again, maybe you've been beating yourself up."

Hunter looked directly into Knox's ice-blue eyes. *Was this some kind of a joke? What did Knox see? How did he know? This is too weird,* Hunter thought. He felt like his instinct was about to end up in the nearby pond.

"Ah," Knox said knowingly, "now I sense some kind of indecision. Every swing tells a story, Hunter. As a journalist, you should know that."

Hunter cleared his throat. "Knox, not to be disrespectful, but the interview is supposed to be about you."

"That's right, but you seem like an interesting fellow. I just like seeing if I can figure people out. So the interview? You want to talk about the glory days of Apollo?"

"Yes sir."

"Well, Hunter Algier, let's play a round. I'll tell you about Apollo and I'll tell you about a great force, a force that took the hopes and dreams of this world to another world.

"I've been to the Moon, but all I did was fly there and walk on its surface. There's much more to the story the world should know. In fact, there's much more the world must know." Knox looked off into the distance. "And soon...it will. With your help, of course."

Hunter watched Knox as he said the last words, unsure of what to say.

Knox looked at Hunter. "Did you ever feel really alive, Hunter?" Knox looked up at the sky. "Up there on the way to the Moon, I felt alive. Looking back at this magnificent blue, tan, and white planet suspended in the blackness of space. Suspended effortlessly by the forces of nature. Looking back at the Earth from the Moon, I realized in both places, there's life and there is death." His intense eyes stared into Hunter's. "There's only a fine line between them. You've got to be smart enough to know the difference, and in some cases be able to cross the line."

As Knox paused to let the words sink in, Phil walked up to the practice tee. "You about ready?" Phil asked.

Knox looked at Phil and then turned to Hunter. "Just you, Hunter. Phil can join us later." With that, Knox started to walk away. "I'll see you at the first tee."

Hunter reached for the golf bag, unzipped a pocket, and pulled out his cell phone. "He's nothing like I expected," Hunter said to Phil as he dialed a number.

"What did you find out?" Phil asked.

"In five minutes? This one is going to take some time. I'd just wish Oscar had told me more," Hunter said, waiting for the call to go through. "All Knox said was the world will soon know more about Project Apollo. Whatever the hell that means."

"That it was faked?" Phil asked.

"If you said that to Knox," Hunter replied, "he would probably shoot you."

Hunter looked at the phone. "Damn, Oscar's not answering his secure line." Hunter put the phone back in his pocket. "I think I can get Knox to talk. I'm going to play a round of golf with him."

Phil looked at Hunter, "Seriously?"

"Well, it's a golf course," Hunter pointed out. "What the hell can happen on a golf course? Knox is our center of attention. I'll keep him contained right here. Just keep trying Oscar. Tell him Knox wants to talk. Apparently just about Apollo. Try to let me know if anything comes up. Text me. But I don't want to cut my conversation short if I don't have to."

"Look, Hunter, you sure? You don't have anything to prove you know," Phil said looking perplexed.

"I'd better go. I'll talk with you in a bit." Hunter picked up his golf bag and started making his way to the first tee as Phil walked back to the car.

Hunter rapidly found his way to the first tee. *The sooner the better*, he thought. When he arrived, Knox was there waiting, primed and ready to talk. "Here's the first thing to consider," Knox said the moment he saw Hunter. "If human footprints are on the Moon, anything is possible. All you have to do is discover the path to make it possible. How's that for a sound bite?"

"Remind me to get you to say that in the interview," Hunter said, putting down his golf bag and pulling out his driver.

Knox stood still and glared at Hunter. "Well, that's what I thought. If you want to sum up the trip to the Moon in a quote or a twenty-second sound bite, you can leave, and you can leave now. If you want to understand, truly understand, we're going to have to start from scratch."

Hunter's face flushed. "My apologies, Commander Long."

Knox backed down. "You're forgiven. Earlier your swing showed frustration. There's no release or transfer into the ball. I can help you lower your score and improve your life."

"I appreciate it," Hunter said. "But I'd like to ask you a few questions."

"There'll be plenty of time for that. Please, you start," Knox said as he gestured to the tee box.

Hunter took a practice swing with his driver. The first hole was a 400-yard par four, dogleg to the right. Hunter tried to concentrate on the game. He took his best shot and the ball flew to the left. It landed near some trees in the second tier of rough. *Not bad*, Hunter thought. He was clear of a large sand bunker.

"It's obvious you know the fundamentals of golf," Knox said as he set up his own shot. "The outline of your swing proves it. But your swing is not smooth internally because you're troubled. Learning about Project Apollo can help you sort things out so you can move on and get what you want, whether in golf or in life."

Hunter thought back to an old commercial he'd seen. *How did it go? If we can send a man to the Moon, why can't we make a better cup of coffee? Something like that.* Knox was sounding like a commercial. Hunter smiled inside at the thought of it and then took a stab at leading the conversation. "You've been very vocal against the current administration."

Knox looked at him. "The president doesn't promote space, neither does anyone in Washington, and that reveals major issues."

Hunter decided to give Knox a little verbal jab as he prepared to swing. "America went to the Moon. We explored it. It didn't solve any real issues back here. It wasn't a solution to our problems. Besides, I've heard all the metaphors in achieving goals. Just when you think you really understand the way the world works, something unexpected happens." Hunter thought back to Angie. "It's back to square one. 'Shooting the Moon' is just Peter Pan advice. I just don't see…"

Knox swung, hitting a beautiful shot that sailed down the fairway in a choreographed flight that took it perfectly to the right. The sound of the impact was sharp and clear, like a gun going off. Knox's swing was silky, effortless, and totally flawless.

The former astronaut paused to take it in; then he spoke, "Many times we have to go back to square one, to find out what it will take to get to square three. Besides," Knox continued, grabbing his bag, "Peter Pan could fly."

Hunter watched the golf ball land far down the fairway. "That was an amazing shot, Knox."

"It was a great shot," Knox quickly affirmed as he started walking, "because it was a complete release and transfer of power."

"Transfer of power?" Hunter asked as he hurried to catch up.

"That's all the golf swing is. A transfer of power." Knox looked at Hunter. "It's vital to remember the release. You're putting everything into the swing and letting go for an instant. You lose nothing by letting go. In fact, you gain everything." Knox stopped walking. "Swing at the ball with your problems, and your problems will disrupt the ball's flight. Swing at the ball with what is right, without fear, and the ball will fly exactly where you want it to go every time.

"But 'without fear' is a big thing. Not something a narrowed perspective can handle."

Hunter was still thinking about the shot. "How do I release the fear?"

"Let go of yourself."

"How do I let go?"

"Easy," Knox laughed. "You let go." He paused to let the words sink in. "Here's an easier way to look at it. No matter where you are in life, you face a line. A fine line. A fine line between standing still, and moving to get exactly what you want. A fine line between holding on and letting go. A fine line between a bad shot and a great shot. A fine line between asking for exactly what you want in life, or just taking what you get. A fine line between staying on the Earth, or going to the Moon. To get whatever it is you want, you must cross the line."

Hunter considered what Knox was trying to tell him. "How do I cross the line?"

Knox smiled. "I thought you wanted to talk about Project Apollo."

***

Phil was by the Land Cruiser, eating an apple, when he finally got through to Oscar on the cell phone.

"Where's Algier?" Oscar's voice expressed concern.

"He's on the course with Commander Knox Long. They just started a round."

"Phil, they're playing golf and you're not with them?"

"Knox wanted to talk to Hunter alone."

Oscar spoke rapidly, "Okay, at least Commander Long is contained. We're closing down the operation. We want to bring him in right now. We believe we have the evidence we need. Several helicopters are on the way. I'm flying down there myself. See you in a few hours."

"Yes sir," Phil said, wondering what had happened. The entire operation had been strange from the start, but ending it like this was unexpected.

***

Oscar put the phone down and looked into the eyes of the president of the United States. The president was clearly agitated. "So you think this entire scenario is possible."

"Yes, Mr. President," Oscar declared forcefully. Then he caught himself, "I would respectfully request we try it my way."

"Understood," the president said, straightening a cuff link.

Oscar looked at the leader of the Free World now in jeopardy, "I'm worried about Agent Algier."

"Commander Knox Long must be stopped. Your agent knew the risks." The president looked at Oscar. "He did know the risks, right?"

Oscar looked down.

"Then I want you to bring McCaully in on this as well."

Oscar tired to hide his disappointment. Commander Robert McCaully usually meant the operation would be messy.

The president snorted at Oscar's reaction. "Listen, do you think I have time for these personal visits to you in the midst of a war and an economy that flip-flops on a sneeze? How long have I known you? Thirty years, Oscar, thirty years. I fully protected you on the India-Pakistan nuclear debacle. I was the only one in the country who knew it wasn't your fault." The president paused, then added. "I'm your biggest fan. Don't let personal feelings of any sort get into it. This is big. If everyone's at risk, no individual can be protected."

"Yes, Mr. President," Oscar said. "We'll take care of it."

The president got up and walked to the door. He paused and turned, "Oscar, one final thing. Something I don't want to have to say in front of the press in the White House Briefing Room."

Oscar looked at the man who'd won his election by a landslide and still had popular support from both sides of the House and Senate.

"If Knox is successful, may God help us all." With that, the president left with a slam of the door.

With the sound of the door ringing in his ears, Oscar picked up the phone to find McCaully. Just outside Oscar's office a helicopter was already waiting for the trip to Pinehurst.

***

Hunter and Knox approached the carefully manicured green of the first hole. Hunter took a practice swing at a chip shot and then asked, "What's it like to go to the Moon?"

Knox scoffed, "Hunter, that question misses the point and that's why we haven't been back. That's not the real question. Of course it's glorious and magnificent. But that's because it's still outside the reality of basic human existence. Only twelve of us have walked there. That makes us rare. But Project Apollo is not the story of a magical or mystical journey to another planet. There's really no magic in the physical action of going to the Moon. The magic is imagining it happening. The magic is creating a plan and schedule. With a dream, a plan, and a schedule, that's how you get what you want. That's how you get to the Moon."

The commander considered his chip shot and said, "Apollo was, at the time, the largest effort ever undertaken by a nation not at war. But it's also a twenty-four-billion-dollar lesson on getting what you want. Apollo is a benchmark, a strategy, an attitude for achievement." Knox paused to look at Hunter. "This is the beginning," Knox said, as he hit a chip shot that rolled inches away from the hole. "It may be difficult for you to understand at first. As we walk and play this course this morning, we're going to talk about the flight plan, the reason, and the goal. We'll cover a lot of ground. This is the basis for everything else, so please stop me if you want to ask a question. Think about Apollo, but let your subconscious mind also absorb the fundamentals of golf."

"Okay," Hunter said. He'd have to go along with Knox for now. Maybe the billionaire would reveal something unexpectedly.

They approached the second hole: a par five, 555-yard dogleg to the left with a fairway surrounded by trees.

Knox put his ball on the tee. "Hunter, it all begins with reason."

"Reason?" Hunter asked.

"In May of 1961, President Kennedy said, 'I believe that this national should commit itself to achieving the goal, before this decade is out, of landing a man on the Moon and returning him safely to Earth. No single space project in this period will be more exciting, or more impressive to mankind, or more important for the long-range exploration of space: and none will be so difficult or expensive to accomplish.'

"Kennedy went on to say, 'We have vowed that we shall not see space filled with weapons of mass destruction, but with instruments of knowledge and understanding. Yet the vows of this nation can only be fulfilled if we in this nation are first, and therefore, we intend to be first.'"

Hunter was fascinated by how well Knox had memorized Kennedy's words. But then again, it was Kennedy's challenge that had put the commander on the lunar surface.

Knox continued, "Everyone remembers when Kennedy said, 'We set sail on this new sea, because there is new knowledge to be gained and new rights to be won and they must be won and used for the progress of all people.

"'We choose to go to the Moon in this decade, and do the other things, not because they are easy, but because they are hard; because that goal will serve to organize and measure the best of our energies and skills; because that challenge is one that we're willing to accept: one we are unwilling to postpone, and one we intend to win.'" As Knox finished, he stared into the sky.

Hunter tried to bring him out of it, "Knox?"

Instantly, Knox started talking again. "Hunter, as reason opened a path for us to get to the Moon, reason opens the path to your own success."

Hunter started to say something, but Knox jumped in. "You've got to have a reason behind your goal, Hunter. Those in life who say they don't have a concrete goal simply don't have a reason to have one. On the other hand, the people who get to the top, and get exactly what they want, have a reason to do so.

"The reason for what you want should be instinctive, because reason is the concrete foundation for your mission of success. Be specific about your reason, be sure about it.

"Reason helps you cross the line. It's the difference between happiness and depression, between a boom time and a recession, between staying here and going to the Moon. A reason starts from within. It can't be generic. It can't be someone else's. It must be yours! Reason leads to passion, passion leads to vision, and vision in the subconscious mind leads to the completion of your goal.

"Once you have the reason, write it down in a forceful way, with carefully chosen words. Keep your written reason close at hand, and close to you heart. Find the right reason for what you want to do, and you'll do it; whether it's run for office, climb

Everest or Kilimanjaro, lead an expedition to the South Pole, or take a dozen strokes off your golf game."

Knox smiled and the two men continued playing the course.

***

Back in the Pinehurst Country Club parking lot, Phil Styles reached in the back of the Land Cruiser. He moved Hunter's green sweater, opened a hidden compartment underneath, and pulled out two Sigma 9mm pistols. He checked the clip of each one.

***

On the course, Hunter was considering his next shot on the par four, 435-yard hole. He stopped for a moment to ask another question. "How do you find a reason if you're frustrated, angry, distracted, or just don't know what you really want?"

Knox frowned. "That's why this is the first step. Finding the right reason is a difficult problem."

"Then what's the solution?" Hunter asked.

Knox chose his next club and words carefully. "That is one of the barriers to crossing the fine line.

"What we're talking about is sometimes difficult to see, and difficult to explain. But I can tell you the right reason cannot be questioned once you have it. The right reason comes from the heart."

Knox paused to consider his shot. "America went to the Moon because we had a reason to. Some say it was political and it was. But the real reason we were able to do it? It's because we could see it. We knew we had to push ourselves in ways we never had. We haven't been back because this country, and the world for that matter, has no reason to go back. At least no obvious reason," Knox said as he laughed.

Maybe Hunter was on to something. He thought about his next question. "Okay, Knox, so how do I find the obvious reason for what I want to do and what would be the obvious reason to go back?"

"It's there. You've just got to see it."

"How do I see it?"

The commander paused to think, then looked at his golf club. Swinging his club in perfect form, Knox said, "To have the perfect form in this game, you must first start with the perfect golf swing in your mind. But that's only the beginning. When you translate the image from the mental to the physical, some finer points may become blurred. All the same, the perfect golf swing begins in your mind, as does the life you want. You've just got to have a reason to see it."

Knox swung. The ball flew a hundred yards and landed about a foot from the hole. The commander had an easy birdie. Satisfied with the shot, Knox looked at Hunter. "It gets back to transferring the power. To hit the golf ball well, you've got to transfer all of your power into the ball. You've got to let go of your 'self' and release. The release lasts less than an instant—and on that edge of infinity, everything changes." Knox pulled out a towel to wipe the end of his club. "Unfortunately, most people are afraid to let go, even for an instant."

"How do I let go?" Hunter asked.

Knox pointed at Hunter's heart. "Easy. You just let go from there."

Hunter and Knox continued the round. For a while no one said anything. Hunter didn't want to waste time. "When you have the reason, what comes next?"

Knox took a breath as they approached the seventh green. "Your goal should be simply stated, with a clear timeline. For going to the Moon, it was simply: man on the Moon safely in a decade."

"Use a slogan?" Hunter was puzzled.

"Use whatever it takes," Knox answered. "But it must light a fire in your soul."

Hunter was still confused.

"Here, Hunter, look at this." Knox reached into his pocket and pulled out an old business card—the front read *Knox Long, Moonwalker. If you really need me, it's not that hard to find me.* Knox flipped it over to reveal writing on the back. *As a tribute to the great game of golf, shoot at least six under par every round.* Knox looked at the card, smiled, and put it back in his pocket.

"It wasn't always that way. I started with a card that read: *As a tribute to the great game of golf, break 100.*

"Here we hit a speed bump. Some people say they have several goals, and don't know what they want to do first. So they wait and they wait. You don't want to wait. You must find a reason to take action on the goal you want most. And you've got to do it, right now. Look at all your goals, and act on the one that's closest to your heart.

"And that brings us back to Apollo," Knox continued. "The Moon is two hundred and forty thousand miles away. There's nothing between here and there, and the vacuum of space is a hostile place. To live in space, I had to use everything I'd learned on Earth to survive. At the same time, I had to be willing to leave the Earth behind. I had to release.

"It's an overwhelming mental challenge to release and let go, but when it's simply stated as 'A man on the Moon safely in a decade,' it wasn't a question of *if*. A man on the Moon was the only option. It wasn't a question of *when*. The deadline was the end of the decade. So the question was simply, *how*? Sounds like a familiar question, doesn't it, Hunter?"

Hunter hit a solid shot onto the green of the seventh hole. "Knox, you also said something about a 'timeline.'"

"The timeline is the deadline for completion of your goal. We'll talk about the timeline this afternoon. For now, let me ask you, what have you gotten out of this so far?"

Hunter picked up his bag and looked at Knox. "We'll, it's important to have a clear vision and reason for what you want, and a clearly defined goal and deadline. You must also be willing to let go." Hunter thought about what he had just said. *Pretty simple and obvious. But if it was so simple, how come he wasn't following this philosophy every day? Why couldn't he let go of the things that haunted him?*

Hunter picked up his ball out of the cup and started walking to the next hole. Everything was starting to change for him, and he knew it.

4

The Goal, Focused Passion, and a Flight Plan

Virginia/North Carolina border: 1031 ET

The lumbering NSA Pave Hawk helicopter was about one hour from the North Carolina border. Inside, Oscar Morrow sat on a makeshift rear seat facing Commander Robert McCaully. McCaully was nicknamed "The Eliminator" by his men. The government used him when they wanted a problem eliminated quickly and efficiently. McCaully was about getting the job done fast. If there was a mess, no worries. In just minutes, McCaully helped plan the ambush to capture Knox Long by using a yardage app downloaded for his phone from a golf website about Pinehurst. McCaully was smart, agile, and precise, at least he was most of the time. Oscar looked at him and wondered what would happen next.

The voice of the pilot came through the headset. "Mr. Morrow, we have a skyfax for you." Skyfax seemed like such an antiquated term for the technology that used triple encryption to secure information.

The pilot reached over his shoulder to hand Oscar the skyfax. Oscar leaned forward to get it. "It's from Nevada operations," Oscar said to McCaully. "They say they've found the missing helicopters, the two Apaches. The VIS hardware and pilots are missing. It says, 'We have reason to believe it was an inside job, start to finish. This kind of technology can be devastating in the wrong hands. We hope Long provides answers.'" Oscar looked at McCaully and said, "If Knox Long is willing to admit to anything."

Oscar crumpled the piece of paper and put it in a small clear plastic bag. He took the bag and squeezed it, breaking a fluid filled pouch inside.

"I sure as hell hope we're not too late," Oscar said as he watched the paper dissolve.

***

Back on the greens of Pinehurst, birds chirped and the sun released its warmth on the two players.

"So you have a reason and a goal. Steps one and two. So let's move on to the third step," Knox said. "A very important step. Focused passion."

"Focused passion," Hunter repeated as he studied the next shot.

"To succeed," Knox began, "the reason and the goal must generate passion. Passion will cause you to take the steps to achieve whatever it is you want. It's a fire in your gut." Knox pointed at Hunter's stomach and then continued. "Passion is about the love of what you're doing; courage and vision; being decisive; having faith; optimism, instinct, and determination.

"But, Hunter, here's something most people forget."

Hunter looked at Knox.

"In our world today, it's easy for people to lose focus. Not being focused costs time. And time is our most precious asset. That's why you've got to stay committed to your real goals. You can't multitask your way to what you really want. You've got to find the exact flight plan. Everything else is a distraction. If you've found your goal and you have all the right reasons, screw everything else."

Knox had Hunter's full attention now. For the first time, Knox appeared agitated. "The universe may want you to get what you want, but sometimes the rest of the world couldn't give a damn.

"Focused passion is about exploration, ingenuity, and eagerness to achieve your goal. It's about the best of what's already past and the best of what's to come; giving a lot, expecting a lot, doing the job."

Skipping the break at the clubhouse turn, they were now at the tenth tee. A par four, 485-yard dogleg to the right through a nasty field of well-positioned sand traps. Knox gestured for Hunter to tee off first. Hunter swung the driver and the ball few in an easy flight. *Not bad*, Hunter thought.

Knox stepped up to the tee as Hunter watched him swing. This time Hunter watched for the release as Knox hit another beautiful shot down the fairway.

Knox looked at Hunter and laughed. "You were probably watching for my release. It's up here," Knox said, pointing to his head.

The two men started walking down the fairway. Knox sighed and continued. "So you have a reason, a goal, and passion. Next you need a path to get there, a flight plan," Knox said. He stopped and looked at Hunter. "Am I throwing too much at you?"

"No, I'm just trying to sort it all out," Hunter replied, even though he was losing focus.

Knox detected it. "Stay with me, Hunter. This information is very important. The basis for everything else. Think about your swing but keep an open mind. You asked earlier, 'How did we get to the Moon?'"

"Yes," Hunter answered, while taking a practice swing.

"The ultimate test of going to the Moon would be broken down into steps," Knox said. "First, NASA and the other contractors involved checked their inventories of accomplishments. Since nobody knew exactly how to get a man to the Moon, the experts focused on detailing out a flight plan and looking at the steps that would need to be taken, including Project Mercury and Project Gemini. But most people forget those pivotal building blocks.

"Driven by passion and mission and country, the scientists began to imagine *how* we would get to the Moon. Then, like most everyone else faced with a problem, they got a pencil and some paper, and started asking the right questions."

Hunter swung, hitting a fairly nice shot towards the green.

Knox watched the swing, and kept on talking. "We asked questions like: Do we take one ship? Do we take two? Do we need to build some kind of contraption in Earth's orbit and fly to the Moon? Do we have two ships in lunar orbit, with only one capable of flying down to the surface of the Moon? Do we blast a rocket to the Moon, land it there, and send the crew supplies until we can figure out how to get the crew back?

"Companies designed plans to get to the Moon, tested them, and designed some more. Prototypes were rejected, prototypes blew up, and prototypes sank. But no matter what happened, everyone involved in the project just kept asking the right questions, in fact, any question asked was the right question. The thing that scared us the most were the questions no one thought to ask.

"Finally, the engineers dreamed and planned the design of a powerful, three-stage rocket called the Saturn V. The first stage would provide the most thrust to get our spacecraft off the ground. The second stage provided the additional kick needed to push us higher and faster. The third stage would be used twice. First, it would put us into Earth's orbit. A short time later, the third stage would be fired again to send us to the Moon. What a ride that was.

"As we coasted to the Moon, our spacecraft separated from the third stage. That left three key vehicles: The Command Module, the Service Module, and the Lunar Module. The Command Module was where we'd spend most of our time and where the key systems were. The Service Module was attached behind the Command Module to provide us with fuel, water, electricity, oxygen, and other critical needs for the trip.

"After three days in flight, we'd enter orbit around the Moon. After a few hours to test equipment, the Lunar Module would take another astronaut and me to the surface of the Moon.

"That's basically 'Moon Voyage: 101,'" Knox said, as he hit an amazing right to left shot around some trees.

"Now back to your flight plan," Knox said. "With your reason, goal, and passion, you begin to write out the steps that will get you to what you want. You do that by asking the right questions: What are the things you already have, right now, to help take you to your goal? What steps have you already taken? What steps will you need to take now and in the near future? What can you learn from other people and what they've done? What can you learn from your past mistakes and past accomplishments? What powerful action will be required as you start?

"Some of the questions will be easy to answer, others will require dedicated research. If you become frustrated, remember: A trip to the Moon is nothing more than a series of steps. The trip to your ultimate goal is just the same.

"A warning: You've got to come up with your own flight plan. Because if you don't, you'll have no choice but to follow the flight plan someone else selects for you. When you do that, you won't be going to your own goal. You'll be dissatisfied."

"But shouldn't I provide support to others?" Hunter asked.

"I'm not saying you shouldn't help other people, but you must be focused on your own goal. That's the key." Knox let the words hang as they reached the green of the eleventh hole.

***

In the skies over North Carolina the Pave Hawk took a momentary dip.

"Sir," the pilot of the helicopter said to Oscar. "We may have a problem. We may need to land. Could be a slight issue."

"Damn," grumbled Oscar. "How long can you keep going?"

"We'll do our best, sir. But I wanted to give you a heads up."

"Shit," Oscar said, as he looked at McCaully. "We don't have time for this."

***

The round of golf was going fast. They were getting ready to putt on the fourteenth hole.

"Hunter, let's move on," Knox said. "We have a reason, a goal, focused passion to get us there, and a flight plan. Let's talk about vision, which, in a way, all comes down to mental toughness.

"Before you implement the flight plan, you're got to test it in your mind. Let me ask you something: what is going through your mind as you hit that putt?"

Hunter paused and thought about it. "I'm looking at the break, thinking about the force it will take to get the ball over that bump in the green."

"But what else?"

"I'm thinking about my line…"

"You're visualizing," Knox said.

"Visualizing?" Hunter asked.

"Correct. Before you hit the ball, you play out where it will go in your mind. If you didn't, you couldn't sink it.

"What was the first step in going to the Moon? We had to know it was possible. We had to see it was possible. Once we had that vision, we were already well on our way. We can never forget that. Sadly, I think some have." Knox paused to let that sink in.

"You've got to run the mental program first, before you can run the physical program. It's the same in goal setting. After you've determined what you want and you've come up with the flight plan, you take each step in your mind, before you take each step physically."

Hunter visualized the putt and saw it go in. He hit the ball…and sank it. Hunter looked at Knox. "Thanks."

"Don't thank me, thank yourself," Knox said. "When designers came up with the flight plan for each Apollo mission, they tested the plan through realistic simulations on Earth.

"During the simulations, we were instructed on what to look out for so we could make the right decisions during the actual flight. By testing the flight plan first through these simulations, the real mission could be refined with lower risk. I slept a lot better too.

"When it finally came time to go, we were ready. We'd seen success in the simulations, and for the most part we'd trained our fears away. In fact, when I landed on the Moon, I simply thought back to one of my flawless performances in the simulator back on Earth.

"You've got to rehearse your plan in your mind every day, and you've got to rehearse for success. If you do, you'll know exactly where you're headed, and you'll be able to tell if you're on the right path. More action will follow. There's a compounding effect."

Hunter thought about it. *It makes good sense: rehearse for success, and you'll be assured of success.* The two men continued to play the course.

As Knox got ready for the next shot over a long stretch of water on the sixteenth hole, he said, "Hunter, you've got everything you need in your life right now to get whatever you want, because you've got the most powerful tool of all. A tool more mighty than the rocket that took us to the Moon. That tool is your mind. Use your brain first, then your body."

Hunter understood the importance of this step. The mind creates both the goal, and the path and focus to achieve the goal. Hunter's expression changed. His goal was to stop Knox Long. *But why? Where was the danger? The Roswell Trinity?*

Knox looked at Hunter, noticing the change in his expression. "Are you okay?" Knox asked.

"Fine," Hunter coughed. "Please continue."

Knox started again. "The ability to imagine and hold on to your goal is what keeps your inner passion alive. By mentally visualizing the flight plan to get to your goal and mentally taking the steps, you show your subconscious mind the way. If your subconscious mind knows the way to achieving a goal and the rewards involved with success, it will lead you to take action."

As Knox finished, Hunter heard a cell phone ring. He thought it was coming from his own bag. He almost started to say something, but then he realized he'd put his phone on vibrate.

"Sorry, Hunter. Hang on." Knox unzipped a large pocket of his bag and pulled out his own cell phone. As he did, Hunter caught a glint from a piece of heavy metal inside. It looked like some kind of gun. Knox looked at Hunter, quickly zipping up the pocket.

Knox touched the front of the phone to answer it.

"This is Knox…Hello, Greg…Okay…Fine…about 50 hours…

"Try the quick fill again just to be sure. Do me a favor and run through plans B and C again with the staff. Check security as well."

Knox listened, and then finally said, "Right, see you soon." Knox touched the face of the phone to end the call and put the phone back in his bag, this time in a smaller pocket.

Knox smiled. "I only barely remember when you could really get away from work on a golf course."

Hunter started to say something, but Knox talked first, "Okay, I've done a lot of talking," Knox said. "What have you learned?"

Hunter answered thoughtfully, "Whether you think you can do something or you can't do something—either way, you're right. What you imagine is what you make real."

"A good basic start," Knox said.

Hunter continued, "You need a reason, a goal, passion for the goal, and a flight plan to get there. But I think your key point is—whatever you imagine is possible, you've just got to take the steps. Visualize those steps in your mind and then physically take action with a dedicated focus. The mind-goal link is what's most important."

"Hunter, you know it, but have you crossed the fine line? Do you really believe what you just said?" Knox asked.

"I'm not sure."

"That's the problem, you've got to be sure. If you want proof of what you can do, look at the things you have in your life right now, evaluate them carefully. Look at your accomplishments and what you've done. Most of the great things you imagined first. You didn't buy those achievements; you paid for them with your thoughts. Material wealth cannot take you to your goal; mental wealth is the only way. It's not about your bank account; it's about your brain account.

"But," Knox said, "some people would still rather use their bank account, or worse, credit. Consider this: A person spends four hundred dollars on a new golf club for their game. They take the club to the course, use it, but never really improve. Why? They think having this high-tech club in their bag will make them hit like the pros. But these people forget it's not what the pros have in their bag, it's what the pros have in their mind. The mental edge.

"If you decide to do something, and the first thing you have to do is spend a lot of money to do it, that should be a warning sign. Having to buy something, to achieve something, is a secret way to procrastinate. In many cases we don't get to our goal because we don't use what we already have.

"The bottom line? Real goal achievement comes from the inside out. Remember: You must mentally achieve the goal first before you can physically achieve it. You've got to know it's possible before you can show it's possible.

"Remember the strategy of Apollo. Once NASA had the vision in place, they built the Saturn V. A marvelous 363-foot, six-and-a-half-million-pound rocket with the power of a small atomic bomb. It had six million parts, operating together like a Swiss watch. Such a majestic rocket. Five hundred million man-hours went into it, with exquisite attention to detail. It was our pyramid for the twentieth century.

"We took this pyramid and left the Earth. We were on our own. We had to trust our spaceship and we had to trust ourselves.

"We were put though simulations so we wouldn't fail. Apollo was designed so it wouldn't fail either. The equipment was sound. If your car's tires were designed the same way, you'd only have to check their pressure once in a lifetime. The insulation surrounding some of the fuel tanks in Apollo was so effective it would take an ice cube inside eight years to melt. And with all this, came redundancy at every stage. Success was our only option.

"Hunter, why can't success be the only option?"

"That's a valid question, Knox," Hunter replied as he prepared for the next shot. They were at the seventeenth hole. A par four, 400-yard straight uphill challenge.

Hunter took a practice swing as Knox continued talking. "Various pieces of the rocket were shipped in from across the United States to the Kennedy Space Center in Florida. That's where we built the Apollo Saturn V spacecraft. We did it in the massive Vehicle Assembly Building, the VAB.

"The VAB was designed so well it was used years later for the shuttle program. The closer you get to this monstrosity, you begin to lose all sense of scale. Walking along the transfer aisle inside the building, on the ground floor, it's hard to believe the roof is 525 feet over your head. Add another thirty feet and you could store the Washington Monument inside.

"The statistics are staggering. The VAB is made from 98,590 tons of steel. The air conditioning it uses can cool three thousand homes. This technology is more than thirty years old. When you were inside the VAB, looking at a Saturn V ready for flight, a strong feeling went through you. You were looking at dreams turned into reality.

"Once the Apollo spacecraft was put together, the team took it from the VAB to the launch pad. Massive transports, called crawlers, did the work. These monstrosities were in use even during the shuttle program. Each crawler generated six thousand horsepower to move the rocket and its support equipment one mile an hour. Everything together weighed twelve million pounds. It took fourteen men an hour and a half just to get a crawler started. The massive machine moved on eight tread belts, with fifty-six treads on each belt. Each tread weighs two thousand pounds. To keep its payload almost perfectly level when going up or down hill, the crawler had a hydraulic system that kept the very top of the spacecraft within the small arc the size of a soccer ball. Driving a crawler would seem like an unexciting job, right?"

Knox didn't give Hunter time to answer. "Wrong, it was run by people who loved the job, even though they were in danger of losing their hearing. That's right. The engines were so loud that workers could only stay on board for a half hour before they had to take a break. It was run by people who said, 'It's a dirty and noisy job,' even though they wouldn't want to do anything else. They were building a pathway to the future and they knew it.

"I ask you this, Hunter, who says we can't handle the heavy loads we're sometimes asked to carry? Who says we can't journey over obstacles that confront us and keep things on an even keel? Apollo shows us we can."

Knox took his position at the tee. They were now at the eighteenth hole, a 405-yard par four with a small stream protecting the green. Knox hit a beautiful shot that followed the course to the right. Two hundred seventy yards. He continued talking immediately following his swing.

"Once the Saturn V was in place at the launch pad, the countdown got under way," Knox said. "The launch was controlled from the impressive firing room at the Kennedy Space Center. The room is designed to keep people focused on the mission. Like the other creations for Apollo, it was even used in the shuttle program.

"I've stood in the firing room and watched people work. First you notice the mission patches framed on the wall. Then you notice the computer screens providing information in every color of the rainbow. Then you see the people. The passionate drive they all have. I remember looking out the window of the firing room, watching Apollo prepare for launch. It was magical, but it was real. The firing room was designed by people with a passion, a reason, and a flight plan with the goal of keeping humanity reaching up.

"Kennedy Space Center is inspirational. It really is larger than life. It's a tribute to our dreams. A tribute to what we've done as a nation yesterday, what we'll do today, and what we'll do tomorrow. It's the front door to the future. And its power is rooted deeply in the force it took for us to get to the Moon."

Hunter thought, *What could be so bad about Knox Long? He was just a man driven by passion. But why wasn't he sharing this passion with the rest of the world?*

"You still want to know how we got to the Moon?" Knox said, breaking Hunter's train of thought.

"I'm beginning to see the path," Hunter replied.

"Remember, Hunter, seeing the path, and walking down the path are two very different things. Consider this: on January 27,

1967, astronauts Gus Grissom, Ed White, and Roger Chaffee died in a fire on board Apollo 1. I'll never forget that day. I was at the Cape. It was a 'plugs out' test. The spacecraft was pressurized with oxygen. Somehow a spark ignited a fire. The men were asphyxiated. But instead of giving up in the face of catastrophic failure, we scrambled to find out what went wrong. We completely redesigned the spacecraft.

"Once the new designs were in, it was time to step out again. First, NASA had to launch the Apollo spacecraft into orbit and test it. That was the job of Walter Schirra, Don Eisele, and Walter Cunningham on board Apollo 7.

"The next step was to see if we could fly around the Moon. Frank Borman, Jim Lovell, and William Anders did just that on board Apollo 8, and gave the world a wondrous Christmas present in December of 1968.

"In March of 1969, we launched Apollo 9 with James McDivitt, David Scott, and Russell Schweickart on board. They tested the Lunar Module in Earth's orbit.

"Two months later, in May, Apollo 10 journeyed back to the Moon. Tom Stafford, John Young, and Gene Cernan took the Command, Service, and Lunar Module to lunar orbit and rehearsed for a landing on the Moon. Stafford and Cernan came within fifty thousand feet of the lunar surface in the Lunar Module Snoopy, but didn't land.

"It was only after all these carefully planned steps that we were ready to land on the Moon by Kennedy's deadline. On Sunday, July 20, 1969, at 4:10 p.m., Neil Armstrong and Buzz Aldrin landed the Lunar Module Eagle on the Moon, while Michael Collins orbited in the Command Module Columbia overhead. At 10:56 that night, thirty-eight-year-old Neil Armstrong stepped on the Moon, and 'For one priceless moment,' the world stopped and watched a dream fulfilled.

"Between 1969 and 1972 we landed on the Moon six times with the missions of Apollo 11, Apollo 12, Apollo 14, Apollo 15, Apollo 16, and Apollo 17. I'm only one of twelve Americans to have walked on the Moon. But we are only a reflection of the three hundred and fifty thousand people and twenty thousand companies it took to get there and the millions of dreamers."

Then Hunter said something he'd regret, "Man, it's a miracle we were able to do it."

Knox turned and looked at him sharply and said, "Some would say miracle. But make sure you're listening, Hunter. Our voyages to the Moon came about by simply asking the right questions, seeing we could do it, and then taking steps until we achieved the goal. The step Neil Armstrong took in 1969 was part of a walk first taken by President Kennedy in 1961.

"Goal achievement is about the steps you're willing to take to get what you really want. You do understand that, don't you?"

"Yes," Hunter said.

Knox looked at Hunter. "As you build the flight plan, you must keep a perspective that makes each challenge manageable. Sometimes that's not easy. If a challenge becomes overwhelming, consuming, and confusing, you may allow it to become magnified, and it will shadow the reason for achieving your goal. If the reason is lost behind a shadow, you'll lose your way.

"If a challenge seems overwhelming, break it down. If a challenge seems consuming, fortify your reasons for solving it. If a challenge seems confusing, look to other sources to find out how other people have handled the challenge successfully. If your goal is in the shadows, shine the light of passion and reason on it.

"Remember the story I started about the person buying a new club to improve their golf game?" Knox asked.

"Yes."

"Let's say that person decides to take another path. They still want to improve their golf game, but this time, they're going to use what they already have. First, they need a reason: they want to win, no questions asked. They set a goal and a timeline: the person wants to win a tournament by the end of summer. They want to win, and they're passionate about it. So they set up a flight plan that includes constant physical and mental practice. To help them visualize what it's like to win, they watch the pros on television or visit a tournament. They watch how the pros swing their clubs, how they handle the competition, and how they relate to others. Then the person takes physical action on the plan. And if they stick to it, with the right motives, they have the best opportunity to win.

"The Bible says, 'Seek and ye shall find.' Seek what's in your mind. Seek the mental images that empower you. Imagine inside what it takes to get what you want and you'll produce the physical actions to get to your goal."

Hunter and Knox were nearing the green on the eighteenth hole. Knox smiled, and said, "To summarize, you've got to realize this: when you work to achieve any goal, know in your mind that you're already there. Think about that. You're already there. That's what visualizing is really all about."

Knox hit a chip shot onto the green. "Remember, the spirit behind Apollo is to be proactive. Don't react to the stuff you don't like, reach out for the goal you want." Hunter took his turn. His swing was better; he was relaxed and concentrating. Knox only smiled and said, "The battle with your 'self' is the biggest challenge."

Hunter and Knox finished the round. Knox had shot eight under par. Hunter added up his score and found he'd shot an eighty-two. His best score ever.

Knox looked at Hunter's reaction to the score and laughed. "You were concentrating on more than golf. Your subconscious mind was focused, so you weren't hung up on all the little variations of golf. Hunter, you were focused on the big picture, and therefore, you shot a corresponding score."

Hunter was feeling good, until he saw Phil waiting for them. The reason for the mission became clear again.

"Hunter, are you ready for the camera?" Phil asked. Hunter started to say something, but Knox stopped him. "No, no cameras yet. Hunter and I have much more to discuss."

Knox quietly said to Hunter, "We'll start another eighteen in an hour. I've got to go back to my room and make some calls and order some room service for lunch."

As Knox walked away, he said, "Remember, Hunter, you're moving on to what you can be, to what you can achieve. This is not just about the exploration of the Moon, it's about the exploration between your imagination and what you make real.

"The countdown to launch has already started. In fact, it's been underway for some time. We've got a great mission in front of us!" With that, Knox turned a corner, and was gone.

"What the hell was that all about?" Phil asked.

"It's a long story," Hunter said, picking up his bag. "Did you get in touch with Oscar?"

"Yes, he wants to close the operation down. In fact, he's coming down to personally pick up Knox himself"

"Where is he?" Hunter asked.

"There's been a slight delay," Phil replied as he led Hunter to the clubhouse.

***

Oscar's helicopter sat in the middle of a field.

"Damn, if Hunter was here he'd have us off the ground!" Oscar yelled at the pilot.

"I'm sorry, sir. It's one of those things. The backup helicopter is on the way," the pilot explained.

"I just hope it's not too late." Oscar looked at his watch.

***

"An hour?" Hunter asked Phil. They were now sitting outside the clubhouse.

"Oscar said an hour at best," Phil confirmed.

"That agency helicopter was always a piece of shit," Hunter said as he looked at the sky, thinking about his conversation with Knox. "Okay, Phil, let's get something to eat."

They went to the grill and ordered the Wednesday special: Carolina Club Sandwiches. As they ate, Hunter thought about the conversation he'd had with Knox. *It all made perfect sense. Have a reason, a goal, and passion for the goal. Create a flight plan to achieve it and then visualize it happening. If you take action on something you already know will work, you can't fail.*

Phil devoured his first sandwich and ordered another one. "You're being pretty damn quiet, Hunter. What the hell was he telling you out there?"

Hunter considered his words carefully. "Knox is intensely focused on Project Apollo and going to the Moon. You should hear him talk, 'Reason, passion, vision.' He says those are the things that got us there. A lot of what he's saying makes perfect sense. He talked about being part of the program. But there's something more. He had a phone in his bag. On the seventeenth hole he took a call and said something about fifty hours and a quick fuel."

Phil was perplexed. "Fifty hours would be close to the five p.m. Friday deadline."

"Yes, of course, but it could be half a dozen things. Then he said he'd see the person on the phone soon."

"Do you remember a name?" Phil asked.

"Greg."

"Greg Mitchell, as in General Greg Mitchell," Phil quickly pointed out.

"I know. He ran Echo Air Force base. Or at least what was once Echo Air Force base."

The cell phone rang. Hunter picked it up and slid the switch. "Algier here."

The voice at the other end of the line sounded troubled. "Hunter?" It was Oscar. "We need a little more time, at least another hour. How's it going? How's our friend?"

"He's not here right now. But—"

Oscar interrupted, "You let him leave?"

"Oscar, he's coming back. I know he is," Hunter said confidently.

"What did you learn?" Oscar asked quickly.

"He's obsessed with Project Apollo, I think he's connected with General Greg Mitchell, and he may be preparing a launch or a flight of some kind," Hunter said, providing the key headlines. "How many units are coming?"

There was a pause on the line. "Delta and Tango." Then Oscar asked, "What's your plan?"

Hunter thought for a moment. "We're supposed to start another round in a few minutes. You'll have to take him into custody on the course. Oscar, don't let them screw this up. And tell them not to blow my cover unless it's absolutely necessary."

"We'll see you out there."

Hunter hung up the phone and looked at his watch. "Phil, there's only two things I know for sure right now."

"Yes, Hunter?"

"Oscar's not telling us everything," Hunter said confidently.

"What makes you say that?" Phil asked.

"Another hunch."

"What's the other thing?"

"Commander Long has a gun in his bag."

5

The Threshold of Time

Pinehurst Country Club, North Carolina: 1300 ET

As Hunter walked to the first tee, he looked at his watch. Only a few minutes left to obtain information on his own. Once Knox was in custody, Hunter could be reassigned to another mission and miss this opportunity. He looked ahead and saw the commander expectantly waiting at the tee.

Knox spoke clearly. "Good afternoon, Hunter. Start whenever you're ready." Hunter put down his bag and pulled out a club. He started to do some warm up swings. The first hole was deceptively simple: 416 yards uphill to a tranquil green surrounded by trees. A small water hazard was the only trouble.

Hunter could hear a helicopter in the distance. *Oscar is close*, he thought to himself.

Less than a mile away, the first of two unmarked army-gray helicopters landed. Four men with semi-automatic weapons hit the ground running. According to Robert McCaully's plan, they would set up a perimeter around the green of the third hole.

Knox turned to Hunter. "What's the quickest way to fail to achieve a goal?"

"I would say simply don't take action to achieve the goal."

"That's right," Knox nodded. "Failure is the end result of procrastination. So even if you have reason, a goal, passion, a flight plan, and vision, it doesn't matter unless you take action.

"Life is about time and how you look at it. Life is not limited, but time is. So don't waste any of the shots you get."

As Knox finished, the sound of another helicopter could be heard in the distance. Knox twisted around to see where it was coming from. Hunter held his composure. Knox turned back to Hunter and gave a subtle smile.

"Okay," Knox said, "before you hit your shot, think about this: What if this was the last time you'd ever get to hit a golf ball? How would you consider the shot?"

Hunter thought about the question. "If this was the last time, I'd be careful about what I was risking. I'd want to hit a good shot, so I'd take my time to make sure it was worth it."

Knox took a look in the direction of the helicopters again.

He knows, Hunter thought. *He knows they're here. And yet he's calm.*

Knox nodded his head, "But what's the bottom line?"

Hunter looked back at Knox and said, "I guess I wouldn't want to waste the shot."

"Then don't waste this one," Knox warned.

Hunter swung; the impact was clean and crisp. It was one of the best balls he'd ever hit. Whether he was nervous, whether he was concentrating, or perfectly distracted, it didn't matter. The only thing that mattered was the pure release. Hunter relished the feeling as the ball flew. It landed with a polite bounce in the middle of the fairway. It was simply perfect. Hunter knew it and he felt a chill. He'd glimpsed another reality.

Knox simply watched. He'd obviously seen something like this before. "My friend, that's the essence of golf: making each shot count. It's the essence of life as well."

Hunter watched as the commander took deliberate time putting the tee in the green grass and setting a new ball on top of it. Knox got set, carefully taking more time. Then, without hesitation, he hit a brilliant shot that sailed down the fairway in a gracefully clean arc. The ball rolled ten yards farther down the fairway than Hunter's.

The two men picked up their bags and started walking.

Oscar's helicopter was the third to land in an area where a new golf course was under construction. Phil ran to the door of the chopper as Oscar slid it open. "Good to see you, sir," Phil said, slightly out of breath. "Hunter and Knox just started a few minutes ago. Delta and Tango Companies are taking up positions around the third hole as instructed." Oscar and Robert McCaully got out of the helicopter.

"Good, Phil. I'd like you to meet Commander Robert McCaully. He planned the operation to retrieve Knox Long."

"Good to meet you," Phil said as the three men started walking to the third hole.

Knox and Hunter were ambling up a hill where they'd play their second shots. "What's in front of you right now is most important," Knox said as he selected a club. "Think about the past too much and you miss the future. Think about the future too much and you miss the present. Live and act right now, with the right motives, and you don't miss out on anything, there's nothing to wait for, and the past and future are always bright."

Walking to where his ball had landed, Hunter paused. "Wait a minute," he said. "If I'm supposed to plan for the future, but also concentrate on the present, how can I do both?"

Hunter tried to hit the shot, but he was more worried about time. *Where would the ambush be?* Hunter took a swing. The ball landed in the deep rough about seventy yards away to the far right of the green.

"You see the impact your concerns had on your shot and your vision?" Knox asked. "Remember, how you hit the ball is nothing more than an amplification of your soul."

"I think my question is valid," Hunter said.

"You want to know how you can concentrate on the present and still plan for the future?" Knox asked.

"Yes," Hunter said as he watched Knox hit a fade that found its way to the green.

By now, Delta and Tango Companies were positioned on one side of the third green. "Delta, Tango have set the trap," a man said into a communications link.

On the other side of the trees, in the fairway, Knox and Hunter continued their walk to the green. "As you mentally compose your flight plan," Knox said, "you must mentally visualize the completion of it in the present. In other words, you're already there. That's why the mental vision of the fight plan is so important."

"I'm already there?" Hunter asked.

"You're already there," Knox repeated. "You're already there because of time."

"Time?" Hunter asked, considering the sand traps by the green.

"Time is life, because time allows you to breathe," Knox said. "To survive right now, that's all you need. Your ability to breathe. So, don't take this breath for granted; cherish it. Now exhale, and mentally move to the next breath and the next moment.

"As you take your next breath realize this: Time is the one thing most people don't really understand until they're taking their last breath. All their life they think about the past and the future and then, only at the end, do they realize their time here is over in an instant. All they really had was right now, this breath. So if you're angry, frustrated, or worried about what's past or what's to come, stop what you're doing for a moment and breathe.

"Take another deep breath and know your life is only as great as you make it right now. It's up to you, you're in control and you're already there. 'Now' is the journey to the future."

They walked up to where Hunter's ball had landed.

"Hunter, you know the fundamentals. When you hit the shot this time, simply focus on right breathing."

Hunter decided not to worry about Oscar for a second. Instead, he concentrated on each breath. He carefully took his time with his swing and the ball took off flying a strategic high trajectory, coming to rest just inches from the second hole.

"Good, Hunter," Knox said, "nice shot. Now, as you focus on breathing, open your mind. Recognize the things life puts in front of you every second, the footholds and pathways offered."

A lookout saw Knox and Hunter make the turn. The soldiers surrounding the green sat motionless with their weapons. Phil, Robert, and Oscar approached a camouflaged makeshift bunker behind a tree.

"What do you mean by footholds?" Hunter asked. They were now at the green of the second hole.

"Chances, opportunities. The ladder to climb to the next level of life," Knox said.

"How will I see the footholds?" Hunter asked.

"You've got to look around and see things you haven't seen before, colors you haven't seen before, sounds you haven't heard. Have you noticed the beauty of this course this afternoon?"

Hunter had earlier, but now he was focused on everything else. He took in the environment. It was a beautifully manicured course and an incredible day, even though clouds had rolled in, bringing the possibility of rain.

"Once you understand the power of breathing and the power of your surroundings, you can really appreciate everything life has to offer," Knox said.

"What's the next step?" Hunter asked.

"The next step is to use time effectively," Knox said, stopping for a moment. "To use time effectively, you've got to have a project that makes you forget about time and focuses you on right now. A goal that gets you up in the morning. A goal that energizes you and gives you vision.

"When we deal with time in spaceflight, we use a 'timeline.' The timeline is by when we have to perform a specific task. It's connected directly into our flight plan for completing the mission.

"We had to be careful to stay on the timeline or ahead of it. In space, a poorly executed timeline would be disastrous. If we fall too far behind the timeline, we run out of air and power, and die. In space, forward movement along the timeline equals life. Procrastination equals death."

Oscar pulled out a pair of mini-binoculars and looked back at the golf course. "They've stopped. They're just standing there talking on the green of the second hole."

Knox continued, "During the mission of Apollo 13, an oxygen tank exploded on board the Service Module. The accident forced Mission Control to abort the lunar landing.

"The three astronauts, and the tens of thousands of people involved in this mission, lost what they'd worked so hard to do, the ability to land on the Moon's surface. From that point on, all that mattered was the crew's survival. Think about that, they'd devoted years and most of their lives to the goal of landing on the Moon, and now it wasn't going to happen this time. But the Apollo 13 team had no time to replay the past, or ask, 'What if things had been different?' They had to concentrate on tracing the steps to get home alive.

"Before the accident, some would have said such a scenario was impossible to survive. But quick decisions saved the day. The control team back on Earth decided the Lunar Module could be used as a lifeboat. To get the crew home, they'd swing the spacecraft around the Moon and use the Lunar Module's engine to send them home. Meantime, with the help of Mission Control, the three astronauts on board Aquarius found ways to extend forty-five hours of life support into ninety hours. Finally, the crew built a box out of masking tape and lithium hydroxide canisters to scrub carbon dioxide out of the air system. This last step would give the astronauts enough oxygen to breathe to get home. So you see, it all came back to breathing.

"Apollo 13 is a lesson on using everything you have, right now. The crew on board the spacecraft couldn't run out and buy a solution. All they had was time, and they confidently used every second they had. That's how they made it home. Death would have come with procrastination."

Hunter and Knox finished playing the second hole as Knox spoke. "Back on Earth it's the same thing. Death may seem like a long way off, but it's not. When you waste right now, you're wasting your life, and eventually you're history. The quickest way to conserve time is to act now to accomplish things ahead of schedule, and move on to the next step. Don't wait. Start taking the steps and concentrate on the things you have now to take you to your goal."

The two arrived at the tee of the third hole.

Hunter grabbed a driver and asked, "What about the time I've wasted in my life?" He was thinking about his ex-wife again.

"Hunter, we're talking about right now. Not what happened yesterday or the day before yesterday. Do you worry about the golf swing you had as a beginner? Are you afraid it will come back and haunt your game?" Knox didn't give Hunter time to answer. "Of course not, because you know you've built on that."

Hunter wasn't so sure. "But sometimes I look at my life and I just want to start over with the things I know now," Hunter said, fixing a divot.

"So do it. Start. Begin. Do it now," Knox paused to let this sink in. "It's about time. Using time now. Not waiting. Hunter, when you hesitate or procrastinate, you're wasting the commodity of time being given to you right now. If you think you should have done something, then ask, 'Okay, why would have that led me to success?' Think about how you can apply that to the present, play off that, and use that. Change your perspective. If you should have done whatever it is you should have done, remember that and move on. There's no logical excuse to waste time. Don't sit there and replay the past."

Knox paused again and looked at Hunter, looking for signs of acknowledgement.

Hunter could feel Knox's ice-blue eyes lock on him. *He knows I replay the past. He knows I can't let go.*

Knox looked away and laughed, "Until time travel is invented, it's impossible to physically relive the past. End of story. But some people can't understand this. They choose to mentally play the past over and over again, wishing they'd done this or that. But wishing for the past eats into the present, and then like a cancer, eats into the future, and kills it. Wishing for the past must be replaced by planning for the future right now."

Hunter hit his drive. The ball veered to the left and came to rest by a set of four sand bunkers.

"But why is it so hard to let go of the past?" Hunter asked.

Knox walked up to the tee. "It's because you've been taught to think about the pain rather than the lessons. The pain has been shoved in your face again and again. When that happens, eventually you're weighed down by too much of the pain and forget the lessons of the past. That means you may repeat the same mistake twice. If you fail, take the lesson, leave the pain, and take the steps that will move you on to the present, where the future begins. Your life depends on right now. You can have a lifetime of yesterdays or tomorrows, but you only get right now, once."

Knox hit his drive.

"Here they come," a member of Delta Company said quietly.

"Everyone get ready," Oscar whispered into a portable radio. "That's one of my best agents out there. We can't blow his cover. And we want to take Knox alive."

Knox and Hunter walked to the middle of the fairway. "What's in front of you, right now, is what's most important, no matter where you are, or what you've done," Knox said. "We all have abundance, because we all have right now. It doesn't matter how wealthy you are or how financially challenged you are, because we all have time."

As Hunter listened, he caught a glint of something in the trees. *They're here,* he thought. *This is it.*

Knox continued, "Time is a commodity, time is a neglected resource. Time is more precious than gold, more priceless than the largest diamond, the largest pearl, or the largest emerald. Forget money as wealth, because time is real wealth. Time is all you've got, and its value only increases as you become more aware of it.

"Keep a record of the time you spend in a journal like you keep a record of the money you spend. Learn from the good investments in time you make as well as from the bad."

By now, Hunter was only half-listening. He looked for a place to take cover if the worst happened. He approached his ball and got ready to swing. He looked again at the green. There was a sand trap towards the left of the green. It would offer some cover. Hunter swung; the shot flew and landed in the trap. *Close enough,* Hunter thought.

Knox looked at Hunter. "Interesting," Knox said, "that was a well-placed shot into that bunker."

Knox hit his shot. It landed with a thud perfectly on the right side of the green. The cards were dealt.

"Don't invest the present into the past," Knox said. "The past is like money you've already spent, you can't get it back. If you look back on the poor investments and get depressed, the present and the future pass by. It's just like golf. You can't let a few bad shots dominate your thinking. You must learn from them instead. Focus on the good shots you've hit, and then think about the good shots you're going to hit.

"And one other thing: don't use the future in the present by saying you'll take action tomorrow instead of today. You can't spend a future you don't have." Knox stopped to make another point.

"Shit," Oscar whispered, "they've stopped again. Just standby."

Knox looked at Hunter. "Consider what some people spend their day saying: 'I'm stuck in this job, and it's not going anywhere.' 'My life is meaningless.' 'My marriage is no good.' 'I can't do well in school.' 'I want time back.' 'I think I'll make that call tomorrow.' If these are the kind of thoughts filling your present thinking, right now is slipping right through your hands and so is the future. It's like having a stack of one-thousand-dollar bills and throwing them on a fire, but this fire offers no warmth, it burns cold as black ice. Before you know it, your stack of money is gone and so is your life! Don't burn the valuable commodity of time!

"Concentrate on your good investments, look at the time you've used well, and begin to act right now to use your time even more effectively. The present is time you haven't spent, time in the bank."

Knox started walking to the green again and did a double take at the trees. He pulled his golf bag over his shoulder in a slightly different way, touching a green button under the main strap.

"Here we go," Oscar said nervously as he watched the men approach.

Knox looked at Hunter. "Children have a lot of time to invest in their future through education and development. This gives them a chance to invest in a great future. Take a look at great athletes or great entertainers and you'll see children who used their time very well.

"My grandmother once told me, 'It's a shame youth is wasted on the young.' That's only partially true. It won't be wasted as long as you have the perspective to see what your experiences have taught you and what they can teach you. If you use that information, and use it well, you will get what you want."

Behind the nearby trees, a sharpshooter set his target on Commander Knox Long.

"One other thing to remember, Hunter," Knox said, "As you get older, time gets more slippery. It's not as magical. The hours seem to go by faster. But the only thing that's changed is your perspective. Move faster than time by changing your mental focus and squeezing the present. Think about that for a second. The real fountain of youth is realizing the value of time, and not letting it slip by. Look for every opportunity to invest time wisely, and act on those opportunities, right now. No matter what you think your plight is—time is all you've really got."

What is Oscar waiting on? Hunter thought as he approached his ball in the bunker. It was a buried lie. Hunter was down in the sand trap considering his shot, when he realized he'd left his golf bag containing his gun about twenty feet away. Hunter tried to fix the problem. "Wait a minute, Knox, I think I need a different club."

"Why? You've got your sand wedge. It's buried," Knox said. "Concentrate and you'll be fine." The commander looked into the sky and said, "Hunter, do you want to know how to cheat time? How to feel great when you turn thirty, forty, fifty, sixty, seventy, eighty, ninety, or one hundred years old? You feel great by making the best of right now, this instant. When you make the best of right now, the present becomes as valuable as the future. You're no longer worried about what time you may have spent in the past because you're content in your heart right now. You're no longer worried about the future because you have a flight plan, and you're having—"

Suddenly a voice boomed from beyond the trees, "Commander Knox Long, we order you to drop your bag and surrender! Hunter Algier, stand clear."

Stand clear? Hunter thought. *That meant they wanted Knox to run. Run where?*

"Again, Mr. Algier, stand clear," the voice boomed.

In an instant, Knox reached into his golf bag, pulled out a weapon, and jumped into the sand trap with Hunter. In the next instant, Knox's gun was pointed squarely at Hunter's head.

"Kill me, and he's dead as well!" Knox yelled back to the trees.

The voice roared again through the trees, "The entire course is secured. There's no way out. Taking a hostage won't work, Commander!"

Keeping the gun pointed at Hunter, Knox looked back at his bag.

The Bermuda grass behind them flew up as a hail of bullets hit the course as a warning. "Sorry about this," Knox said, pushing Hunter down into the sand trap.

"What the hell?" Hunter shouted. *What the hell is Oscar doing!*

"I would have certainly allowed these folks to play through," Knox yelled as he raised the gun and squeezed off a round of bullets into the woods. "I remember when golf was a quiet game."

Knox reached out of the sand trap to grab the strap of his golf bag. As he pulled the bag to the trap, it was blasted with bullets. One of the bullets ricocheted off the bag, nearly hitting Hunter in the head. Knox grabbed the bag, unzipped it, and pulled out a radio. He turned it on and spoke into it, "Fox, this is Hound, we're at the third green, just listen for the gunfire. The situation is extremely hazardous. We'll be dead as soon as I run out of bullets!"

Hunter heard a woman's voice through the radio. "I'm already on my way," she said.

Knox looked at Hunter. "Ever do any stories that would piss off anyone?"

"No," Hunter said, half-forgetting he was supposed to be a journalist.

"I guess they are really after me," Knox said. "Obviously we'll have to continue our conversation elsewhere."

There was more shouting from the woods. "Give up, Commander!" Knox answered by squeezing off another round of bullets from his gun.

A return round of gunfire hit the course from the unseen enemy. Knox fired another round, then a car, a Range Rover Land Defender, broke through the trees on one side of the course heading directly for Knox and Hunter.

Knox yelled, "There's Fox now!" The Range Rover stopped in the middle of the green to block the line of fire. A woman got out with a large automatic weapon and sprayed bullets into the woods.

Knox pointed the gun at Hunter and began pushing him to the car. "You're our ticket out of here."

Hunter ducked in the car just as another round of bullets was sprayed in his direction. A second later, Knox got in. The woman fired off a final round and jumped into the driver's seat. She hit the accelerator and Hunter was slammed into his seat.

Oscar yelled, "Hold your fire!" Seconds later it was quiet, except for the sound of disgruntled birds flying over the makeshift battlefield. The green had over a hundred new divots and the damage would take some time to repair. The normal sweet aroma of the course now had the added smell of gunpowder and smoke. Oscar took out his radio. "Attention all units. Knox is on his way. He took Agent Algier with him. Hold your fire, I repeat, hold your fire. We're going in pursuit."

Two men in a small helicopter hovering over the left edge of Pinehurst never heard Oscar's message. They had mistakenly written down the wrong radio channel for the operation. One of the pilots looked in the direction of the gunfight that had happened moments before. Smoke was rising from the trees. "Oh shit," one pilot said. "There's trouble. Let's go."

The other pilot replied, "Why in the hell haven't they contacted us?"

As Fox drove the Range Rover up the path, Hunter looked at her. He'd seen her before. Then he realized it was Knox's daughter, Kathy Long. The photo of her in Oscar's office the day before hadn't done her justice. Moments later, the Range Rover broke clear of the trees. Two helicopters sat in the middle of a field. Kathy was headed right for them.

Kathy speeded up and crashed into one of the helicopters. She backed up, and hit the other helicopter with the heavy metal bumper of the Range Rover. "I saw these on the way in," she said. "That should slow them down for a while."

"That's my Fox, always thinking. Let's fly," Knox said.

Moments later they'd left the course and turned on to one of the main roads. Hunter heard the sound of another helicopter. *It's probably a backup in case anything went wrong on the ground*, Hunter thought. If Oscar was really trying to let Knox escape, it would be in his best interest to make the chase look as real as possible.

Knox also heard the sound of the helicopter overhead. He turned his head to look up and out the window. "Well, they won't shoot at us here," Knox said, looking at the helicopter. "There's too much traffic."

The sniper in the helicopter leaned out the window with a semi-automatic weapon and fired the first round at the fleeing Range Rover. Lethal fire. Three cars swerved off the highway. A bullet pierced the window and hit Hunter in the arm.

"Damn!" Hunter yelled. *What the hell is Oscar doing?* Knox turned to Hunter and saw he was bleeding severely. Knox handed him a cloth. "Here, apply direct pressure." The commander paused for a second, and then said, "Hunter, I know you're in pain, but I've got to ask you to hand me that gray tube behind your seat." Hunter looked over his left shoulder and saw the gray tube. In pain, he lifted it up and gave it to Knox.

"Good. Now open that suitcase back there and hand me one of those rockets," Knox said, as he made adjustments to the tube.

Holding the pressure on his arm, Hunter found the suitcase and opened it as best as he could. There were four sleek "rockets" packed in foam rubber. Hunter knew they were surface-to-air missiles, but there was something different about them. Right now at least, there was nothing he could do to stop Knox. Besides, the people in the helicopter had shot him.

"Fox, roll down all the windows," Knox said. "When I say three, stop. And then get ready to drive like hell."

"One," Knox said as Kathy pushed a button to roll down the windows automatically. She cranked on the car's air conditioner to full.

"Two," Knox said, as he opened the sunroof, Hunter buckled his seat belt.

"Three!" he yelled. Kathy slammed on the breaks, throwing Hunter forward in his seat. The helicopter buzzed past overhead. Knox unbuckled his seat belt, took aim with the tube through the sunroof, and pulled the trigger. The car filled with thick smoke. Hunter covered his ears for the blast. But he heard nothing.

"Hit it!" Knox yelled. Kathy accelerated, throwing Hunter back in his seat. The smoke quickly cleared. Hunter leaned over to look outside the window. The helicopter was still there in the middle of the air. It just wasn't moving. Hunter had seen his far share of strange things in the air, but this was like nothing he'd seen before.

Knox looked at the helicopter and answered. "The surface-to-air rocket releases a pulse that freezes anything in flight. Once the energy dissipates, they'll come down, with only their pride injured. If the pilot is good at autorotation that is."

Kathy drove on as fast as she could. No one said anything for a few minutes. Hunter was in pain from the bullet.

Knox turned around in the passenger seat and looked at Hunter. "Hunter, you came here to learn about Apollo. Don't worry. You will. But you came here looking for more, didn't you? Come on, tell me, I know you did."

"Yes, Knox, I did. I wanted to know who Knox Long was. A man who walked on the Moon. A man who helped change the course of human history. Now…well now…" Hunter was shaking from loss of blood.

Kathy was driving on the open road. She was quiet, but determined. "Kathy, stop the car," Knox said. She stopped. It started to rain.

"Hunter, we'll turn around and leave you where you can get medical attention. We have enough time to do that. You'll be safe. But Kathy and I may not be safe."

Hunter looked at him and said, "Those people just tried to kill us."

"That organization has already killed ten of my people. If they'd wanted us dead, they would have done the job. It's just a direct warning to stop what I'm doing," Knox said.

"Stop you from what?" Hunter asked.

"Hunter, it's too soon to tell you," Knox looked at Hunter's arm. "But I owe you the full story. So I'll share what I know. That's what these people are trying to prevent. What you're about to find out will send shockwaves around the world. It's also going to change the course of human history and our evolutionary path. So I need your help. Are you in or out?"

Hunter looked at Knox, not knowing what to say.

"If you go home," Knox said, "the questions you want answered won't be answered. You may never even know the right questions to ask. This is your chance, Hunter. What I'm asking you to do is release."

Then Knox said something he'd said earlier. "Live in the future by waiting to do what you need to do right now and you miss the present. Live in the past by looking at what you've already done and you miss the future. Live and act right now and you don't miss out on anything, there's nothing to wait for, and you don't make any mistakes. Hunter, don't spend the rest of your life asking, 'What if I had?'"

This is it, Hunter thought. The threshold. The beginning of a journey or the end of a journey. The choice was his. He had more questions for Knox. Besides, if he went back now, he could be killed. *But why? Was it The Roswell Trinity? Did he know too much about it?* Then again it was always there. All he had to do was see it. And what about Knox? *Why hadn't Oscar told him they'd already tried to stop him? Stop him from what?* For now, he'd have to find out on his own. "Okay, I'm in," Hunter whispered.

Kathy smiled.

"Then the timeline moves on, and so do we," Knox said. "Not because it's easy." The Land Rover started to accelerate once more.

"Exactly where are we going?" Hunter asked.

Knox said, "Well tonight, you're going to meet a very good friend of mine. She just happens to be sixteen feet long." Knox smiled.

6

Departure

Moore County Airport, North Carolina

The Land Rover made several turns and then arrived at the airport. Kathy parked the Land Defender in front of a large hangar. "Let's hope they don't know we came by jet," she said to Knox. "But it seems quiet."

She got out of the car and ran to a small door built into the hangar. She unlocked a padlock, opened the door, and went inside. Knox helped Hunter out of the car. As the hangar door rapidly moved up, the sound of clicking and creaking filled the air.

The hangar door opened to reveal a sleek new jet. Hunter recognized it instantly. It was a new Ahrens 750, the fastest private business jet in the world, with a range of about seven thousand nautical miles. *We could be going anywhere*, Hunter thought.

The jet was white with blue stripes. Kathy noticed Hunter's expression. "It's even better than you think, Hunter. This one has at least one very special modification."

In the distance, Hunter heard sirens. Kathy jumped on a small tractor and quickly pulled the aircraft out of the hangar. As it rolled out, Hunter noticed the letters "N.B.I.E." on the tail of the plane.

While Kathy opened the passenger door, Knox moved the Land Defender and then the tractor into the hangar and hit the close button. As the hangar door closed, Hunter looked at the back of the Land Defender; it had a vanity license plate with the letters "NBIE" as well. One at a time, they climbed the steps to get in the jet. The aircraft was richly appointed in dark teak and tan leather seating. Hunter looked around and saw flat-screen monitors throughout the cabin. Instead of magazines, a display glass was in every seat.

Knox and Kathy went up front to the flight deck. As they prepared for takeoff, Hunter looked over their shoulders. The entire flight deck was glass, autopilot, weather radar, and, surprisingly, some equipment he'd never seen before.

"I'm glad we topped off the tanks when we landed, we can go to battery power, but it won't be as fast," Knox told Kathy as they were reviewing a checklist.

"Exactly where are we going?" Hunter asked.

Knox looked at Hunter and said, "South. Please, find a seat and buckle up. We're going to get out of here as soon as possible. Kathy will be back to help you with your injury in just a few minutes."

Hunter sat down and buckled up as Knox closed the cabin door.

A short time later, the jet was off the ground, pulling several Gs on takeoff. From his window seat, Hunter watched the ground disappear as the plane went into the clouds.

Hunter looked at his watch: 1635. He made a mental note of the time. His window view was now completely obscured by clouds, giving him no idea which direction the plane was traveling. With the door to the flight deck closed, he couldn't see a compass.

Hunter looked at his golf shoe for a long time. Then, with some hesitation, he began to tap the toe. He tapped it in a very orderly pattern, like he was listening to a favorite song.

A short time later, Kathy Long walked back from the flight deck with a medical kit. Hunter looked at her. "Sorry about the blood," he apologized. Her face was flawless. She was beautiful.

"It's not the first time I've seen it," she said, pulling up Hunter's sleeve. He caught a whiff of her perfume. Her hair was perfect. Her brown eyes deep.

Kathy examined the arm. "The good news is the bullet went clean through. The bad news is you've lost a lot of blood." He felt her soft breast touch his arm as she worked on the injury. Kathy reached into the medical kit and pulled out a hypodermic needle. "This will take away some of the pain and promote healing." She put the needle into the wound and gave Hunter the injection.

Immediately, Hunter felt a tingling sensation in his arm. In a matter of seconds the pain was gone.

"What is that stuff?" Hunter asked, suspecting it to be a derivative of ZR5. One of the elements in The Roswell Trinity: instant healing.

"You'll find out," Kathy said. She finished dressing the wound, gathered up her medical equipment, and went back to the flight deck.

***

Oscar walked through the police line on the highway and examined the wreckage of the helicopter. He looked at Robert McCaully and whispered, "I wonder why they still went after Knox?"

A solider wearing white gloves ran up to them. "Sir, our flash investigation indicates the pilot's radio was tuned to the wrong channel. The crew's in bad shape, but they will survive. We should be able to ask them exactly what happened within a few hours."

"That explains that," Oscar said to McCaully. "At least we were successful. He ran. Now we can follow him. Let's get back to Washington, we should be able to track the jet from there."

Seconds later, another soldier ran up to Oscar and handed him a note. Oscar took a few seconds to read it. He turned to McCaully. "It's from Hunter. He's using a special transmitter in his golf shoe. He says, 'Thanks for the bullet.'" Oscar looked at the wreckage of the helicopter, then continued, "'Escaped in plane. Kathy Long with us. Heading south and taking notes.'"

***

With his arm feeling better, Hunter picked up a piece of glass. As he held it, it came to life. *Knox Long Aviation Unlimited* the glass read as it turned opaque. He touched it again and it listed magazines and newspapers from around the world. He put the glass down and it instantly went transparent again.

The sun had set and Hunter could see stars in the black sky. Just as he was getting his bearings on the stars, Hunter heard a clicking sound. Knox opened the door to the flight deck and walked back to where Hunter was sitting.

"How are you feeling?" Knox asked.

"Better," Hunter answered, rubbing his arm.

"Hunter, I know it may be difficult to concentrate. But it's time to finish our conversation concerning time. We have just enough time to talk about it before we get to our destination."

"Where exactly are we headed?" Hunter thought it was worth a shot to ask.

"I thought I told you. South," Knox said.

"That's all you'll tell me?"

Knox looked at Hunter. "For now, that's all you need to know. In the meantime, I have a few things I'd like you to consider.

"The first thing is this: Imagine an hourglass filled with sand, the hourglass is your life. The sand is time. You stand at the middle of the hourglass. When you're born, the glass is flipped over and the grains of sand begin to fall. The grains of sand at the top represent the future above you. That sand falls and becomes the past below you.

"How well you do in life is determined by what part of the hourglass you focus on. Look down at the sand that's already passed, and you miss the sand to come. Look at the top of the hourglass at the future, and you miss the sand that's in front of you right now. But look at the middle of the hourglass, and something incredible happens. You begin to seen each grain of time passing by, and all the opportunities.

"What happens to the grains of sand from top to bottom is up to you in the present. Be proactive and have a plan. As sand comes from the future to the present, nurture it and use it to aggressively pursue what you want. Keep the value of the present and let the sand pass. Once the sand passes, it's gone. The past falls below you. Don't try to hold on to it, because if you do, you'll miss the other grains of time that are always coming at you. Take the value from the present and let it pass.

"You're always running out of time. Procrastinate and the sand still falls. You've got to make the changes in your life right now. If you wait seconds, seconds become minutes, minutes become hours, hours become days, days become weeks, weeks become months, months become years, years become a lifetime, and that's it. Your story is over. The sand runs out.

"It's about taking action now, in all aspects of life," Knox said, looking at Hunter's arm. "From goals to personal health. Consider the expense of health care. People who invest in preventative health care create their own value and add sand to the top of the hourglass on their own. It can be as simple as brushing and flossing your teeth, or as demanding as being in shape for a marathon. Wouldn't you rather invest in exercise and self-development now, rather than paying the high cost of treatment and undergoing intense discomfort later?"

Knox took a deep breath, and then said, "People who live the best lives have a no-nonsense attitude toward life. They love life because they've beaten time by squeezing the center of the hourglass. They do that by using every second. When they squeeze the present, the sand appears to fall more slowly.

"Squeeze time. Get all you can from it. Start in the morning. Great things happen in the morning at the start of a new day. Realize how great life is in the morning. Learn something early in the morning. That's how you really feel young.

"They say people who worry about time and worry about getting old aren't living their lives to the fullest. That's right. That's because people who are worried about time are frustrated, and when you're frustrated you look at the nearest clock. If you're not committed to realizing your goals, you'll spend your life watching a clock. And if you concentrate on the passage of time, an amazing thing happens to you. You'll grow older.

"People who are happy don't think about time. When these people arrive at their goals, they could care less about how much more time they've got, or how old they are, because they've beaten time."

Knox continued, "Time passes by. It's a law of nature. What you've got to do is be the person you want to be right now.

"Set a goal and set a timeline to achieve it, and never waver. Because the more you waver, the easier it becomes to waver. Just do whatever it takes to complete the mission. Don't compromise.

"We call it the timeline in the space business. But it's also called a 'dead' line, as you well know from journalism. In goal achieving, if you don't meet the timeline, you're dead. Set your goal and stick to it.

"The past has made us what we are right now. But right now makes the future, what will be. It's today's investment. That's what you should think about.

"New Year's resolutions should become New Day's resolutions. Each day make the resolutions that will cause you to evolve into something more.

"Hunter, let me ask you this. What if those people had shot and killed us?"

"It would have been over," Hunter said.

"If that was it, and you had to cash it in, how much would your life have been worth? Were you getting everything you wanted out of it? How would you be remembered? For the contributions you made? For the smiles you brought to people's faces? Or would people have asked, 'Who was he?'"

Knox paused, but only for a second. "Well, Hunter? Had you done it all? Were you truly satisfied? Were you developing your talents and looking for new talents? Were you using every grain of time God gave you? Were you closer to your goals? Were you following a flight plan?"

Knox didn't give Hunter a chance to answer, instead he said, "Every year 'experts' come up with an average life span for humans. Let me let you in on a little secret: the average life span for true achievers and those who get everything they really want is right now!"

Hunter looked out the window into darkness. *Was he getting the most out of life?* Work took much of his attention. He'd never taken the time to heal the emotional scars from Angie.

A buzzing sound broke his concentration.

Knox reacted rapidly and said, "That's all I have to say about the timeline. Tonight, over dinner, we'll discuss the next part of the countdown. We'll be landing soon. You may want to get a few minutes of rest. How's your arm?" Knox asked.

Hunter shook his head. "It's feeling better, Knox. Won't they follow us?"

"Believe it or not. There's no possible way they can. You're flying in the world's first personal invisible jet."

Hunter looked at Knox. It was all adding up. Apparently Oscar was right, Knox was responsible for taking two elements of The Roswell Trinity: stealth technology and instant healing.

Wherever they were heading now, Hunter was sure it would lead to the third part of the puzzle, the instant acceleration engine, XIA.

"We'll be landing in about fifty-five minutes," Knox said as he made his way back to the flight deck. He went inside, shutting the door behind him.

Hunter began tapping his shoe once again as the invisible jet flew on into the night.

—STAGE TWO—

7

Passionate Risk

In the Skies over Virginia: 2050 ET

Oscar and McCaully flew in the badly dented helicopter back to Virginia. Kathy's Range Rover did moderate damage, but not enough to ground the aircraft.

The pilot in front handed Oscar a piece of paper. "Sir, another Skyfax."

Oscar put on his glasses to read the note. "It's from Hunter. He says, 'Plane has stealth. But you know that by now. Still headed south. Still angry about the bullet. Landing in 55 minutes.'"

McCaully reacted by shaking his head and looking out the window. "We were right about the radar. Knox installed the VIS hardware from the helicopters on his jet. Which means he can replicate the process."

Oscar rubbed his face, "Damn, it's been a long day."

He pulled a map display glass from a pocket of the cabin. "Knox's plane is the A750, which means it can travel fast and far," Oscar said, activating the digital map. "All we know is he's heading south." The men looked at display under the dim passenger light of the cabin, hoping they would find an answer.

***

Hunter looked out the window of the plane. Through the inky darkness, he could see the flaps were down on the wings, meaning they were on final approach.

The A750 landed with ease, a testimony to Knox's piloting skills, or for that matter, maybe Kathy's skills. Hunter carefully studied the view outside the window. He could see only the white lights of the runway. Those white lights gave way to blue lights as the plane taxied to a hanger. Hunter immediately began tapping his heel. After several minutes, the jet rolled inside a lighted hangar, its engines slowly winding down to a restful whisper. Hunter looked at his watch: 2058. They'd been in the air for more than four hours. The lights came on, and the door to the flight deck opened.

Hunter heard Knox talking to Kathy. "I think they let us run. The president will do everything he can to stop us. We have four rocket launchers at the house. Even so, we don't have a lot of room for mistakes. We'll need to be ready."

"What about our guest?" she asked, looking back at Hunter.

"I'm sure he can handle it," Knox said as he flicked a switch.

Kathy pulled herself out of her seat and left the flight deck. "Hope you enjoyed the flight," she said to Hunter as she turned a metal handle to open the jet's door. In a matter of seconds, warm, humid air blew in from the outside. "It's still hot down here," she observed.

Knox punched some final buttons, and then got up from the pilot's seat. "We're here," he said to Hunter as he left the flight deck.

"Wherever here is," Hunter replied.

"When the time is right, we'll tell you. But for now, I want to introduce you to a friend of mine and then we'll eat. I'm hungry and you must be as well. Let's go."

Hunter followed Knox down the short stairway of the jet. As soon as Hunter stepped on the airport tarmac, it was obvious they were in a tropical location. The flat land and humidity revealed at least part of the mystery. He could also smell the ocean and see palm trees under parking lot lights in the distance.

A large black BMW was waiting for them. Knox shook hands with a man who took the luggage out of the back of the jet and put it into the trunk of the car. Moments later, Commander Knox Long, Kathy Long, and Hunter Algier got in the car and left the airport.

Hunter noticed more palm trees and dense foliage along the side of the road. He even noticed a cactus. *It feels like an island*, he thought to himself.

Knox, always eager to take advantage of time, picked up where he had left off while he drove. "Hunter, now that you know about time, it's time to prepare for the departure to your goal. So let's spend some time talking about the basic supplies you'll need."

Hunter looked at the commander and said, "Knox, you want to continue this now?"

"Why not? We don't have a lot of time, besides you said you were in, right?"

Hunter looked out the window, wondering what his options really were.

"Right?" Knox asked a second time.

"Yes," Hunter said.

Knox said, "Apollo carried us to lunar orbit, took us to the surface of the Moon, and then returned us safely to the Earth. What did we need?"

Knox waited for a moment and then answered his own question. "We needed the basics. The spacecraft, energy, propulsion, guidance, communication, heat, and light. The machine had to be as fit as each astronaut was.

"And each Apollo spacecraft was fit for the most part, but let's go back again to the mission of Apollo 13. Shortly after nine p.m. on April 13, 1970, an oxygen tank exploded in the Service Module as the spacecraft was making its way to the Moon. Losing power and life support, the crew had to power down the Command Module Odyssey and climb into the Lunar Module Aquarius to stay alive. James Lovell, John Swigert, and Fred Haise became focused on doing whatever it took to survive the trip back home," Knox said.

"How did the accident happen?" Hunter asked as the car hit a bump in the road. Hunter was listening, but he was also evaluating the flight time, trying to figure out how far they'd flown. *It had to be more than a thousand miles. Which would put them in Cuba? No. Somewhere in the Caribbean?* He tried to remember something he'd read about Knox and the Caribbean.

"The oxygen tank in question was dropped at a factory several years before it was installed in the Service Module," Knox said. "When the tank was dropped, and it was only dropped about two inches, a tube inside the tank became loose. During a test, the tank was filled with oxygen. When the test was over, because of the loose tube, the tank could not be emptied properly. Technicians had to use heat to empty the tank. When they heated the tank, a vital switch in the tank was damaged, but nobody knew it. In flight, that damaged switch led to the explosion, and the flight to the Moon became a fight for survival.

"Even with this unexpected disruption to the mission, the crew of Apollo 13 survived. With the correct flight plan, they knew they could get home. We can learn a lot from Apollo 13," Knox continued as the car made a sharp turn.

"That the flight plan is the key," Hunter said.

"Exactly, Hunter."

Hunter thought about what Knox had said. Watch out for the five-dollar bolt in the million-dollar bridge. If that bolt is damaged, you lose the integrity of everything else. Folklore has another explanation: *For want of a nail, the shoe was lost; for want of a shoe, the horse was lost; for want of a horse, the rider was lost; for want of a rider, the battle was lost; for want of a battle, the kingdom was lost.*

Knox paused for a second to glance out the window and then he looked back at Hunter. "To protect your flight plan, you need to protect your body. You need to treat it like the precision-tuned instrument it is. The power, the life, has got to be secure. Don't let poor maintenance interfere with your goal; use positive daily maintenance to achieve your goal. Take care of the body you've been blessed with.

"There's plenty of information about how to take care of yourself. Your body and mind should be in shape, well rested and free from drugs. Your body can't fail you on the way to your goal. You'll be going into new territory and things may get hostile at times."

Talk about new territory, Hunter thought to himself as he looked outside the window beside Knox. The tropical jungle around the road seemed to be getting denser.

The commander continued, "We talk about the technology of Apollo, but look at your body. Notice how everything works in harmony. What's even more amazing is that you can improve it. It's not hard to find out what you need to know to get and stay in shape. There are resources everywhere to tell you, and most of them are free. The hard part is making the best use of this information.

"Another great thing about the human body is that once you get it into shape, your brain records the mental image of what it's like to be in shape. After that, the subconscious will make every effort to keep it that way.

"To become physically fit, you've got to be mentally fit as well. You've got to be mentally fit to take the stress. The stress of the obstacles you'll run into, the stress of mistakes."

Hunter appreciated what the commander was saying. But it was getting late and Hunter was tired. He was afraid he would miss some vital slip by the commander, so he raised a hand to interrupt.

"Isn't there a better way?" Hunter asked. "Can't we avoid stress altogether?"

"Avoid stress and you avoid the potential for growth. You can't be comfortable and live life to the fullest. You must be stressed to a certain degree because stress ensures your survival. If you don't handle stress, or try to avoid it, your body and mind become weak.

"A quick example. When you lift weights, you encourage muscle growth. Growth means strength. If you don't push, your muscles will atrophy. It's just the way nature works. You've got to use what you're given.

"It's the same with acting on a plan. If you don't act on a plan, you may be safe, but you're not growing. If you act on a plan, even if you make a mistake, you'll learn and you'll grow. So you probably won't make that mistake again."

The word *mistake* stuck in Hunter's mind. *Had he made a mistake traveling this far with Knox? No, it was his job. But who should he trust? Oscar Morrow or Commander Knox Long?*

The car turned left into a driveway. Hunter saw a lighted building in the distance. "Welcome to my home away from home," Knox said, and then laughed sarcastically. "At least now you know where you are."

The house ahead was high-tech and modern, a three-story frame with a flat roof. The windows were brightly lit. The house was circular. Hunter guessed it was built to survive a hurricane.

Knox looked at his home, "As you head to your goal, Hunter, you'll have to generate power to get there. It's got to come from within. It was the same for Apollo. Just a few seconds before liftoff, the spacecraft switched to full internal power. From that point on, it generated its own electrical supply. It became a miniature world of its own.

"The source of your strength," Knox said, "the reason and passion for what you want to do cannot be generated by other people; all they can do is offer support as you make your way. Your power has got to come from inside."

"That's much easier said than done, Knox. Sometimes it's difficult," Hunter responded. "How do you stay totally motivated?"

"By getting excited about the plan I want to complete," Knox replied. "In the space business, there's a lot of talk about 'the right stuff.' Well, what makes people successful, what really takes them to their goal is they see beyond, to the conclusion."

"How?" Hunter asked as the car slowly rolled up the driveway.

"It's like we talked about before. They're driven by reason, passion, and vision. It's fundamental motivation at the subconscious level. Believe me, if you have that, you'll feel great every morning.

"Any questions?" Knox asked as the car stopped.

"How will I know if I'm going in the right direction to my goal?" Hunter replied as he opened the car door to get out.

"Look at Apollo," Knox said. "The guidance system on board the spacecraft was defined as something that automatically adjusted the vehicle to a pre-determined flight path. Essentially it knew where it was going and where it was by knowing where it came from and how it got there."

Kathy led the way to the house, while Knox continued talking. "To guide you properly, your subconscious must be focused on the goal at hand. Getting focused means realizing you're already at the goal. Meantime, you've got to know where you came from, what you did to get this far, and where you're going from here. This should be measured by looking at your flight plan.

"You know what this means, Hunter?" Knox asked.

Hunter shrugged.

"Life is really rocket science. And rocket science isn't that tough. It's just a matter of steps."

"How do I keep track of how much time until I reach my goal?" Hunter asked.

"Keep a journal of what you do that coincides with your flight plan. Record the thoughts that push you on to your goal so you can look at them for reference. Our missions to the Moon were carefully documented in every way. You must document your life as well. This allows you to see how far you've come. It also allows people to look at the different paths of success and apply those paths to their own lives. Record your life. It will contribute to you, your family, or it could benefit a complete stranger sometime in the future," Knox said as he opened the front door of the house. Kathy and Hunter walked inside.

Hunter was amazed. Knox's home was a masterpiece. A monster-sized aquarium packed with exotic saltwater fish dominated the living room. It served as the centerpiece of the room and must have had four thousand gallons of water in it.

A stream, complete with more fish, ran along one wall. There were even mini-waterfalls. The second story was open to the first floor in a grand atrium. The floors were hardwood with a stone walkway in the center. The furniture was a natural color to match the surroundings. The ceiling was about thirty feet above their heads. The miniature stream that ran along the foot of one wall ended in a moon pool. Hunter guessed the moon pool led to the ocean. It was surrounded by benches and scuba gear.

Hunter looked at the brightly colored fish. "Knox, fish and water everywhere. Why?"

"Astronauts tend to love the sea. Maybe it's an instinctive knowledge of our eventual evolution—from the sea to the land and then to the stars."

Knox looked at Hunter's arm. "How are you feeling?"

Hunter had forgotten about his injury, he looked at the arm and said, "Fine, I guess."

"Okay, then it's time to talk about perspectives. You're a diver, right?"

Hunter looked at the equipment and nodded. "Yes, Knox, for most of my life."

"Well, we're going diving. I need you to meet a friend of mine."

Hunter knew that anything could happen, and there was just no sense in saying no. Besides, he was intrigued.

Knox handed Hunter the appropriate dive gear. "We won't have to swim far."

Knox provided Hunter a special covering for his arm. Much to Hunter's surprise, the bullet wound was already beginning to heal. But then again, that was the power of ZR5.

As they got dressed, Knox handed Hunter a small orange tube with a piece of glass on one side and an antenna on the other. "Here's a high-intensity light and tracking device, just leave it on the entire time. We'll follow the lights to a sandy bottom at thirty feet. We'll be using full-face masks, so just ask me any questions. All the data from the dive will be displayed in your face mask. We shouldn't have to wait long once we get there."

Once the scuba gear was on, they entered the water and swam through the connecting concrete pool to the opening of a reef and then went to a depth of about fifteen feet. The house was right on the ocean. Hunter looked ahead and spotted the area they were swimming to, a perfectly round circle lit by other lights on the sandy bottom. He looked at the depth in the heads-up display on his mask. They were now at thirty feet in the center of the lit area. He looked over at Knox, who made a gesture to stop.

"Okay, Hunter. We're here," Knox said through the underwater communications device. "She's usually good about showing up."

Knox and Hunter kneeled in the sand.

Knox spoke between breaths. "Hunter, the most important thing we can do in life is change our perspective. Once you're stuck in a rut, nothing changes. We hold on to ideas and false beliefs for far too long. Our fear takes over, and we become stuck. The only way to get what you want, what you need, and what you desire is to blast through your fears. No questions asked. As you're about to see."

Hunter was getting nervous. Here he was on the bottom of the ocean after running from a gunfight and a four-hour flight to anywhere in the Caribbean. *The water was crystal clear, so it had to be the Caribbean.* At that moment, he saw movement just outside the light in the blackness.

"She's here." Knox said.

Hunter tried to wrap his head around what he witnessed next. A shark, a very big shark, swam into the light. Hunter recognized the species as a tiger shark, with distinctive stripes and big cow-like eyes. The shark was swimming directly to Knox.

"Hunter, I'd like you to meet my friend, Thalassa, a sixteen-foot-long tiger shark."

Knox extended his hand towards the nose of the shark. "While most people see a terrifying shark, I see a big friendly dog." Knox rubbed the shark and its eyes went white as the creature flashed its nictitating membranes.

Holy shit, Hunter thought to himself.

"Sometimes you've got to change your perspectives to find the truth. Good Thalassa.

"Many people hate sharks. They think they eat people. The fact of the matter is—healthy oceans need sharks. If Thalassa wanted to eat us, it wouldn't take long."

Knox gave the shark a last rub and then the impressive animal swam by Hunter, looking at him with enormous brown eyes. Hunter looked deeply into the eyes of the animal and detected respectful intelligence. He was compelled to touch it on its side. When he did, the connection with this massive shark sent shivers down his arm. He wouldn't have thought it was possible, and yet, here he was.

With that, the shark swam out of the light and back into the darkness.

It reminded Hunter of a dream. *A dream that was turning into reality.*

Knox said, "I hate to come home without giving some love to Thalassa. But it's time to go. We must eat and talk about next steps."

With that, Knox turned around and started swimming for the reef that would lead back to the house. Hunter took a last look at the darkness and then swam to follow Knox.

***

A short time later, after a quick shower and a change of clothes provided by Kathy, Hunter went to the dining room.

The dining room was a tribute to Apollo. Mission patches were hung on one wall. Paintings and pictures of the landings on the Moon decorated other areas. Knox explained that some of the paintings were original paintings by Apollo 12 astronaut Alan Bean. There were models of the Saturn V and the Command, Service, and Lunar Modules. In one corner, displayed in a glass case and carefully lit, were several gray rocks.

"Knox, are those—" Hunter started to ask.

"Yes they are," Knox replied.

"Did the astronauts get to keep some?"

"These were stolen from a display in California shortly after the first landing on the Moon. Eventually, they fell into my hands. Someone at NASA owed me a favor and helped me track them down.

"But the Moon is much more than just a place to find rocks," Knox said as he picked up the model of the Saturn V. "Forty-one rockets powered the Saturn V, and these rockets all did different things. Some provided as little as seventy-two pounds of thrust for fine adjustments, others provided as much as 1.5 million pounds of thrust to escape the gravity of Earth.

"While rockets took Apollo to the Moon, it's the actions you take that will get you to your goal. From the large acts that will get you off the bench to take action, to the small acts that provide small course adjustments."

Hunter looked at the model of the Saturn V and asked, "So how are these personal rockets powered?"

"Motivation, heart, guts, drive, ambition. But the key rocket power is passion."

The commander put the model down, and pointed to a picture of the Saturn V taken shortly after liftoff. "Passion is a pure fuel that can drive you to the most remote star."

Knox gestured for Hunter to sit down at a large table. "Take the word 'burnout' for example," Knox said.

"Burnout is defined as, 'the point when combustion ceases in a rocket engine.' Only with continued passion will you make it to your goal. If you say you're burned out, it's because you've lost the passion. But passion can be rekindled with the right motivation."

As Knox talked, a woman brought in water, a plate full of spiny lobster tails, and an assortment of fruits to the center of the table.

"Thank you, Shannon," Knox said.

"Please, Hunter, help yourself," Knox insisted. At that point, Kathy came in from another room and sat down with them. Hunter, feeling somewhat hungry, filled his plate and listened to Knox.

"As you make your way to your goal," Knox said, taking a few lobster tails for his own plate, "you've got to remember that information is power.

"On board Apollo, we used information provided by the computers in the spacecraft. We also had constant communication with ground control. You've got to do the same. Use each source of information available to you and look for information in new areas. This will help you answer a question you've got to consider at each stage. That question is simply: Is your final target still worth it?

"You must also watch the people around you. See if they have information that can be used to readjust your flight plan. This also allows you to save time and avoid potential mistakes."

Knox gestured to the food. "By the way, these lobsters were caught last season, but we have a technique to perfectly preserve seafood and preserve taste—one division of my company is focused on sustainability, using the resource but not abusing it. How is the food?"

"Very good, great. Thanks," Hunter said.

Knox changed the subject. "The tiger shark you met tonight."

"I was going to ask you about that. How did you?" Hunter started to ask.

"I truly believe, the way the we look at an animal, like a shark, is the way we look at the Earth. Do we accept something we don't understand? Sharks have a role on this planet, like we do. But people don't want to take the time to learn. If we continue removing them from the sea, we will destroy the planet. The oceans need sharks."

Hunter was having a hard time thinking about the real mission. The ambush on the golf course had only happened a few hours ago, and now here they were discussing sharks. There was no arguing with the fact Knox had shot some kind of a missile at the helicopter. But the commander was no cold-blooded terrorist. For Knox to take aggressive action like that he'd have to have a strong reason, a good reason. Knox said they'd killed ten of the people working for him. *But why?* Hunter was ready to give anything to have five minutes with his boss, Oscar Morrow.

***

Oscar was now back at his office waiting for the latest word from Hunter. Tomorrow was October 24, the last full day before the deadline of five p.m. on October 25.

While he waited, he examined a detailed map of South America for places where Knox could hide. A soldier ran in with the latest message from Hunter. Oscar took it from the man, read it, and immediately dialed McCaully's number.

"Hello," McCaully said on the other end of the line.

"Here's the latest: Hunter says they've landed in a tropical location. I've got the time this came in. At least now we have a basic radius to determine how far they traveled. Encouraging news, I think."

"I'll be right over," was all McCaully said.

***

"Now let's talk about heat," Knox said.

"Heat?" Hunter asked, looking at his empty dinner plate.

"The heat of life, for lack of a better way to put it," Knox said. "People who've been burnt or rejected too often don't want to get near the flames of challenge anymore, and that puts them out of the running for true success. If you stay away from the flames of challenge, you'll be chilled by a future that's already gone. But if you stay close to the fire, you'll feel the warmth of a better today and tomorrow.

"For instance, say you have a great idea. But you also have an intense fear of rejection. Trying to stay away from rejection may prevent your great idea from ever being realized. You're rejecting yourself and that's the slowest burn there is."

"How can I stay close to the heat without getting burned?" Hunter asked.

"That question brings us back to Apollo," Knox said. "Returning from the Moon, our Apollo spacecraft entered Earth's atmosphere at a blazing speed of 36,194 feet per second. As you may remember from high school physics—that kind of speed, moving through molecules in the atmosphere, causes intense friction. That friction leads to heat, about five thousand degrees worth.

"A heat shield protected us. The shield is on the bottom of the Command Module facing the atmosphere as the spacecraft comes back to Earth. The shield takes the heat, and keeps us at a comfortable seventy-five degrees inside. The heat shield is ablative, meaning bits and pieces of it break off to dissipate the heat.

"It's really an amazing design: a fiberglass honeycomb injected with a resin that covered the bottom of the spacecraft.

Three hundred and eighty thousand holes in the honeycomb had to be filled in by hand and carefully checked. If a hole wasn't filled in perfectly, a dentist's drill would be used to bore it out, and workers would start over.

"The heat shield had to be handled with care. Once the spacecraft was on its way to the Moon, we'd put ourselves into what's called 'a passive thermal roll.'" He put down his fork and picked up a model of a spacecraft behind him and twisted it. "The spacecraft actually traveled to the Moon like this, like a rotisserie chicken, to keep the heat shield and the ship evenly heated and cooled. Workers were afraid if the shield, or for that matter the entire spacecraft, got too hot or too cold in space, there would be damage. So each side rotated in and out of the sunlight.

He put the model back down and picked up a model of the space shuttle. "The heat shield has always been a part of the space program. There were thirty thousand silica tiles on the outside of each shuttle, to take the heat. It was amazing to watch workers care for each numbered tile as they prepared a shuttle for flight. These silica tiles were designed better than Apollo's heat shield because they could be reused.

"As you make your way to what you really want, the friction of life will cause things to get hot, but you can design your own shield. If it's working properly, bits and pieces will simply take the heat and break off. You'll lose nothing in the process, and you'll keep your cool. The more you learn, the better you can design your heat shield."

"What do you mean by 'design your heat shield'?" Hunter asked.

"Your personal heat shield is designed with self-confidence, a well-defined goal, a flight plan, and the effective use of resources at your disposal. You'll have to work on your heat shield. It takes time to construct.

"One other thing," Knox said. "It's cold in space, and it may be cold on the way to your goal. To heat things up, you've got to give off warmth. Warmth expressed in the form of care and compassion."

Knox opened a box of cigars and offered one to Hunter. "Then there's the element of light," the commander said as he lit Hunter's cigar.

"Light allows you to see everything you need to see, the beauty and the danger. Light helps guide you. But this light has got to be internal as well. What you're really searching for is illumination."

***

Oscar turned on a light as McCaully spread five maps out on a large conference room table. They had A750 jet specifications spread out on the table as well. Oscar made a few calculations on a tablet device.

"Cuba?" McCaully asked.

"Intelligence recorded no landings. What's south of Cuba?" Oscar asked.

"Ummm," McCaully looked at another map. "The Caymans."

"The Caymans?" Oscar repeated the words. As he did, he remembered. "'Cayman Brac. Of course!" Oscar yelled.

McCaully looked puzzled. "How's that?"

"Cayman Brac is like a second home to Knox Long. Stayed there for two months after he returned from the Moon. Fell in love with the place. It's that passion some of the astronauts have for the ocean. Outer space and inner space, I should have known."

McCaully looked at Oscar. "What the hell are we waiting for?" he asked. "Let's go."

* * *

"There are a few more factors we need to discuss," Knox said. "The first is risk."

Knox got up and pushed in his chair. "Ask me or any other astronaut about the risk of a trip into space and we'll tell you the payoff is worth it. We're professionals and we make our living by turning every risk into a success."

He walked over to a photo hanging on a paneled wall. It was a picture of a burned-out spacecraft. "I use this as one reminder to never take anything for granted," Knox said.

Hunter got up to take a closer look. At the bottom of the photo was a plaque that read, In Memory of Apollo 1. Beside the picture was a portrait of three astronauts.

"When we talk about risk, we need to talk about the mission that paved the way to the Moon. Apollo 1."

Knox looked off in the distance and spoke slowly. "The day: January 27, 1967. A Friday afternoon. I'll never forget it. I'd gotten married the Saturday before. No time for a honeymoon, of course. Pad 34, Cape Canaveral. A full-scale simulation of the February twenty-first launch of Apollo 1 was underway. In a simulated 'plugs-out' countdown with the crew on board, the spacecraft was operating on internal power with its own atmosphere. That's what 'plugs-out' means.

"Anyway, it was a long day full of communication problems. Everyone was edgy. At one point, Gus Grissom asked, 'How the hell can we get to the Moon if we can't even talk between two buildings?' That was one of the last things he said. At 6:31 in the early evening, an electrical spark in the oxygen rich atmosphere of the Command Module caused a fire to sweep through the spacecraft. The blaze killed forty-year-old Gus Grissom, the second American in space; thirty-six-year-old Edward White, the first American to walk in space; and thirty-one-year-old Roger Chaffee, who was training for his first flight." Hunter looked at the photograph of the three men.

Knox continued, "NASA never expected to lose these men on the ground. Six other astronauts had been killed, but either in car accidents or plane crashes. This was the first time we'd lost men because of a problem related to a spacecraft.

"Before he died, Colonel Grissom told his wife, Betty, that if there was an accident, it would probably be on the first mission, his mission. Ironically, he even summed up the fire that would kill him before he died. He said, 'We want people to accept it. We are in a risky business, and we hope that if anything happens to us it will not delay the program. The conquest of space is worth the risk of life.' Basically, he knew an accident could happen, but he trained fears away by being ready for any problem, and he did the job with pride. That's how he handled it. That's how we all did."

Knox pointed to the image of another one of the astronauts. "Ed White was a man who said the saddest day of his life—the saddest day—was when he had to end America's first spacewalk during the Gemini 4 mission. He considered being first on the Moon a duty to himself and to his country."

Knox gestured to the last astronaut in the picture. "And I remember the passion in Roger Chaffee's words when he talked about going to the Moon, even this many years later. He talked about seeing a full Moon when he was flying at night. He would say, 'It's just big and bright. You look up there and say to yourself: I've got to get up there. I've just got to get on one of those flights.'"

Knox looked away; the words affected him. Hunter looked at the picture again.

"We were preparing to fly a spacecraft with numerous flaws," Knox continued after a moment of silence. "We overlooked the fact that a pure-oxygen environment is highly flammable. Overlooked the fact that all the items in the spacecraft had to be fireproof, no questions asked. We overlooked the fact the hatches would have to quickly open to protect the crew. The hatch for Apollo 1 was extremely difficult to open. In fact, the crew used to joke around about using it for weightlifting because it was so heavy and difficult.

"So anyway," Knox said with a catch in his voice. "We all knew there were problems with the spacecraft. Memos were written and we worked to get them fixed. Some of us just had the attitude to 'blow the bolts,' and we'd take care of problems once we were in space.

"But maybe we weren't thinking about the overall flight plan. Kennedy's challenge was to 'safely' send a man to the Moon. It's like I've been saying, before you achieve the goal, you must see the vision. That was perhaps the basic problem with Apollo 1. Vision was blocked by frustration.

"Apollo 1 serves as a warning that you must have vision for your goal. If your vision is blocked by frustration, take time out to redefine the flight plan. Apollo 1 teaches other lessons as well. Before Apollo 1, we'd gotten spaceflight down to a 'science' with the Gemini Program. Because of that success, we took certain things for granted. When things get routine, the rewards are lowered, but the risks increase—the risk that your learning curve will decrease, the risk that you'll overlook something you can't afford to overlook.

"Another key lesson of Apollo 1 is that we must learn from the past mistakes we make, and we must share our mistakes with others so they can learn. Sometimes we can't afford to make the same mistake twice.

"The astronauts of Apollo 1 put us on the Moon. Their ultimate contribution, and what we learned from the accident, created the way.

"When Italy's president expressed his regrets over the Apollo 1 tragedy back in 1967, he predicted the future: 'The courage of your great country will prevail, because America always will give scientists and heroes to the world.' And we did. We finally focused on the vision. The accident uncovered flaws in the spaceship. A hundred and fifty thousand people worked twenty-two months to make more than a thousand changes in the design. We would get to the moon."

Knox looked at Hunter and said, "When you shoot for your goal, there's risk. Accept it, live with it, but instead of worrying about it, focus on the reason, the passion, and the vision. If you find yourself lacking in vision, something needs to be corrected. Go back and look at the steps of your flight plan. Find out which step needs to be reworked or replaced. Plan until you get a vision of making it work. Then release the passion and take action.

"People who succeed, evaluate the possible risks, look at the balance sheet, determine if the goal is worth it, and if it is, they go for it."

Hunter looked at the pictures from Apollo 1 and then glanced at some of the other memorabilia in the room. "Knox, I think I understand what you're saying. But these men sacrificed everything for the goal. Is that what it takes?"

Knox puffed on his cigar and said, "Some people will talk about sacrifice or the price that must be paid. When people talk about sacrifices, think about contributions, and contribute to your own goal, first. Then think about how that will help the others around you. Build, accumulate, and contribute. Don't just sacrifice. Consider the price you'll pay if you don't achieve your goals. Think about the price others will pay.

"As you work on your goal, you'll run into obstacles, sure. It's hard, yes. But you're setting the trend for a better life. You're building on past successes and contributions. Part of the path has been cleared. You get to pick up where other people have left off, and if you hang on, you get to finish. And if reaching your goal helps other people reach their goals, what more could you give?" Knox asked, putting down his cigar. "Let's go outside."

Knox opened a sliding glass door to a massive wooden deck. It faced the ocean. Knox dimmed the outside lights so they could see the sky. It was full of stars. The Moon reflected off the water as they sat down at a table. The woman who had brought them dinner, brought out coffee. Kathy walked out to the deck a few seconds later. "Beautiful night," she said, as if she was seeing it for the very first time.

***

In the NSA Dragon Jet travelling five hundred knots, Oscar was on the phone making final arrangements. "Mr. President, I'm asking Special Forces to provide us with four C-130s with full battalions at Cayman Brac first thing Friday morning. I want to get them there tomorrow but there's not enough time to do it safely. I'm on my way to set up the operation now."

"Don't screw this up, Oscar," the president threatened on the other end of the line.

Oscar swallowed hard, "Agent Algier is keeping me informed, we're on track this time." But it had already been two hours since Hunter's last report.

***

Hunter took a deep breath of the salt air on Knox's porch and looked out at the ocean and then up at the stars. Knox looked at the Moon and said, "Now some final details, Hunter. There comes a time to change what's attracting your attention, a time when you must make a polar shift. The polar shift is always to the positive and it always alters your perspective.

"A major polar shift happens when you realize that you can dramatically change your life and the lives of others in an instant. It happens when you realize you can forget the pain of the past. The shift turns a comfortable life into a life with an edge. The shift pushes people through challenge. It turns fear into bravery, panic into calmness and night into day.

"The shift can be small or large, and it can begin right this second, by looking at something in your life from a different perspective—like the tiger shark tonight.

"For some people it can be as simple as taking a weekend adventure to get away from what they usually do. Or it can be as simple as breathing fresh air, standing in the rain, or just enjoying life. Hunter, you made a polar shift when you decided to join us."

The words "join us" forced Hunter to think. He'd never even thought about being a double agent. He wondered if he had inadvertently become one.

Knox continued, "Shifting sometimes requires a major change in perspective. Like a flight to the Moon. That's what a stage-one launch is all about. Because when you light the first stage on the way to what you really want, suddenly you realize your goal is not just a dream. It's something you really can achieve.

"Look at a child's imagination, ambition, and drive. They go for what they want because they haven't learned the limiting lessons yet," Knox said. "They haven't been told, 'Hey, you've got to watch out for this, you've got to watch out for that.' Or, 'There's a possibility that you may not be able to do this,' or, 'What if the worst happens?' or, 'I don't know if that's such a good idea.' After years of this, the brain begins to develop limiting benchmarks. The child begins to think he or she can fail. They may find it hard to compete.

"When you attempt to do something grand, know that everything you do will be a step towards success. Forget limiting beliefs and ask good questions to bring you closer to your goal. Questions like: What if the best happens? What if I get everything I always wanted?

"Use good answers as well: Okay, when I get everything I wanted, I'll teach other people how to get everything they want. After that, I'll get everything else I've always wanted. And so on.

"Visualize where you want to be and begin the polar shift. Change your outlook and perspective." Knox reached up in the air with his hands, "Imagine the future as a grand place and make it so. That's the real secret of life.

"Remember, you can either move forward in life or backward. There's no way to maintain a constant velocity without constantly working to maintain speed or go faster. There's always some other force acting on you.

"Find the reason. Be passionate. Break the rut. Break the barriers."

Knox paused and looked at Hunter. "I think you're ready to learn about what comes after all this." Knox glanced at his watch. "But it's late. Considering the trouble we had in Pinehurst, tomorrow won't be easy. Kathy will take you to the guestroom."

"Goodnight," Knox said, as he left. Kathy and Hunter were left alone, sitting on the deck.

"What does he mean, 'Tomorrow won't be easy'?" Hunter asked.

She smiled and said, "Hunter, you'll soon see everything he's saying is true. Just pay attention. Your role is critical."

"My role?" Hunter asked. "My role in what?" Kathy looked striking under the starry night.

"No more questions," Kathy said. "You should get some sleep. Knox is right. Tomorrow will be a long day."

She looked at the sky and then got up. "Follow me. You've got the best room in this place for a good night's sleep." Hunter took a final look at the wonderful sky and then followed Kathy into the house. One thing was for certain, he was beginning to feel incredibly attracted to her.

As Hunter followed Kathy to the guest bedroom, hundreds of miles away, on the NSA jet, Robert McCaully and Oscar Morrow were planning the assault on Cayman Brac.

8

Knox's Resolution

Thursday, October 24

Cayman Brac: 0659 ET

The shadow of the Great White Shark passed over Hunter. He only had a few moments left. Without fear, he let the inevitable approach. Then he spied a small cave in the reef. Just big enough for him to enter. He swam inside. The shark would not be able to follow…

Hunter dreamed comfortably in an oversize bed. The room he was in was immaculate. As the new day approached, sunlight beamed through a window. A large clock sat on a dresser. The display changed from 6:59 to 7:00.

Music began playing. Island music.

Hunter opened his eyes and came out of the cave of his dreams, away from the shark. It was strange he dreamed about a great white shark, when the encounter he had the night before was with a tiger shark.

An accented voice came on the radio. "The time is seven O'clock. It's seventy-three degrees and sunny. Now more of the hot island sounds."

"Damn," Hunter said half-asleep, "it's not a dream." He got out of bed to turn off the alarm. He fumbled with the clock for a second before finding the off switch. Hunter looked around the room. "This really is no dream," he muttered. He thought about the shark. He'd been able to escape by entering the cave…

Hunter stretched and walked over to a window. He pulled up the shade to look outside. An enormous orange sun was rising over the ocean. Then he noticed Knox on the beach—on the beach, hitting golf balls into the ocean. "How the hell does he get them back?" Hunter said to himself.

Hunter stood back from the window feeling like something was wrong. He was forgetting something. He walked to a mirror and looked at himself. Then he looked at the bandage on his arm. He didn't feel the pain anymore of the bullet wound he'd received as they were making their escape. He reached up to pull off the bandage. As he removed the bandage, he noticed there was no trace of injury. Not even a scar. It was like it had never even happened. ZR5 had worked. He'd seen two parts of The Roswell Trinity in action: invisibility and instant healing. He still had to find out about the third: the XIA rocket and instant acceleration.

The island music suddenly triggered a memory in Hunter from all of his research. *Cayman Brac. We're on Cayman Brac. Knox's home away from home. I should have known.*

Hunter went back to the window and looked to see Knox selecting another club. A surprise knock at the door made Hunter jump. He turned around to find his pants, quickly pulling them on before opening the door. Kathy stood there, holding a cup of coffee. She also had a large machine gun slung over one shoulder.

"Good morning," Hunter said. Dressed in shorts and a bikini top, she looked as impressive as when he first saw her, even with the heavy weapon. Hunter looked at the gun. "Expecting trouble?" he asked.

She avoided the question. "Good morning," she said as she offered him the cup of coffee.

"Thanks, Kathy," Hunter said, taking the mug. "My arm. It's healed. Or was that just some kind of a dream?"

Kathy ignored that question as well and smiled. "Knox is already on the beach."

"I saw him," Hunter said.

"He wants you to join him as soon as possible. Those clothes should fit you," Kathy said, motioning to a chair.

Hunter went back to the chair to get a polo shirt and his shoes. Hunter pulled on the shirt and followed Kathy back down to the first floor to a sliding glass door. The inside of the house was just as impressive during the day. The sunlight played off the water in the aquariums and danced on the ceiling.

"I hope you slept well," Kathy said. "There's no telling what will happen today."

"Certainly. But I thought the jet was—" Hunter started to say.

"Knox is waiting," Kathy interrupted.

Hunter walked out the door and down a path to a perfectly manicured golf tee on the beach.

"Good morning, Knox," Hunter said.

Knox gave Hunter a quick once over. "I hope you slept well."

"Yes."

"The arm has healed, I take it," Knox said knowingly.

"Yes. How—" Hunter started to ask.

"Good. Because I have a feeling it's going to be a big day today. On the eve of the world changing forever."

"Knox, why?" Hunter asked, knowing the warning the president received was for tomorrow.

"Great things happen in the morning," Knox said, changing the subject. "Don't just stand there, hit a few." Knox pointed over to clubs set up by a fence. Hunter walked over to get a club. As he did, he also noticed three rocket launchers and four suitcases.

Knox hit a ball over the ocean. There were flags floating in the water to mark the distance in yards. As the ball hit the water, he looked at Hunter and saw the concern.

"We've got to be ready to roll," Knox said. "The trouble we had in Pinehurst is just the beginning. But they can't stop me."

"Can't stop you from doing what, Knox?"

"It's still too soon to tell you. Don't worry though, we're heavily armed and can escape from here if we need to. Now let's hit a few while we still have time."

Hunter looked at his arm again.

"Knox, back to my arm for a moment. The, bullet wound has totally healed. What was that substance Kathy injected me with yesterday?" He had to ask, even though he knew the answer.

"Which do you want to hear about, medicine or Apollo?" Knox asked mockingly while taking another swing. The ball flew over the water.

From deep water, Knox and Hunter were just two tiny points on the beach. The water was calm. The ball hit the water and quickly sank. From under the splash, something stirred. Something just beneath the surface—waiting.

Back on the beach, Knox watched Hunter warm up. "What a grand time the early hours are," Knox said. "To wake up and go outside as the sun is getting up, the sky a crisp blue, the clouds not exactly sure which direction they'll go for the day. Go outside on a cool, crisp morning and you can see your breath, like a Kentucky thoroughbred practicing at dawn at Churchill Downs. You're ready to run. You're alive."

Hunter took a deep breath as all the familiar questions started going through his mind. *What is Knox up to? Why didn't Oscar tell me everything? Think and don't get too close,* Hunter told himself.

Knox set up another ball and swung. Another beautiful arc. Hunter could see the passion in each one of the commander's swings.

"Knox, how do you collect all those balls?" Hunter asked, gesturing to the water. "I mean, isn't it a waste hitting them in the water?"

"They only look like golf balls," Knox said. "They're really made out of compressed fish food."

"What?" Hunter asked.

"That's right, fish food. The fish on that reef out there," he pointed to the line of flags, "are probably the best fed on the entire island. Why waste a good golf ball, when you can practice and feed the fish?"

Knox looked at Hunter. "Come on and hit a few. It may be our last chance for a while," Knox said as he took another swing.

"I love the morning. It's a great time to decide how the day will go and how you'll continue on the way to your goal. Each day is a gift.

"You've got to have intense drive in the morning. You've got to have passion for your dreams. You've got to have the passion to turn them into reality."

"I agree," Hunter said. He had to find out more as quickly as possible and he was running out of time. "It's like you were saying yesterday. Reason, passion, vision."

"That's right, Hunter. But remember the passion must be strong. You must have passion from the time you open your eyes at the beginning of the day, until the time you close your eyes at night. Don't be blinded by fear or hostility. Don't be blinded by the past. There's so much waiting to be seen, so much waiting to be explored."

Hunter hit a few balls in the water while Knox continued to talk. "Great missions start in the morning. Our voyage to the Moon started in the morning. We ate steak and eggs for breakfast and caught a ride to the launch pad. Steak, eggs, and a trip to the Moon.

"What an incredible morning that was. To see the Saturn V rocket sitting on the launch pad at the Kennedy Space Center with vapors steaming off of it. What a magnificent sight, it was a live beast ready to fly. I walked up to the rocket the morning of my flight, and you know what went through my mind?"

Hunter looked at Knox.

"I could only think about the hard work and dedication that went into that creation," Knox said. "I wasn't afraid. It was up to me to fly the dream of a generation to the Moon. My heart was already on the lunar surface. My body simply had to follow."

Hunter looked at Knox and said, "It must have been incredible."

"It was a massive creation for a massive undertaking. A dream turned into reality because of discipline. A dream turned into reality because the right questions were asked and the right steps were taken.

"The best of what we could do. A creation to take us to the heavens, to take us beyond our comfort, to put us in a totally hostile environment where we could still live and work. Apollo's Saturn V was the vision of a country, a vision of those who dreamed of leaving the Earth to explore the heavens. Saturn V was a skyscraper built with a delicate touch. A skyscraper built for human evolution.

"The Saturn V did not come easy," Knox said, putting down his club. Sitting in the sand was a model of a Saturn V rocket. He picked up the model and gave it to Hunter. Knox continued. "The Saturn V was broken up into three stages, as you can see by this model. To construct the three stages it would take hundreds of thousands of people and millions of hours, the largest peacetime project in our history. At the facility where stage one was built, the assembly area was as big as four football fields. We rode bikes to get around.

"The five engines at the bottom of the first stage were eighteen feet tall, fourteen feet wide, weighing ten tons each." Knox looked at Hunter. "Ever balance a golf club on the end of your finger?"

Knox demonstrated by taking his driver and balancing it upright on the end of his finger.

"That's what it was like to fly the Saturn V! Four of the five F-1 engines were attached at the end of an X at the bottom of the first stage. The F-1s would carefully steer the rocket through winds and away from the launch tower."

Knox pushed the driver up in the air and then caught it.

"The structure of Saturn V looked mighty, but the side of it, in some places, was as thin as a shoe sole. In fact, the first stage was really just a flying balloon of fuel. It weighed 288,000 pounds empty and 5,022,674 pounds when fueled.

"At liftoff, more than five tons of kerosene and ten tons of liquid oxygen mixed in the five combustion chambers every second. Every second! All together, the five engines would generate nearly 180 million horsepower!"

Hunter listened to the passion in Knox's voice.

"The roar of the rocket's engines was like nothing the world had ever heard before. The only thing any louder constructed by man was a nuclear blast. The only thing louder in nature was a meteorite that hit the Earth in 1883. It was the sound of man reaching for his goal, the sound of technological evolution ripping at our DNA. It was a fundamental, bone-shaking sound, the sound of courage, bravery, ambition. The sound of achieving. With such a sound came a shockwave you could actually lean against.

"The flames of the Saturn V first stage were a fifth of a mile long at takeoff. The astronauts were riding on 7.5 million pounds of burning thrust, the force of a generation."

At the other end of the island, a solider put a small amount of plastic explosive around a heavy-duty padlock. Next, he carefully took two small wires and fastened them into the compound around the lock. He took the other end of the wires and attached them to a small electronic device in his hand. He turned his back and pushed a red button on the device. With a flash, the padlock was gone.

"We're in," the soldier said into a communicator as he opened the door to Knox's jet hangar on Cayman Brac.

Two miles away, Knox and Hunter continued to hit golf balls into the ocean.

"What's the most dangerous part of a trip to the Moon?" Knox asked Hunter while setting up a shot.

"Landing on the Moon?" Hunter said. The answer seemed obvious.

"Liftoff and the first twelve seconds of each mission," Knox corrected. "If the spacecraft hit the launch tower, it would have caused a massive explosion.

"But after those first twelve seconds were over, time flew by, and so did the Saturn V.

"At one minute and twenty-one seconds after liftoff, the gleaming white spacecraft was already at an altitude of more than forty thousand feet, traveling at almost two thousand miles an hour. Before long, Apollo was traveling at fifty-four hundred miles an hour, consuming forty thousand gallons of fuel per minute.

"The first stage of the Saturn V took the Apollo spacecraft from zero to fifty-four hundred miles per hour in about two minutes and forty seconds.

"In only three minutes, the Saturn V was fifty-seven miles away from the launch pad."

Knox stopped and looked at Hunter. "If I were to say that stage one was the same as leaving for your goal, would you agree?"

"Yes," Hunter quickly answered.

"Why?" Knox asked.

Hunter said, "Well, it takes tremendous force to achieve a goal. Focused force. Positive force."

Knox said, "Well, that's true, Hunter. But how would you sum it up in a word?"

"Drive?"

"That's part of it, yes. But I'm talking about the main strength and thrust to get you to your goal."

Hunter thought about it for another second and then the answer came to him. "Passion?"

"That's right. Passion. Passion for your flight plan. Just look at Apollo. It took passion to go to the Moon. And it will take passion to achieve what you want to achieve."

"How do you define passion?" Hunter asked. "I thought it had more to do with love."

"Love, yes. But passion is also that burning in your gut that pushes you. It's strong, pure and fundamental. Passion is the feeling that, whatever it takes, you're going to achieve your goal. Passion forces you to focus. Strong passion means success is the only option. You need passion to leave the past and achieve your goal. You need passion to achieve liftoff.

"To control the passion, you've got to have a framework to work from. The framework is the written flight plan and the mental image of what you want. This framework will help you focus.

"Passion can be dangerous. Too much at once and it explodes out of control. Not enough and you can't break the gravity that's holding you back.

"To get started, passion for the goal must outweigh everything else in your mind. Remember, it took seven-and-a-half-million pounds of thrust to lift the six-and-a-half-million pound Saturn V off the ground.

"Even though you need an enormous amount of passion at liftoff, God's given you the gift. Yes, passion is a gift. Give your flight plan the power of passion and there's nothing you can't do. You've got to find a way to tap the passion. If you're depressed, if you have a problem with how you're feeling, then you haven't found what you're looking for yet. You still need a reason. And the reason brings passion."

Hunter thought about everything he was facing. "Knox, I've been thinking about yesterday when you were talking about reason. I've spent many years of my life looking for a reason. I've achieved some goals but they aren't really what I wanted. I think my real goals are too high."

"That's your problem, Hunter. You think your goals are too high. Listen, the trip to the Moon was nothing more than a carefully planned way to achieve a dream. If you plan your life the same way, you can get whatever it is you really want."

"But how do I make the passion last?" Hunter asked.

"Remember, Hunter, reason is why you're motivated to do something. If you're motivated by intense reason, you'll find the way."

Hunter shook his head, "I know. But sometimes I'll work on something for a while, get it going, and then say, 'To hell with it.' Or worse, I just feel like, 'What's the use?' I get frustrated and defensive. I'm afraid of rejection. I just sit there and think, 'Why bother?' 'What will change?' I just can't seem to find a way to complete what I must complete. I look for distractions. I don't focus. I—"

Knox lifted a hand. "Your reason becomes clouded by fear. No clear reason, no passion, no vision. If that happens, frustration and depression kick in and stagnation develops. You'll be focused on a hundred moving targets, and not one of them will bring satisfaction. It's a very common scenario. Remember the lesson of Apollo 1. The goal of getting to the Moon was clouded by the immensity of the challenge."

"How do I stop it from happening?" Hunter asked, trying to understand.

Knox took a breath of the ocean air before answering. "Reorganize, refocus, and get your reason back. Remember, whatever it takes, you'll finish. Fear is the dragon that keeps you from doing what it is you really want."

"But fear is a real problem," Hunter interjected.

"Think about our conversation yesterday. You've got to train your fears away by seeing the right path. You've got to find out the real reason you're afraid. And then you've got to face it. You've got to face it, Hunter. That's all there is to it."

"But sometimes I feel all possible paths to what I want are blocked," Hunter said. "I lose the reasons for wanting whatever it is I wanted."

Knox paused and looked at Hunter. "Find stronger reasons. If you really want your goal, you'll open any roadblock. But you've got to want it." Knox pointed to his heart. "And you've got to want it in every part of your heart. Your heart must be connected to the goal. There is simply no other way."

Hunter and Knox were both quiet for a while as they looked at the ocean. The surf was calm. After a time, Knox turned to Hunter and said, "Your passion has got to be to the bone. You've got to breathe it, taste it, feel it. When you do, you'll notice both a physical change and mental change. You'll feel energized. A polar shift will occur and force you to take action."

"But, Knox, how do I find passion that deep?"

As Knox started to answer, Hunter heard a door open and Kathy ran out of the house to the beach. "Knox, I don't know how, but you were right, we were followed!" she yelled. "The alarm just sounded, someone broke into the hangar, found the plane, and they're trying to break into it."

"How much time?" Knox asked calmly.

"Ten minutes at best. I'll get everything ready," Kathy yelled, as she ran back to the house.

"Knox, who found the plane?" Hunter's heart dropped. He knew the answer—Oscar.

Knox avoided the question and picked up the conversation. "We don't have a lot of time. Please hit a few more."

Hunter knew he had to stay calm. So he hit another golf ball into the ocean. The ball flew, feeding the fish at the 165-yard flag.

Knox grabbed a handful of balls for himself and continued, "You had asked: 'How do I find passion that deep?'"

Hunter shook his head. "Yes."

"I can tell you that passion is pure power and only works when it's natural. Drugs can't give you passion because they weigh too much for your fabulous rocket. They may take you up, but when the effect is gone, gravity, that natural law of nature, slams you back into the ground, and there's damage." Knox picked up some more balls and dropped them in front of Hunter. Then he picked up the rocket launcher.

"Likewise, you can't rely on other people for passion," Knox said, working on the rocket launcher. "Don't get me wrong. They can help push you on, but if they decide to leave, you've got to have what it takes inside your own mind to continue on." He put down the launcher and opened the suitcase to remove a missile.

"Apollo moved against gravity," Knox said as he loaded the missile into the launcher. "You must move away from your past, a rut, or a comfort zone. The past can hold you down like cement and bind you to where you are now. A rut can take you into an endless spiral or a dangerous comfort zone.

"If I were to incorporate a change in your grip," Knox said, reaching into another bag, "it would be up to you to use the new grip and break the rut of using the old and familiar grip. However, after a lesson, a lot of people will revert to the old style because it's what they're most familiar with and less painful than making a change. But their game may not improve. They're stuck in a rut." Knox pulled out two large automatic weapons.

"Hunter, forgive me for asking. But can you handle one of these if we need you to?"

"I think so, Knox," Hunter said, for the sheer reason he didn't know what else to say.

"Good," Knox replied.

Knox was quiet as he finished working on the rocket launcher and Hunter hit a few more balls into the ocean.

Hunter agreed with most everything Knox said, but would he remember it all?

A calm came over Knox. He looked down at the ground.

"What is it, Knox?" Hunter asked.

Knox then looked at the horizon and smiled. "When you begin your journey to your dream, the first step is the most important, the most spectacular part of it, in a special kind of way. You're leaving the gravity of the past directly so you'll need more passion to break free. That also makes it the most difficult and dangerous part of the mission. You've got to use the right amount of passion. You've got to find the goal that lights a fire in your soul. It's in front of you, Hunter, you know it is."

"But what if I'm scared of taking that first step?" Hunter asked.

"It takes force and planning," Knox said. "It takes risk and courage. That's why so many goals never get off the ground or have only limited success. People are scared of what will happen if they light the first stage. They simply haven't planned away their fears.

"But with a written and visualized flight plan, success can be seen in advance. And once you've seen success and the fulfillment it brings, you'll be eager to take the first step to turn your dream into reality, whatever it takes.

"When you take the first step, and you realize you're headed for what you really want, the passion builds. It may seem like you're starting out slowly, but the Saturn V had to move that first inch to get to the Moon. And you've got to take the first step to get to your goal. You build upon each step until you're moving faster and faster. Eventually, you move away from the gravity of the past and push skyward."

Knox looked at the sky. "What a great feeling to know the power of momentum," he said. "What a great feeling to know you're on your way."

The commander reached into his pocket and pulled out a piece of paper. "Keep this, Hunter. Next time you're feeling down, read it."

Hunter looked at the paper:

Once you have the reason and the passion, the first stage can be as simple as a phone call. As simple as a letter. As simple as a meeting. As simple as saying, "Hello."

Unleash the passion and take action by taking a physical step to your goal. By doing so, you can change your entire life in a matter of seconds.

Your imagination can take you anywhere. Through physical action, you can turn your dreams into reality. It doesn't matter how big the first step is, as long as you take it, and then take another.

What are you doing just sitting there?

Take the step.

After giving Hunter a chance to read the note, Knox said, "The people who put Apollo together planned everything carefully. So have I, Hunter."

Hunter looked at Knox. He didn't want the commander to get caught. Hunter wanted to know what Knox knew. *How can I tell Knox who I really am?* In a heartbeat, everything had changed. Hunter thought back to Knox describing a polar shift.

Knox said, "We only have a few more minutes, so listen and swing carefully.

"When it came time for the Saturn V to launch, we had most of the flight plan laid out. During the launch, we monitored the vital systems.

"Once you start the first stage by taking action, the majority of your flight plan should be ready, with a vision of success in place. Your main job becomes watching for the unexpected questions and finding out how to answer them.

"And when you start your mission, remember the lessons of the past—but leave the weight of the pain behind. The more weight you carry, the more passion you'll need to achieve your goal. For Apollo, one pound at the top meant an extra eighty pounds of fuel at the bottom. So companies were given financial incentives to cut every pound they could.

"You need to give yourself the incentive to forget the pain of the past. If you're weighed down by too many negative memories, you may never get to the future that could be."

Knox took a look at the concern on Hunter's face. "Why make things harder than they have to be? Shed the excess weight of painful memories and move on.

"Now is the time for you to focus on your goal. Your brain is always hungry and ready to learn. Don't pacify it. Challenge it. Find the right reason and find the passion to achieve your dream.

"This is a launch; it's a change in your personal evolution. It all begins by visualizing your dream and then taking the first step."

"I understand that, Knox," Hunter said. "But what if I'm too uncertain of the outcome?"

"In life, there comes a time to act on what you really want, no matter what—a time when you measure the pros and cons and then take action. Be ready to face risk. Life is not designed to be 'routine.' It's designed to be 'flown' and enjoyed no matter what you face. Don't be pacified! Have passion!"

At that moment, a massive explosion could be heard in the distance. Moments later, a huge fireball could be seen floating over another part of the island.

Hunter looked at the fireball but remained calm. Oscar's team must have destroyed Knox's jet.

Knox looked and shook his head, "They tried to get into the jet. I hate to lose it, but as you can see, it was secure."

Hunter looked at the fireball. Even though he wanted to help Knox now, he'd probably given everything away by sending the messages from the plane. Now Hunter could fail both Oscar and Knox.

"We all face our challenges," Knox whispered, watching the remnants of the fireball.

Kathy ran out of the house. "There's no time left, Knox. We've got to go, now! I'm getting the cart. You'll have to tell him."

"Tell me what?" Hunter asked.

"I wasn't sure you'd be ready for what you're about to see. But it looks like I have no choice.

"Let's go," Knox said, taking a final swing and dropping his club.

Oscar walked up to what was left of the hangar on Cayman Brac. He turned to McCaully. "That's what I was afraid of—explosives and traps. Who did we lose?"

McCaully said, "Elton Campbell. He was a good man, but expendable."

"Let's stop wasting time," Oscar said. "Let's go get him."

"The helicopter is already on its way," McCaully said. "And the second surprise has been waiting off shore now for the past hour."

"What about Hunter?" Oscar asked.

"If my men are expendable, so are yours, Oscar," McCaully said as he walked away.

Hunter saw the helicopter first. It was near the fireball, and headed their way. Knox looked at the approaching helicopter and said, "I only wish I knew how they got here so fast."

Knox picked up the rocket launcher, keeping it by his side. The helicopter was getting closer.

"In the space business," Knox said, "we call this launch commit. You're committing to leave, taking a risk."

The helicopter was getting larger and louder.

"Once you begin moving," Knox continued, "it's up to you to decide when to stop. Keep your reason clear, your passion pure, and know you'll get exactly what you want."

From around the side of the house, Kathy drove up in a high-speed golf cart. The vehicle was larger than usual and fit four people.

"I can tell you the people in that helicopter have been told to succeed in their goal of killing us," Knox said as he raised the rocket launcher to his shoulder, waiting for the right moment.

A battery of bullets hit the sand—but they didn't come from the helicopter; they came from the water. As the sand flew, Hunter looked at the surf. Two divers with automatic weapons had surfaced at the one hundred-yard marker. Hunter dived for one of the guns. Knox knelt down, still keeping his attention on the helicopter.

Then Knox turned, took aim, and fired the missile at the surf. The two divers submerged, but it was too late. A large red blast marked the spot where the divers had been.

"Poor fish," Knox said. The danger from the water was gone, but he'd lost his one shot at the helicopter bearing down on them.

"Hunter, stay down," Knox said. Hunter ducked just as he heard another blast. This time it came from behind him.

Hunter looked up to see a trail of smoke lead directly over his head to the helicopter. The aircraft exploded in a ball of fire and fell to the beach. Hunter turned his head to see Kathy taking the rocket launcher off her shoulder.

"Let's get the hell out of here," Knox said. "I won't be needing this anymore." He threw his launcher in the ocean and ran for the golf cart. Hunter was on his heels.

Hunter jumped on the cart and Kathy hit the pedal, driving like she had in Pinehurst. Knox looked back at the beach where the helicopter had crashed.

"Where are we going?" Hunter asked.

"You'll see. Remember, Hunter, movement to the goal is fundamental to success, you can't let people stop you from getting there." Knox reached for a radio on the dash of the cart.

"This is Hound to Security," Knox said into the microphone.

"This is Security, go ahead, Hound," the radio crackled back.

"Good to hear your voice, Greg," Knox said. "How big is the problem?"

"We think there are two teams on the island. We're sending in a team to close up your beach house now."

"Okay, Greg, tell them to be careful. Have everyone ready to push ahead."

"Okay, Hound. We'll see you when you get home."

Knox looked at Hunter. "Remember, life is rocket science, and rocket science needs to be broken down into steps. It's just like your golf game. Concentrate on the fundamentals, relax, and breathe, and you'll hit the ball well every time."

Hunter was nervous. If the "Greg" on the radio turned out to be General Greg Mitchell, Hunter's cover would be blown in a heartbeat. He'd met General Mitchell at Echo. But he couldn't turn back now. How would he explain that he allowed two helicopters to be shot down? There was no going back.

Knox must have seen the concern on Hunter's face. "Let's say you take the first few steps and everything is looking good," Knox said. "You've had one success, but then maybe you think, 'How long is this going to last?' It's almost like it's human nature to think about the bad instead of the good."

Knox looked at Hunter. "Sometimes we're caught looking at the negatives simply because it's easy to. Being positive all the time isn't easy. Being positive takes vision, and vision comes with reason and passion."

The road started getting bumpy. They were approaching the cliffs of Cayman Brac. Hunter looked ahead. "Kathy? Knox? Did you know we're about to run out of road?"

As they approached the base of the cliffs of Cayman Brac and the end of the road, Kathy suddenly turned the wheel and drove into a cave. She switched on the cart's headlights and increased her speed as the path smoothed out. The cave was cool, dark, and damp.

McCaully and Oscar were under a tent at the island base camp that had been established close to the airport. McCaully turned to Oscar. "There's nothing left of the helicopter."

"Dammit," Oscar said. "There's no way for Knox to get off this island. Let's just secure his beach house, find him, and be done with it. What we want is somewhere close by and this island isn't that big."

Back in the tunnel, Hunter could hardly see Knox, but he heard his voice. "Look at the scale of Apollo. Think about what it required to get Apollo off the ground. The first stage instruments took nine hundred measurements in a matter of seconds to keep the spacecraft on course. Think about all the fuel involved in the first stage: four and a half million pounds. Think about how high and how fast it went in such a short time. Apollo was thirty-eight miles over the Atlantic, traveling at fifty-four hundred miles an hour in two and a half minutes. All these grand perspectives, all these marvelous scales. We traveled to the Moon, two hundred and forty thousand miles away, in a ship only 363 feet long.

"Apollo's second and third stages were fueled by liquid hydrogen and liquid oxygen. These fuels had to be kept at chilling temperatures: 423 degrees below zero for the liquid hydrogen, and 293 degrees below zero for the liquid oxygen. At these temperatures, the super-cold fuel would stay condensed and take up less room. The cold fuel also helped stiffen the side of the rocket to make it stronger. Everything had a purpose. Apollo was a celebration of precision. A celebration of what people could do working as a team.

"The men and women who worked on Apollo were driven in unbelievable ways. A lot of time people put into it went unpaid. People worked without eating, without sleeping. What drove these people? They knew they were turning a dream into reality. The flight plan and reason fed their soul."

The tunnel ended with a large cave lit by a hole in the ceiling. Kathy stopped the cart, found a flashlight, and got out.

Hunter watched her walk over to a wall as Knox continued talking. "Have you ever been working on something that was so exciting that you lost all sense of time? That's the kind of passion you need for your goal. Your goal should motivate you from the time you first come up with it, until you complete it."

Kathy opened a panel on one of the cavern walls to reveal a bank of lights and a keyboard. She began typing.

"Let's go," Knox said as he got out of the cart.

"Go where?" Hunter asked.

As Hunter got out, Knox said, "Having the reason and the passion to achieve your goal freshens and invigorates your soul, moving you and pushing you on in all regards, through all obstacles. People who've done great things have many common traits but above all else, they had an undying passion for what they were doing. Perhaps Apollo 7 astronaut Walt Cunningham put it best: 'Everything else is parsley.'

"Nothing would keep us from our goal. And once you realize the same thing, nothing will stop you from achieving your goal.

"What you may have to do may be difficult and challenging, but thank God it is. Isn't the journey what it's all about anyway? The challenge to leave where you are, to get where you want to go?"

Hunter heard a low humming. Before his eyes, the wall of the cave altered its shape to reveal a door.

Knox looked on proudly. "Something I call 'solid holography.' I'm still working on it."

Kathy opened the door and walked into another room. She came back and started to unload the cart.

Knox continued, "Remember, you've got to have a timeline at liftoff. You don't want to go through all this effort and leave the past without making it to your goal on time. You don't want to get out there and run out of fuel before you turn your dream into reality. Decide when you'll get what you want. Know about how long it should take. Set the timeline. Be reasonable, but be ambitious. The tighter you set the timeline, the better the chances are that you'll act right now.

"Small changes today take you to a dramatically different tomorrow. There are so many things out there waiting to be challenged, so many ways to help yourself. Realize all of the possibilities. With the passion to achieve, you will get to your future."

They walked to the door and went inside a small square room with another door at the opposite end. Kathy shut the door to the room. Lights came on and another panel opened. A label at the top of the panel lit to indicate they were in AIRLOCK ELEVATOR ONE. Then a display screen lit up: PLEASE WAIT. A computer voice also said, "Please wait."

Knox walked to another panel that had just opened and said, "As you begin the journey to your goal, you must also remember the next generation. Do something to teach someone younger than you how to reach. Teach them at an early age. The world's children must be taught that with the right reason, they can and will achieve their dreams. Pay attention to their dreams and give them encouragement. You've got to make sure their dreams aren't broken. So many dreams may be tossed aside because children have things coming at them so fast. You must foster their creativity, their ability to bring fresh perspectives. You've got to push them forward. When you do, they'll help you as well by making you see things with childlike wonder. And if you don't have children, encourage the child within yourself."

The airlock made a hissing sound as it began to move.

"Remember, there are three ways you can go," Knox continued. "You either accelerate and learn, decelerate and crash, or coast into a grave."

The computer said, "Descending and pressurizing."

"So let's light the spark," Knox said.

"You're getting ready to do something great. The challenge is set. The stage is set. Powered by passion, your spirit soars. Because now you realize you really can achieve your flight plan. You can take the first step and begin to move to tomorrow, to your future, right now.

"The higher you climb, the broader your vision. With each new vision comes a new reason for achieving your goal. With each new reason, the passion is intensified. You're on your way."

Knox turned to Hunter and said, "You've started the adventure of heading to your future. Isn't it wonderful to think of the possibilities of what could happen, of what's beyond that door?"

Hunter looked at the door of the airlock. Feeling somewhat guilty about everything, Hunter said, "Knox, I haven't done anything. I just followed you. I had nothing to do with this."

"Oh, but you did, Hunter. You made all this come true by making a series of decisions. We could have left you in Pinehurst. Understand whatever happens from this point on, you're responsible for your own actions. You hold the power to do whatever it is you want to do. So, what are you waiting for? Come on. Your time is too valuable. You need to get going. You need to build your momentum. Incorporate what you have right now into what you want tomorrow."

Hunter heard a release of pressure. The sign now read, READY, then: PLEASE ENTER. A moment later, the computer said the same thing.

"Come on, it's time to take the next step," Knox said.

Knox opened the door, and Hunter walked with him into another world.

Hunter looked around and couldn't believe it. It made everything else seem like a dream. He'd never seen anything like it. Hunter looked back at Knox and hesitantly smiled, realizing the commander really did have answers to questions he didn't know how to ask.

Knox looked at Hunter and smiled. "Isn't it great to leave the past for the future? Isn't it great to say goodbye so you can say Hello? Aren't mornings great? Isn't passion great? Isn't it great to be alive?"

"Steak, eggs, and a trip to the Moon," Hunter said as he looked through a massive cavern to see the gargantuan stages of a Saturn V rocket.

Hunter looked at Knox and then again at the rocket and laughed.

The power and reality of Project Apollo now belonged to Commander Knox Long.

9

What We Think, We Make Real

Unbelievable... Hunter thought as he caught his breath. His heart raced.

The massive cavern in front of Hunter was divided into three sections. The giant stages of the Saturn V sat in the middle, separated by huge yellow support vehicles, surrounded by dozens of busy workers. Hunter noticed each stage of the Saturn V had "N.B.I.E" painted down the side.

In the left part of the cavern, dwarfed by the stages, there was a kind of gray-glass office building, four stories tall. Through picture-glass windows, Hunter could see people working on computers inside.

In the right section of the cavern there were more workers, cranes, equipment, and several large storage tanks. Hunter also recognized a full-size Lunar Module, Command Module, and Service Module. Robots appeared to be doing most of the heavy lifting. The cavern was buzzing with activity. It was also brightly lit, making Hunter feel like he was outside on a sunny day. The air was cool and dry.

Hunter turned to Knox and took a deep breath. "This is the most incredible thing I've ever seen."

"What you see is the result of hard work, careful planning, and execution. Nothing more," Knox said as Hunter turned to look back at the huge cavern.

"But how, Knox? How did you do this?"

"I think it's time to begin the tour," Knox replied.

Kathy smiled, "Sorry, Dad, I'll have to miss this one. I've got a few navigation problems I want to finish and I want to tweak one of the displays." It was the first time Kathy had acknowledged Knox as her father.

She kissed Knox on the cheek then said to Hunter, "Try not to be too amazed, because if you are, you'll miss the point." She waved goodbye, walked over to the main building, and went inside.

Hunter and Knox walked to the center of the cavern. "To begin with," Knox started, "you came through an elevator airlock back there. We're six hundred feet below the surface of Cayman Brac. The pressure is higher in the cavern to keep out the heat, humidity, and salty air. The atmosphere in here is perfectly controlled, perfect for the equipment, perfect for my team.

"The building Kathy just went into is administration. There you'll find accommodations for workers and guests, plus Mission Control and Operations."

"But how?" Hunter asked, still in awe.

"Remember, Hunter, I'm not the first. This was all done once before, more than forty years ago. I'm just continuing what should have been continued. Follow me."

"What does N-B-I-E stand for?" Hunter asked

"Not because it's easy, borrowed from President Kennedy when he first challenged us to go to the Moon."

"No shit," Hunter whispered.

The scale of the cavern was incredible. Knox looked up and said, "First of all, this is one of the biggest natural caverns in the world, and well-concealed. In fact, my geologists assure me that we're the only people who know about it. It's five hundred feet to the top, a thousand feet across, and nine hundred feet wide. It's almost a natural box. We made very few changes."

"And yet you say the temperature and humidity are perfectly controlled?" Hunter asked.

"Yes," Knox said. "In fact, we have a separate department to handle that. Basically, we use seawater to cool this facility. Water is pumped through pipes to dissipate the heat, and there are sensors everywhere to measure temperature. Where we don't have sensors, we use thermal imaging to look for hot or cold spots. Being underground helps as well. We're well insulated."

"Where do you get your power?"

"Ocean currents, tides, and waves."

"For this much energy?" Hunter asked, looking at the enormous lighting system on the ceiling, high overhead.

"Yes, we've learned how to harness the ocean's energy very effectively. I'll show you sometime," Knox said.

"Because we're in a cavern, lighting is very important. It's white laser light controlled by a computer and works on a timing system at the right spectrum to keep people content and working at their best."

Knox and Hunter walked to a white Saturn V stage sitting in the middle of the cavern surrounded by workers.

"But, Knox, what about the money? Who financed this?" Hunter asked as he looked at the white and black stage.

"The ocean did that for us as well."

"The ocean?"

"I'll explain later. In the center of the cavern here, as you can see, we have the three stages of the Saturn V. They are separated for now. We're getting ready to stack them into a launch configuration."

"Launch?" Hunter's eyes got wide.

"That's right. The biggest stage is stage one—"

"Knox," Hunter interrupted. "Where are you launching to?"

Knox looked at Hunter and smiled, "Where do you think?"

"But…"

"Why not? I've got the talent and the equipment," Knox said. "Besides I've found something up there I want."

"What?"

"I'll tell you later.

"Hey, Pete," Knox said to one of the workers, another distinguished looking man in his 60s. "How's everything?"

"Coming along fine, Knox. We've been able to cut another fifty pounds," Pete said as he showed Knox a blueprint displayed electronically on a large piece of glass.

"Perfect. I'm glad that new alloy is doing the trick. Good job." They shook hands, and the worker went back to his business.

Knox patted the side of the first stage and said, "Three minutes into the flight and the Saturn V was more than fifty miles high over the Atlantic Ocean, traveling sixty-two hundred miles per hour.

"Then it was time for staging, the mechanical act of dropping the used first stage and igniting the second stage. To make this happen, explosive bolts that connect the first and second stages were activated. The stages came apart," Knox said as he gestured with his hands. "Then the first stage fires eight retro-rockets to slow it down. It's left behind."

He turned to the second stage. "At that point, four small rockets on the bottom of the second stage fire to kick the fuel to the bottom of the tanks," he pointed to the back of the stage, "and five J-2 engines begin to generate thrust.

"The astronauts describe staging as a violent maneuver. When the first stage cuts off, the astronauts are jerked forward because the force of flight is no longer directly behind them. When the second stage kicks in, the astronauts are thrown back in their seats as the spacecraft picks up speed.

"The J-2 engines develop one million pounds of thrust and burn for about six minutes. They take the spacecraft to a height of over a hundred nautical miles and to a speed of over twelve thousand miles an hour. The engines are powered by liquid hydrogen and liquid oxygen. A very powerful combination that burns about thirty to forty percent more effectively than other fuels."

They walked back to the front of the stage and Knox pointed to bright orange tanks inside.

"Hunter, if you'll look here, you'll see the fuel tanks in the stage. Liquid hydrogen tends to catch fire when it comes into contact with air, making leaks dangerous. In fact, during the Apollo program, engineers used brooms to find leaks. They'd wave a broom over a tank and if the broom caught fire, they'd found their leak. Now we use self-sealing tanks.

"Liquid hydrogen also needs to stay very cold. The tanks in the second and third stage are kind of like giant thermos bottles to keep the liquid hydrogen and the liquid oxygen at their proper temperatures of 423 degrees below zero and 293 degrees below zero, respectively."

Knox walked over to a bench by the second stage and sat down. "As you can see, we're well on our way to putting this baby together," he said as he leaned back.

Hunter looked at Knox, then back at the second stage. "Will it work?" Hunter asked.

"Yes," Knox said confidently. "Success is our only option."

"How did you come up with all the details so quickly?" Hunter asked. "When did you start working on this?"

"Project Apollo was well documented. It was just a matter of making improvements and putting the right team together. Overall, because of current computer technology, we have a much more reliable system. Putting this project together, basically what you see here in the cavern took five years."

Hunter sat beside Knox on the bench and looked at the first and second stages. It was extraordinary.

Knox looked at him. "As you make your way to your goal, Hunter, you'll go through stages. Stage one gets you off the ground and on your way. As we've talked about before, sometimes that's the most difficult part, but it's not the only time there's potential for trouble on the journey. You must be ready to let go of stage one when the fuel is gone so you can move on. Keep the momentum and take another major action to get to your goal. Don't rest or you'll be pulled back."

"What do you mean, 'pulled back'?" Hunter asked.

"Sometimes people hold on to things that help them begin their flight. They hold on for too long. They keep thinking how great the first action was, but when the fuel or passion is gone, they return to where they were or, worse yet, they get stuck.

"This is why many people lead quiet lives of desperation. They ricochet from gravity to gravity with a series of stage-one launches. But to really get going, you've got to light the second stage. You've got to accept the risk and move on with your flight plan.

"If you find yourself stuck, do a restart. Go back and develop a better flight plan and kick in the first stage again! Start over as soon as possible; you don't want to be drifting around for too long."

"How will I know when to move to the second stage?" Hunter asked.

"You'll know because you'll feel like you're looking for something. Maybe you feel like you're coasting. If so, you won't feel the passion of the first stage behind you anymore. When that happens, light the second stage."

"How will I know if I've taken the proper action to move on?"

"You'll know because your vision will expand. As you move toward your goal, you become more fulfilled with life. As you become more fulfilled, you'll look back and see the beauty of your life and the beauty of what it took to get this far. Seeing the beauty drives you to want to accomplish even more. The cycle builds."

Knox got up and gestured for Hunter to follow. They walked around to the back of the first stage. "Thanks to composite material, we can build this stage horizontally instead of vertically. In the Apollo days, if you tried to build the first stage horizontally, the sides would actually warp because of its size."

Knox pointed to the monster-sized engines of the first stage. "Each of our engines is about the size of a dump truck. You're looking at the five F-1 engines. We've made some improvements, but these babies have always been reliable. And they'll help me explain my next point."

The engines were both imposing and impressive. They actually looked like giant props for a movie. Knox looked at them and said, "As you make your way to your goal, you've got to make sure you're in control of your emotions. You must stay in a forward-moving state with positive momentum. You do this by focusing on the reason for what you're doing. Whatever it takes, the reason is all that really matters. With that in mind, remember: getting angry or negative will make the drive for your engines inefficient and unstable. When that happens, you slow down and become more susceptible to gravity."

Knox gestured to the F-1s. "These engines are eighteen feet tall and fourteen feet wide. Once we light them, if instability develops in a combustion chamber, the engine will destroy itself in a matter of seconds. When they designed these engines for Apollo, engineers put bombs inside to try and develop instability during test firings. Eventually, they created an engine that could correct an unstable situation in a tenth of a second. Our engines do it in even less time.

"The lesson, Hunter? If you're hit with problems on the way to your goal, try to clear them up immediately. Don't let instability interfere with your passion and drive for what you want. Don't let instability destroy your engines.

"And with that, Hunter, I think you've earned a break," Knox said as he gestured to the office building.

Hunter looked and saw Kathy standing in front of the building. "Kathy will take you to the cafeteria for lunch and then to your room. Get some rest. I'll meet you back here at six, just before dinner. We have a few more details I want to go over. For now, I should deal with a few key items that need my attention. See you at dinner."

Hunter nodded his head and watched as Knox walked to the area where his men were working on the Lunar Module and the Command and Service Modules. Kathy walked over to Hunter.

"Hungry?" she asked.

"Yes," Hunter said.

Hunter and Kathy entered the administration building and took an elevator to the second floor. They walked down a long hall into a large cafeteria. "Not Because It's Easy" was painted along one wall. Hunter was confident he would finally get to know more about Kathy. *She doesn't seem to say much. She just watches her dad.*

The two went through the service line with about fifty other men and women. Hunter noticed the different languages being spoken and how everyone seemed to be content and focused on their work. Kathy and Hunter each filled their plates with an assortment of food and sat down at a long table by a picture-glass window. From this view, he could see all the activity on the cavern floor. Hunter looked out through the glass and saw Knox working with some people by the second stage of the Saturn V.

"Kathy, tell me, how did he do it?" Hunter asked, looking into her eyes.

She looked out at her father on the floor of the cavern, then back at Hunter. "He simply found the best people. The most motivated people. People who still believed in the dream and ready to make it happen again. Dad will tell you that bringing people together for this was the hardest part. But once he had the team, everything else seemed to be created overnight." Kathy looked out the window again. "He jokingly calls us all, 'Futurenauts.'"

"Futurenauts?"

"People on the edge of tomorrow. People who know that our species is made up of explorers. We travel to where the action is. If we are to survive and continue to evolve, our common destiny is reaching up and out. Reaching the next goal. The men and women who work here are devoted to opening up the path for everyone else. Even if it's just another footstep beyond."

"Kathy, why is he showing me all this?" Hunter asked, unable to eat.

"He likes you and trusts you. He says you have a strong heart and a strong will to do what is right."

Do what is right... Hunter cringed at the words. He looked down at his shoe. He hadn't sent any messages since the flight. With everything he knew now, he didn't want to be part of some secret government bureaucracy responsible for stopping Knox Long. He had to know why Knox wanted to go back to the Moon. *Project Apollo had been squandered. Why should Knox be prevented from using what had already been created? Should my agency act as judge and jury? Should I?* His mind was swimming in questions.

"Hunter, are you okay?" Kathy smiled.

Hunter quickly cleared the thoughts from his mind and said, "What about the people trying to stop him?"

"No big deal. We hate to lose the jet, but there are other ways off the island. In fact, pretty soon there will be another way and the whole world will know about it," she said as she looked at the stages of the Saturn V.

"We've tried to be reasonable. We've tried to avoid conflict, but the organization working against us refuses to leave us alone. Even in conflict, we sought out a peaceful resolution. I'm saddened, and I know my father is saddened by the lives lost. We didn't want it to be this way. We just want to conduct our business without being stopped by anyone."

"Why does your father want to go back?"

"I'd better let him tell you that."

After Hunter and Kathy finished lunch, she took him to his guestroom on the third floor. The room was something you'd expect for a president or head of state. It had everything except a television or telephone. Kathy walked across the room and opened the curtains of a large window overlooking the floor of the cavern. Then she opened a door that led to a library.

"Copies of most everything ever written about Apollo or going to the Moon are in this room," she said. "My dad wants his team to know the topic. He spends a lot of time up here as well. You're welcome to look around."

Kathy started to walk towards the door and said, "That does it for now. I'll be back to collect you at five forty-five." Hunter looked at his watch: 1405.

After she left, Hunter looked at Knox's collection of books. He picked up an old book, *From the Earth to the Moon* by Jules

Verne. He opened it and saw that Verne's signature was taped inside the cover. On another shelf was a book called *Reconstructing Apollo*, written by Knox Long. Hunter remembered it was the first book he'd read by Knox. He sat down and began to read. An hour later, he put the book down and fell asleep...

* * *

"Getting inside the house isn't as easy as we thought it would be," McCaully said to Oscar, looking at a diagram. "Basically we're looking at top-down booby traps. One mistake and it will make the jet explosion look like a picnic." Soldiers continued to bring in high-tech equipment, turning the tent into a command post.

"How long until we can get in?" Oscar asked.

"At least several more hours. At least."

"Knox Long knows how to plan that's for sure," Oscar said, looking at his watch. It was already 1500. They had little more than twenty-four hours before the deadline. "Whatever it takes, we've got to find Knox."

***

The shark was still trying to enter the cave. Hunter swam deeper into the darkness, and then suddenly, a fast moving current pushed him from underneath. As he moved up quickly, the surrounding light grew brighter. In an instant he was pushed out of the cave into brightness, a brightness he'd never experienced before...he was going up and up and up....

A loud sound shattered Hunter's dream. He looked at his watch, and tried to shake off the sleep. It was 1730. Kathy would be back at 1745. Just enough time for a shower and shave. Hunter heard the loud sound again and went over to the window. A giant crane was lifting the first stage of the Saturn V into vertical position.

Hunter was running out of time. After showering he found some clothes with a note attached saying they should be his size. Hunter got dressed and sat at the edge of the bed. He'd made up his mind that during the next meeting with Knox he'd reveal that he was an agent sent to find out what had happened to the XIA engine, the stealth helicopters, the planes at the boneyard, and the medical files at the National Archives. There was no other choice; he had to speak up first. Besides, when General Greg Mitchell recognized Hunter, it would all be over.

At exactly 1745, Kathy knocked on his door. She looked stunning in a deep blue dress. Hunter wasn't sure what to say. *She would be so easy to fall for. I am falling for her. Focus.*

Kathy seemed to realize she'd thrown him off and smiled. "My dad will be ready in fifteen minutes. Meet him by the construction pile over by the Command and Service Module," she said. "I'll see you at dinner."

A short time later, Hunter made his way across the floor of the cavern. The first stage was now upright. After walking around the second stage, Hunter saw Knox waiting for him.

"Follow me," Knox said.

Knox was quiet for a few minutes as they made their way across the cavern. They walked up to two chairs by a pile of neatly stacked construction materials. "Here, Hunter, have a seat." They both sat down.

"Hunter, it's time to add the next element that will take you to your goal. We've talked about it already, but I haven't directly pointed it out to you yet. It's the difference that truly makes the difference, it gives life meaning, it's the reason I'm here."

"What is it?" Hunter asked.

Knox took a deep breath, "It's the edge."

"The edge?"

"There's always been a lot of talk about having 'the edge.' It's a cliché to say the least. But do you have any idea what really makes up the edge?" Knox asked.

Hunter shook his head.

"It's that point shrouded in mist. Between heaven and hell, between mind and body, between life and death, between the real and the imagined, between night and day, between getting everything you've ever wanted and not getting everything you've ever wanted, between staying on the Earth or going to the Moon. He pointed to the first stage, now standing upright.

"The edge gives you the advantage in the heat of competition. It's the line where playing ends and winning begins," Knox said. "The edge is what you're trying to hone in on."

A worker walked over. "Sorry to interrupt, Knox. I thought you might like to see this," the man said as he handed Knox a slip of paper.

Knox quickly read and signed the paper. "Charlie, just make sure the coupler accepts yaw and roll d-c body rate signals from either gyro assembly and make sure the computer 'go' program is involved in the loop."

"Thanks, Knox. Sorry I had to interrupt," the worker said as he took the paper and left.

"The edge is what it's all about," Knox continued.

"How do I get the edge?" Hunter asked.

"If I directly answer that question, I destroy the edge. I can only describe its shadow in the following way: having the edge is the knowledge that nothing will stop you from the goal you're focusing on. It's the ability to program the subconscious to help you get what you really want, whatever it takes.

"Having the edge is also having something at stake."

"Having something at stake?" Hunter asked.

"If you have something at stake, then you have risk. If risk is involved, you won't take unnecessary chances and you'll do whatever it takes to succeed. Risk gives life, because life will do whatever it takes to survive.

"You're given a sharp edge at birth. The first twenty or so years of your life you either keep the edge sharp through positive reinforcement, or make it dull through negativity.

"But if you think your edge is dull, you can sharpen it. America sharpened its edge with Project Apollo. We had the reason to go and the vision to go. With passion, we did whatever it took to get to the Moon.

"Here's another example: Let's say you're trying to make a difficult sale in business. But before you take the physical footsteps, you take the mental footsteps, and you make the sale in your mind. With that vision, you're happy and confident. After that, just know that whatever happens, you're taking a step in the right direction. That's true even if you don't make the sale that time. Eventually you know you'll do it. As long as you act, you don't lose anything.

"Having the edge, and getting the edge, is the ability to continue taking the steps to what you really want, even when the path seems blocked, or you're rejected.

"It's like having what some like to call 'the right stuff.' A test pilot may put it all on the line, but he or she has no question about capability. Therefore, everything can be put at stake, and with the edge, it can be brought back in an instant.

"Here's another example of the edge, and this is why we've come here." Knox went to the construction pile and picked up a thick black plank about twenty feet long and three feet across. He put it in front of Hunter.

"This is a composite that my chemists here cooked up. It's one of the strongest substances in the world and one of the lightest." Knox put the plank down and walked away. He came back with a small box. He opened it. Hunter saw an incredibly large diamond inside.

"Hunter, this diamond is worth approximately two and a half million dollars, maybe more." He put it at the opposite side of the plank. "The diamond is yours if you walk across the plank."

Hunter got out of his seat and walked across the plank without even thinking about it. He picked up the box and looked at Knox.

"Good. How about double or nothing?"

"Fine," Hunter said.

Knox walked away and came back with another box. "The diamond in this box is worth three and a half million dollars. So this will be worth more than double." Hunter gave Knox the first box. "All you have to do is walk across the plank and take both boxes."

"Okay," Hunter said.

"Wait a second," Knox held up a hand and then turned and waved. At that instant, a massive crane picked up the plank and took it high into the air. A moment later, the crane delicately placed the plank between two scaffoldings. Then a robot arm, attached to another machine, came down in front of Knox. He placed the two boxes in its grip. The robot arm lifted the boxes, maneuvered them into position, and carefully put them at one end of the plank.

"Follow me," Knox said. They climbed a stairway on one of the scaffoldings. The plank had been placed on the scaffoldings about a hundred and fifty feet above the cavern floor. When Hunter reached the top, he looked down. A fall would be lethal.

About a foot of the plank was on their scaffolding, another foot was on the other scaffolding, twenty feet away. The boxes containing each diamond were on the far end of the plank.

"Well, Hunter, all you have to do is walk across. Since you're a hundred and fifty feet up, a fall off the side would be deadly. Taking those diamonds could change your life. Which do you concentrate on now, the goal or the danger?"

Hunter looked across at the diamonds.

Knox said, "Chances are you're no longer just thinking about the money, you're thinking there's a possibility you could fall. If you see yourself falling, chances are you will.

"What you need to do is rehearse," Knox said. "Rehearse for success. Close your eyes and see yourself walking across and reaching the goal. Do it again, and again. See yourself reaching the goal, reaching those diamonds. When you begin to concentrate on the goal, you begin to have the edge. With the edge, you begin to bypass all the people who are still thinking about falling off the plank. The more you mentally practice walking across, the more you sharpen your edge. If you can walk the plank knowing that success is your only option, then you can get to the positive goal you really want.

"Now millions of dollars in diamonds is a lot to offer. It's very tempting. So what I want you to do is put your goal on the other side. Okay, here's your reason at this side of the plank: there's your goal at that side. Is it still worth it to walk across? If not, you'd better come up with another reason and another goal. Remember, it's got to be worth the walk."

Knox waited for Hunter to make a move across. Instead, Hunter just looked at the boxes. Wealth, death, or safety? Finally, Knox sat on the scaffolding. "What happens to some people is that they get stuck in comfortable lives, and it's their fault."

The metaphor struck Hunter in the heart and Knox knew he'd hit the mark. "Hunter, people who don't achieve their goals are afraid to look into their souls."

"But why?" Hunter asked as he sat down beside Knox.

"Because somewhere in their minds they know they could get whatever they want, but they're still concentrating on falling halfway.

"The bottom line: their goals aren't worth the walk. To those people, failure is an option. They concentrate on the negative, decide to stay put, and become frustrated.

"But people with the edge visualize the plank and walk across it every day. They consider the elevation and distance, weigh the risks, and if the payoff is greater, they go for the payoff. They take the walk in reality. Besides, they always make sure the payoff is greater; they don't have time for anything else.

"People with the edge have a vision for success. This vision gives them the ability and the capacity to get what they want, physically and mentally. People with the edge don't waste any time. They visualize and move out. People who have the edge look at comfort and laugh. They'd rather walk across the top. For them, comfort is somewhere down the road, as soon as they find the tallest building or the loftiest goal.

"Hunter, what do you want?"

Knox waited for Hunter's answer. When Hunter didn't give him one, Knox said, "You've got to find out what you want. Make sure the risks are worth it. Make success your only option. Don't delay."

Hunter looked at the two boxes twenty feet away, and then down at the smooth rock floor of the cavern a hundred and fifty feet away. Success was closer by a hundred and thirty feet and yet the floor seemed closer.

Knox went on. "People with the edge will say, 'Do everything you can today, because tomorrow you'll do something better.' Or 'Do everything you can today, because this could be the last day of your life.'

"Remember the story of the servants and the talents? Three servants are given talents. Two of the servants are given several talents. They invest them and bring back more talents. Then there's the one guy who's only given one talent. He buries it because he's afraid it will be taken from him. When his master finds out, he becomes angry because the servant didn't do anything with the talent. He didn't invest it. His master tells him to give it to someone else who will make better use of it. If you don't use what you're given, it will be taken away from you. And if you lose the great things you're given, then what good is all this?"

"Knox, are you telling me to take chances?" Hunter asked, looking across at the diamonds.

"Necessary chances, yes. Unnecessary chances, no."

"How will I know the difference?"

"If you walk the edge for the wrong motivations, in the end it won't be worth it, and gravity will pull you down with a vengeance. So ask yourself: 'Is it worth the walk?' If the answer is yes, then it's a necessary chance you need to take. Plan it out and take it."

Hunter looked at the boxes from the safety of the scaffolding.

Knox got up. "It's easy to become comfortable and think we can maintain our lives without taking any chances. However, by doing so, instead of producing, we consume, and we begin to use up everything we've got. Chaos is always at work."

"Chaos?" Hunter asked, getting up.

"A good explanation is 'the butterfly effect.' It goes something like this: Weather does not repeat itself and is to a great extent unpredictable. That's because smaller changes are always cascading through the weather system. Basically, the flap of a butterfly's wings somewhere in South America today could cause slight weather changes that get bigger and bigger until it rains over your house next Tuesday.

"You've got to keep up with the chaotic changes in life, and you've got to be willing to adapt to survive. If too many people become complacent, extinction is the next step. The nature of chaos is out there changing everything about life everyday. We've got to be ready to adjust, because what works today may not work tomorrow. Space travel, leaving the Earth, is about leaving our comfort zone in the most intense way. It's about evolving as a species through the chaos that departure can and will bring.

"Chaos in everyday life leads to stress. Stress either forces us to evolve or pushes us out of the picture. The ability to handle chaos-related stress determines your ability to survive. It's true with all life forms. To move ahead, they need to be stressed and challenged. Without stress and chaos, life stagnates.

"As you move to your goal, you will be confronted with stress. It's tough, but you've just got to hold on to your dream. That's the biggest challenge: the ability to hold onto a dream and achieve it, in the face of chaos. That's what the edge is really all about, seeing the steps to your goal no matter what happens. So once again, it all comes back to the flight plan. The pathway."

Knox looked over the edge of the scaffolding. "Don't live your life in fear. Life is meant to be cold, rainy, foggy, hot, sunny, snowy. We've survived this long because we've been built to take it.

"We've had these breakthroughs in medicine that have allowed us to be comfortable. The breakthroughs have helped us avoid the stress of physical pain. But what about the people doing drugs that aren't in any physical pain? It's because they're in mental pain. They can't find true peace of mind because they don't know what they really want. They try to get the edge with drugs, and what they don't know is they're really jumping off a cliff.

"And then some people think they can buy their way to happiness. You can't buy the things you really want. You've got to produce them with your mind first. After all, isn't the book always better than the movie? That's because when you read a book you produce the movie in your mind. The writer may have written the words, but somehow it becomes your vision.

"Well, Hunter, you don't have to walk across for the diamonds right now. I'll leave them up here. When you think you're ready, go for it."

Hunter looked at the plank.

"You know, Hunter, I asked Kathy about you walking across. She thinks you'll do it. In fact, she's sure you will.

"Kathy?" Hunter asked.

"She says you have a true and strong heart. If there's one thing I've learned at this age, never argue with your daughter about that kind of stuff.

"And she thinks you're doing fine. We're throwing a lot at you at once," Knox said.

Knox started walking down the steps. Hunter followed, looking back at the boxes containing the diamonds. *Maybe tomorrow I'll try,* he thought, *but not yet.*

"We've talked about a lot," Knox said as they walked down the steps. "But I haven't even told you how grand the view is from Earth's orbit yet. It's time for stage three. We'll talk about that tomorrow. For now, let's have dinner."

Hunter and Knox went back to the cafeteria and waited in line with several other people. Being with Knox was like being with a celebrity. Everybody wanted to shake his hand and give him the latest information on what they were working on.

After filling their plates, Hunter followed Knox to a room adjacent to the main dining room. It was a conference room with a large black marble table in the center. On one side there was a bank of television monitors with different views of the cavern and all the equipment. Four people in security uniforms watched the screens. On the other side of the room, a massive model of the Moon stood about twelve feet tall. It slowly rotated, revealing a carefully laid out map of the surface. It seemed to float in the air. Hunter realized it wasn't a model. It was a full-motion hologram, the best he'd ever seen and another example of Knox's solid holography.

Knox sat at the head of the table. "Please, Hunter, sit here, to my right." Hunter sat in the seat beside Knox. The room began to fill with people. Kathy came in and sat directly across from Hunter, to Knox's left. She smiled and Hunter smiled back.

When everyone was seated, Knox touched a button on the table. The lights dimmed slightly and the room got quiet.

"Ladies and gentlemen, thank you for joining me tonight," Knox started. "Let me introduce you to Hunter Algier. He's the journalist we've chosen to record our journey back. As you may know, Hunter's written some excellent articles for News Now." Knox raised a glass to Hunter, and the other people around the table did the same.

"I'm glad we're all here together at this important stage of our mission. Of course, General Mitchell and his security team couldn't join us tonight. They're dealing with some of the trouble we've had on the island."

Hunter breathed a sigh of relief. He would have time to tell Knox who he was before General Mitchell recognized him.

For the most part, dinner was quiet. Occasionally someone would ask Knox about a construction or scheduling issue. At those times, the conversation was fast and highly technical. For the most part, Hunter was able to keep up with the discussion.

Two hours flew by.

When Hunter got back to his room after dinner, he found a note taped to the bathroom mirror in his room. It read: Meet me on the Observation Deck. Just take the elevator.

Attached to the note were directions on how to get to the deck. About ten minutes later, after going through another elevator airlock, Hunter found himself on a deck built on the cliffs of Cayman Brac. There were other workers looking at the night sky. After a while, they left and Hunter was the only one on the deck. He didn't mind being alone, looking at the starry, cloudless sky. Hunter looked at the almost-full Moon. He thought back to when he'd first met Knox, just two days ago. His life had changed forever, in an instant. The Moon was no longer just a light in the night sky; it was once again a destination.

Hunter heard the top hatch open behind him. It was Kathy. Her hair was gently blowing in the breeze. Looking up, she said, "It's an amazing sky. It's a shame more people don't get to see it like this. After two days of my dad, I thought you might like someone else to talk to. What have you learned?"

"What do you mean?"

"Do you see the pathway of Apollo?" she asked as she sat down.

"I don't know, Kathy. I just don't know. Everything Knox tells me makes sense. I've seen his creations, and they are stunning." Hunter looked into her eyes. "It's obvious what you imagine can be turned into reality. But I keep asking myself, 'Do I really have what it takes?' I know I want more. But what do I want, and do I really have the reason to want it?"

Kathy sat down beside Hunter. "Sometimes you've just got to let it come to you. Listen, I've heard all the lessons. My dad has taken me on the golf course as well. You know how sometimes you sit there and really try to hit the ball and it turns out bad?"

"Yes," Hunter said.

"And then one time you'll approach the ball, in tune, focused subconsciously, and the ball really flies, but you have no idea how you did it?"

Hunter nodded his head.

"That's what you've got to do now, Hunter. Let your subconscious mind and your heart be your guides. You have a strong soul. It will tell you what to do next."

He took a long look at her. A crust over his heart was breaking. A crust formed so long ago for so many reasons. He wondered if she felt the same. He started to ask a question, but she stopped him. "Hunter, tomorrow he'll tell you about the third stage. Listen to what he says carefully."

With that, she got up and left.

"Goodnight, Kathy," Hunter said, and he was alone again, under the stars of Cayman Brac.

***

"I don't care how you do it, just do it!" Oscar yelled, looking at map showing a possible pathway to Knox's house.

"You know it's not that damn easy, Oscar," McCaully said. "The house is wired five ways to hell. I can't afford to lose anymore of my men for whatever information Knox may have inside."

"I know," Oscar said, "but we are less than twenty hours away from the deadline. We still don't know what Knox is planning and we can't afford to screw this up."

At that instant, Phil walked inside the tent. "Sorry I couldn't get here earlier. My flight was delayed."

"Please sit down, Phil." Oscar said. "I have reason to think Hunter may have joined Knox. He hasn't reported in all day. What did he tell you at Pinehurst?"

"Nothing, Oscar. He spent most of his time on the course with Commander Long."

Oscar sighed. "Depending on what happens, we need to be ready to take Hunter into custody."

McCaully looked at Oscar and Phil sharply, "We may even have to kill him." He let the words sink in and turned back to the map.

10

The Shoe Drops

Friday, October 25, 2002

Cayman Brac: 0710 ET

That night Hunter found sleep difficult, his mind troubled by a hundred memories. Strangely, for now…the shark had left his dreams. It was replaced by Angie, his ex-wife.

Hunter met Angie at the agency. She was sharply intelligent. Her intensity about everything was infectious. Her smile was a gift she used judiciously: she could instantly light up a room with her lips. He had loved her with all his heart. At the height of their relationship, he would ache to see her, ache to hear her voice. He loved her unconditionally.

He dreamed about the day he turned Angie in. The day he found ten million dollars in cash in a canvas bag. Enough for them to live the rest of their lives comfortably. Angie had sold environmental information to the New Soviet Union.

Siberia had become an environmental nightmare during the cold war. The United States had come up with a plan to help the Russians deal with the problem. But the plan was halted when communist radicals overthrew the government. Relations held for a while until reports of a new weapon filtered back to the West. The New Soviet Union was working on a process called 'Digital Decapitation,' a way to instantly disable computers. The electromagnetic pulse, or EMP, from a nuclear weapon would cause the same effect. According to reports, the Soviets had found another way to shock computers worldwide. As relations chilled, the United States withdrew its offer to help with the environmental problem. Angie was outraged. She felt the environmental offer to help clean up Russia went beyond politics. It was, after all, one world. In an act of defiance, she gave a computer with all the information to Soviet agents. Her intentions were noble, but they had also given her ten million dollars. The fact that she didn't ask for it didn't matter. The damage was done on so many levels.

By the time Hunter found the money, it was too late. He couldn't do anything to help his wife. Two days before he was scheduled to take a routine lie-detector test, he turned her in, knowing he wouldn't pass, pleading for them to go easy on her.

Hunter was interrogated for nearly four weeks about his connections to the crime. Hunter couldn't answer any questions. Angie had left him in the dark for his protection.

Hunter tossed and turned again. He remembered walking through the cavern with Knox...

"Will it work?"
"Yes, success is our only option."
Hunter was now standing on the edge of the scaffolding. *"Hunter, what do you want?" Knox had asked.*
Lunch with Kathy... *"Creation is beautiful,"* *she had told him.* *"My father created a pathway to the future. That's all he ever wanted to do."*
Hunter remembered Oscar's warning: *"Knox is a dangerous man, so be prepared. But he's cocky; he doesn't think he can make a mistake. I want you there when he does.*
"Stop by weapons requisition before you leave."
Then Hunter was falling off the scaffolding...falling... No, he wasn't falling, he was weightless...

Hunter woke with a start and sat up quickly on the edge of the bed. He looked out the window of his room to the floor of the cavern. Even this early in the morning, workers continued stacking the rocket.

Hunter looked at the massive stages of the Saturn V. He was missing something. Something about The Roswell Trinity. Where was the XIA rocket? How was Knox planning to use instant acceleration? Hunter found his shoes and picked one up. By now, Oscar and other agents were on the island. If he sent a message, they could probably triangulate his position.

He looked at the shoe. *Does it end here?*

Hunter set the shoe on the side of the bed and put his face in his hands. "Shit," he muttered. "I've got to tell Knox." Then he threw himself back on the bed with enough force to cause the shoe to drop to the floor. The shoe, deactivated until that point, hit the ground hard enough to send out one signal…

* * *

Oscar sipped an early morning cup of coffee by himself under the command tent as the October Caribbean sun climbed into the sky. He looked at the radio, waiting. Phil and McCaully had left for Knox's house about an hour before, after McCaully and his men had finally found a way through the elaborate security system. The plan was to have the house explored and investigated by 0800 that morning. It was now 0715.

At that moment, a soldier stormed into the tent. Oscar dropped his cup of coffee.

"Don't you knock? What is it?" Oscar said, trying to clean up the mess.

"Our monitors have picked up an energy reading from the north end of the island."

"What?" Oscar froze.

"It fits the profile of what you gave us. It's the transmitter in Agent Algier's shoe."

"Damn! Knox must have found out who Hunter was and killed him. Where was the signal from?"

"Underneath the cliffs of Cayman Brac."

"No shit?" Oscar said.

"The echo would indicate there's some kind of a large cavern there. Make that a huge cavern."

"Of course!" Oscar shouted.

***

Hunter was alive and well, still leaning back on the bed. Then he sat up and realized the shoe had fallen off the bed. "Shit!" But it was too late. As he reached down to pick up the shoe, the door to his room swung open. Three armed men rushed in with guns aimed squarely at Hunter. Kathy followed them in and looked at him.

"Hunter, we detected an energy transmission coming from this room." Kathy looked at the shoe in his hand. "From some kind of transmitter."

Kathy took the shoe from Hunter and slammed it on the ground. The heel of the shoe came off to reveal a maze of electronics. Kathy looked at Hunter sharply. The men pointed their guns at Hunter's face.

"Who are you and who do you work for?" Kathy demanded.

Hunter put his hands in the air.

***

Back at the command tent, Oscar and the men were now huddled around a large computer screen. A technician stared at his monitor. "We have a second transmission, a larger one but the same format. The way that echo bounces around…definitely a cavern."

"We've got to get in there," Oscar said.

***

Hunter looked at Kathy. "Kathy, it's not what it looks like."

"You liar. We trusted you. My father trusted you. Now you're going to destroy it all." Kathy looked at the shoe. "That's how they were able to follow us so quickly. Everything we worked for."

Kathy looked at Hunter with cold eyes. "I'll ask you one more time. Who do you work for?"

As tears started to roll down her cheeks, Kathy took a gun from one of the soldiers, cocked it, and pointed it at Hunter's heart. As her finger was about to squeeze the trigger, another hand surrounded hers and pulled the gun gently away.

Knox Long looked at his daughter, and then looked at Hunter. "That's not the way to solve this problem."

In the security center of Knox's cavern, General Greg Mitchell was watching a bank of monitors. Lieutenant Shaw from Echo Air Force Base was standing beside him. They'd arrived on the island shortly after the blast destroyed Echo.

A door opened and Kathy and Knox walked in, followed by two armed guards escorting Hunter. His eyes quickly focused on General Mitchell.

Knox pointed to Hunter. "Greg, I need to know exactly who this man is. He says he's Hunter Algier of News Now. But we now know that's not the case. He's been transmitting information through this special device." Knox held up the shoe.

General Greg Mitchell nodded to Knox and acknowledged Hunter. "Knox, this is Hunter Algier. He's a writer, but unfortunately he's also a tactical aviation specialist for the National Security Agency."

"Hello, General Mitchell," Hunter said.

Knox's eyes rolled up. "So I guess I should have introduced you to him first."

Greg said, "Sorry you didn't."

"Tell me more."

"His branch deals with all kinds of aviation-related sciences. He helped me out on a few projects at Echo Air Force Base."

Knox laughed and looked at Hunter. "Why shouldn't I kill you right now?"

Hunter looked at Knox squarely. "My mission was simple. Find out as much information on you as possible. Shortly after we started talking and after I was shot, my mission objectives became unclear. I think I've been had as much as you have."

Knox stood inches away from Hunter's face, carefully considering his words. "Access the central computer, Greg," Knox said. "Give me the full story on Mr. Algier. Have a seat, Hunter. This could take a few minutes."

The guards motioned for Hunter to sit down.

"Knox, one other thing," Greg said, looking at a monitor, "Our men are entering the camp on the island. Now, about Agent Algier."

* * *

Oscar was in another tent when a team of four of Knox's men moved into the camp. In a rhythmic, silent pattern they began to knock out all the men in Oscar's unit with a quick-acting gas.

* * *

Phil Styles and Robert McCaully entered Knox's house, followed by two more men from the unit. McCaully spotted a man walking up steps to the second floor. In a heartbeat, he tackled him and quickly incapacitated him by breaking his arm.

McCaully looked at the face of the injured man. It was a face he recognized in an instant. "Sam Harris. Apache feather," McCaully said. "You're a long way from Area 27 and California, son. You're absent without leave and so is a few billion dollars worth of equipment. Where is Commander Knox Long? If you don't cooperate, I'll kill you right here." McCaully pulled out a gun.

Harris moaned in pain, "I don't know what you're talking about." McCaully stepped on his arm. Harris yelled in pain.

As McCaully put handcuffs on Sam Harris, Phil gestured to other agents entering the house, "Check for microphones and cameras. Disable whatever you find."

***

Back in the cavern, Knox finished reading the information on Hunter. "Why didn't you stop me sooner, Hunter? You know why? I think you see what's really going on here." Knox looked at Lt. Shaw. "What's the status of their operations camp?"

Shaw looked at the latest readout on his computer. "Our unit has the camp secured. Everybody knocked out."

"What about the house?" Knox asked.

"Harris should be online on his computer," Shaw said, tapping a few keys. "Why isn't the house secured and vacant?" Knox asked.

"We had to send Harris in, but we probably shouldn't talk about it here," Greg said, looking at Hunter.

"Go ahead and tell me. Hunter may never see the light of day again anyway."

Greg looked at Knox. "We made a mistake in clearing the house last night. We moved too fast. Jon in engineering discovered we were missing a set of geological charts, charts of the cavern. They were in a drawer in a desk on the second floor of the house. We sent Harris back to get them."

"Charts of the cavern?" Knox asked.

"They were first put there when we were setting up the cavern about five years ago. They were on the list to scan into the computer, but we had to push back because we needed a larger scanner." Shaw tapped the keyboard. "Harris should have radioed in by now."

Knox glanced at the computer screens. "What about views inside the house?"

Shaw tapped a key and looked at his monitor. "Someone's disabled those cameras. They must have done it a few seconds ago."

"What about sound?" Knox asked.

Shaw pushed another key on his computer. "Nothing."

Knox looked at Hunter. "Your associates are finally starting to get it together." Knox turned back to Greg. "Recommendations?"

Greg looked at Shaw, and then back to Knox. "We send in a team to destroy the house to get rid of any other evidence." Greg paused. "Sorry, Knox."

Knox leaned back against a wall and thought for a second. He looked briefly at Hunter, and then at Kathy. He gave Kathy a gentle smile and then picked up a phone to dial a number. After waiting for the call to go through, he said, "Central Control, this is Knox. Stack the rest of the rocket and ready for launch. Evacuate all the heavy equipment from the cavern."

Greg and Kathy looked at each other in shock as Knox gave the final word. "Prepare for the quick fuel." Knox hung up the phone. "They're not going to stop me," Knox said, looking off in the distance. Then he turned to his daughter, "Kathy, supervise the rest of the stacking and the quick fuel." Knox looked at Greg. "Above all else, stay on the timeline. I'm going to get Harris. If I'm not back in an hour, your orders are to destroy the house and proceed with the mission. If these people want a war, give them one. We're too close now."

Knox looked at Hunter. "Agent Algier. What are we going to do with you?"

Hunter remained silent.

Knox looked at a security guard. "Give me the hypo."

One of the soldiers gave Knox a small hypodermic needle with a flashing red light at one end. "It's a matter of trust, Hunter." Before Hunter could react, Knox injected him with the hypodermic needle.

"I've just put a squadron of nano-bombs in your bloodstream. They're small but highly lethal. At the touch of a button, those bombs will explode, causing massive internal bleeding that will be impossible to repair. You'll be dead in a matter of minutes or seconds, depending on where the bombs are in your bloodstream when they detonate. That will also determine the pain. You're coming back to the house with me."

Knox turned to Greg. "Activate countermeasures to secure the cavern. As I said before, above all else, at all costs, stay on the timeline."

"Okay, Knox," Greg said, swallowing hard.

Knox gave his daughter a gentle hug. "I love you. You mean the world to me. Promise me you'll complete the mission."

"Dad, you're the key."

"No, Kathy, you are. You're the next generation. I would have never gotten this far without you."

Kathy's eyes started to well with emotion. Even so, she cleared her throat and gave her father a confident smile. "I'll finish the mission."

"Hunter, let's go," Knox said.

Hunter and Knox left the conference room. As they walked across the floor of the cavern, Knox was silent. Hunter finally had to say something. "Knox, I won't make excuses."

Knox looked at Hunter. "I know, Hunter, that's why I like you. We're so alike."

"Knox, I followed your career ever since I was a kid. I watched you walk on the Moon. I watched you become a national hero. Why did you turn on everything?"

"We all make choices. Each choice takes us down a separate road. This is the road I've chosen," Knox said.

"But why, Knox?"

"I had to do it, Hunter, I couldn't wait."

"But where does it end? You said these people killed ten of your men. Do you really think you can succeed? They're ready to do anything to stop you."

"Remember, Hunter, it's the mission they're after, the plan. Think about it. If one person is able to go into space or to the Moon independently, and that person doesn't represent a country, wouldn't you expect a lot of people to be envious?"

"Yes," Hunter said. "But you were well on your way secretly. Why did you go after The Roswell Trinity? You practically gave yourself away."

Hunter and Knox approached the airlock.

Knox motioned for Hunter to go inside. "The Roswell Trinity was held secret for too long by the U.S. government. It was mired in too much hocus pocus about UFOs and aliens. When I found out about it, and that it was becoming a reality under Senator Langston's oversight committee, I knew I had to stop it. Too much was at stake.

Knox punched several buttons on the wall to open the airlock. "In the wrong hands," Knox said, "The Roswell Trinity can be used to take over the world. If one country has it, there is no balance of power. They were right to end it the first time around in 1949. When I knew that Operation Crystal was ready to test the VIS technology, I knew I had to disable Roswell. I knew I also had a peaceful use for the technology. To help our civilization evolve into something better instead of destroying itself."

"But why not use your connections and your allies? Why fight the people who could have listened?" Hunter asked as Knox closed the elevator airlock door and pushed the button marked "PRESSURIZE."

"That's a two-front war. It was difficult enough to protect the cavern and build the rocket. I didn't want to have to fight the military as well over Roswell. The most cost-effective solution for my team was to just take it." Knox turned a switch.

"Five minutes till pressurization," the machine said.

"Knox, if you go back to your house and members of the agency are there, they'll kill you."

Knox looked at Hunter. "Harris is a young kid, about twenty-four. He's more of a hotshot pilot than he is a covert soldier. If he doesn't talk, they'll kill him. I can't live with that."

"Don't you worry you'll lose all this?"

"That I'll lose this?" Knox looked at Hunter sharply. "What you've seen in the cavern can be replaced. If I lose this, I'll do what I've always done. I'll start again. Besides, some things in life take priority over others. Family, friends, and finishing the job you set out to do, without compromise.

"Did I think this project would be easy? No. Sometimes I think I was hoping it would take everything I had left. But now I'm going to see it completed. If I lose this facility, I'll continue. Success is my only option. I'm already there."

Knox looked at Hunter. "I read your resume back there in the cavern. You're thirty-five years old and you spent most of your life going from one city to the next, looking for answers. Except you didn't find them.

"Here's the answer, Hunter. Life is about going after your personal dreams with the people you love. You can't serve any person, any country, or any organization. If you truly want to be happy, you've got to serve your own dreams and yourself. That's what I've spent the last few days trying to tell you. Life waits for no man. It starts now, Hunter. The past is over and that's as good as it gets."

Hunter looked down. "I know that now, Knox."

The two men didn't say anything for a few minutes as the airlock hissed to adjust the pressure. Hunter finally spoke up. "I take it most of the men and women working for you worked at Echo Air Force Base."

Knox smiled. "Yes. There's a reason most of them came on board with me. They believe in a better future for the world. They know the truth is up there waiting." Knox paused and looked at Hunter. "But why am I telling you this? You were trying to stop everything."

"Pressurization complete," the computer reported.

"What would you say if I told you I changed my mind? I want to join you," Hunter said.

Knox smiled, "Then your past really would be over."

11

Choosing the Path

Hunter felt Knox look into his soul with his penetrating eyes. "I believe you. I know you, Hunter, better than you think. You're a smart man. Smart enough to know what I've built here represents the best of what we can do."

"I also know this is only the tip of the iceberg, Knox," Hunter said. "I want to see the rest of it. I want to be a part of it."

"Where you want to be and where you see yourself are good indications of how mentally and physically strong you are. They're also good indications of how far you'll go."

Hunter and Knox walked out of the elevator airlock. Hunter noticed he didn't feel any of the apprehension he'd felt when he first walked into the cavern. His perspective had changed. The polar shift was complete.

Knox reached into a locker on the floor of the airlock to find grenades, two machine guns, and a small piece of glass. He placed them in the back of the electric cart.

"We'll take the cart back to the beach," Knox said.

* * *

Kathy walked up to the microphone on the floor of the main cavern. "Attention," she said. "This is what we've spent the last five years preparing for. Begin the quick fuel. Refrigerate the lines and make sure the fans are ready to ventilate. I want full capacity in one hour. This is it, make it count."

The workers in the cavern hurried toward their posts as Kathy ambled back to the administration building.

***

Hunter and Knox made their way out of the tunnel in less than two minutes. They drove along the rocky path they'd used to escape just the day before. Eventually, Knox pulled the cart beside a massive tree. He got out and picked up a machine gun and the display device he'd gotten out of the locker. "Hunter, take the grenades. But be careful."

Hunter looked at Knox.

Knox smiled. "It's a matter of trust."

"How do we get back inside the house?" Hunter asked.

"Just watch," Knox said.

The two men walked past the palm tree to the wreck of an old ship that had washed ashore. Knox reached down to remove two large pieces of wood from the front of the boat. As he did, he revealed a door inside. He pulled out a key from his pocket and unlocked the door. It made a creaking sound as he pulled it open.

"This tunnel," Knox said, pointing inside, "will take us under the house. We'll come up under the kitchen."

Hunter followed Knox into the tunnel. Knox punched a button on the wall. Small lights came on to illuminate the floor. The two men walked about fifty yards. The tunnel ended with a ladder leading to a hatch on the ceiling.

"This is it," Knox said.

Knox slung the machine gun over his shoulder and pulled out the small piece of glass. "This is a heat sensor and motion detector."

He turned it on and pointed it up. After several seconds, three dots and an outline of the house appeared on the screen. One of the dots was flashing. "That's Harris. He's by the artificial stream in the living room. He's not moving, but he is alive."

"How can you tell it's him?" Hunter asked.

"All of my employees are tagged," Knox said.

Hunter had been tagged himself on two previous missions. "Tagging" involved a small device used to electronically keep track of key people. The tag was usually inserted just under the surface of the skin.

Knox carefully climbed the ladder. When he reached the top, he opened a hatch. He motioned for Hunter to join him. A few seconds later, Knox and Hunter were in the kitchen.

Knox looked at the motion detector. "They're in my office on the second floor," he said quietly. "They're looking for any information, but I didn't leave a lot. Hopefully it won't matter anyway. Harris should be in the next room."

Knox and Hunter made their way around the stone path to the living room. After rounding another corner, they found Harris tied up on the floor with masking tape over his mouth. Knox pulled out a knife to cut the rope off Harris's hands and wrists. Hunter carefully pulled the tape off Harris's mouth, gesturing for him to stay quiet.

"Good to see you, Knox," Harris whispered, "Sorry about this..." He was in a great deal of pain.

"Don't worry, Harris, we'll get you back," Knox said. "What about the chart of the cavern?"

"It's over there by the couch."

"That's a relief," Hunter said, looking upstairs, "Can we get it and go?"

"There's a problem," Harris said, looking at Hunter. "They scanned and sent it out."

"I figured as much," Knox said. "That means they're looking for a way to get in the cavern right now. Let's get out of here."

They carefully picked up Harris and walked back to the kitchen. "I think they broke my arm," he groaned.

Then a cry came from upstairs, "The bastard's not telling us the truth!"

Hunter recognized the voice instantly as that of Commander Robert McCaully.

Knox looked at the motion detector. The dots were moving.

"Hunter, give me a grenade," Knox said. "Get Harris in the tunnel."

Knox took the grenade and carefully pulled the pin out of the top. He then picked up one of the ropes used to tie up Harris and wrapped the end of it to the kitchen door knob. Then he took the other end of the rope and tied it to the grenade. Very carefully, he closed the door leaving just enough pressure on the rope...

"When they open the door, this house will be vaporized," Knox said as he helped Hunter lower Harris into the kitchen tunnel. "We've got to move as quickly as possible. The tunnel should be able to handle the blast, but no promises."

Once inside, Knox closed the hatch and climbed back down into the tunnel as fast as he could. Hunter and Knox supported

Harris as they walked. Knox looked at the motion detector. It was getting fuzzy but he could see the dots still moving. Then the dots started to move wildly.

"Here it comes. Brace yourself," Knox said.

One of the dots started to head to the right, to the kitchen door, then stopped.

"Damn, Hunter. Your men are good," Knox said. "They didn't fall for it. We've got to move."

Knox, Hunter, and Harris scrambled out of the tunnel by the shipwreck and started walking for the cart. Then they heard a voice from behind. "Stop! Drop your weapons! Hands up!"

When Hunter saw who it was, he was relieved. It was Phil.

Phil looked at Knox. "Move and I'll shoot."

"You call this a photographer?" Knox asked Hunter.

Phil looked at Hunter then back to Knox. "As a representative of United States, I hereby place you under arrest on charges of international terrorism and murder. Mr. Algier, please step away."

Knox just smiled. "You're out of your jurisdiction, son."

"I don't think so, sir," Phil replied.

"We'll see," Knox said.

Phil looked at Hunter. "Step away, Hunter."

Hunter held his ground while Knox lifted the point of his shoe off the ground and kicked his heel back. Nothing happened.

"Agent Algier, please step away," Phil said, not noticing the movement Knox was making with his foot.

Hunter still didn't move.

Knox lifted the point of his shoe off the ground again and kicked his heel back. This time a dart shot out of the shoe in a puff of smoke. Phil Styles was hit by the projectile in the leg, and fell to the ground with a thud.

Knox turned to Hunter. "You're not the only one with state-of-the-art shoes."

Hunter looked at Phil on the ground. He would have done anything to protect him. Phil had saved his life at least four times.

Knox noticed Hunter's concern. "Don't worry, he'll be all right. Let's go."

Hunter looked back at Knox. "Trust me, Hunter."

Hunter and Knox made their way back to the airlock without incident. Knox took out a radio and called for a medical team.

When they came out of the airlock and back into the cavern, Harris was given a shot of ZR5 and then taken away on a stretcher.

Hunter looked around and noticed the cavern was somehow different. The first and second stages of the Saturn V were stacked. The rocket was now a monstrosity in the middle of the cavern. Greg ran from the administration building yelling, "Knox, we're on the timeline and working to stay that way."

"Good, but they got the chart," Knox said in return. "Push everything up. Have the key players meet me in my office in fifteen minutes."

"Okay," Greg said. "Building the rocket is not a problem, but Harris was our pilot and ZR5 takes at least 24 hours to heal a bone fracture. There's no one to take his place on the flight."

"Let's move to plan B," Knox said as he started walking to another part of the cavern. "I have one more thing to show Hunter before the meeting."

"Okay. See you in the conference room," Greg shouted as he went back to the administration building.

"Hunter, follow me quickly," Knox said. "It's time for a look at the third stage."

Hunter took a look around and saw people everywhere scrambling to get the rocket ready for launch. "Knox, there's time to do this?"

"You've got to understand the whole story if you're going to take the next step with me."

As Knox and Hunter approached the massive rocket, Knox said, "The second stage of the Saturn V burned for six and a half minutes. By the time the third stage kicked in," Knox pointed to the third stage, "we were already a hundred and five miles high, traveling at a speed of fifteen thousand miles an hour." As Knox talked, he helped a worker connect and adjust a cable. After finishing the task, he pointed to the back of the third stage. "Because Apollo had come this far, escaping the gravity of the Earth, we only needed one J-2 engine to get our spacecraft into orbit." As Hunter looked at the single engine, Knox said, "At this point in flight, the Saturn V had already lost ninety-five percent of its original weight.

"Overall, the third stage performed three important functions: it took us to Earth's orbit, gave us the push we'd need to get to the

Moon, and provided storage for the Lunar Module." Knox pointed to the Lunar Module being lifted off the ground by a crane.

"The third stage burned for almost three minutes. After that, our spacecraft would be 'parked' in Earth's orbit at a velocity of seventeen thousand five hundred miles per hour.

"After the third stage boost to Earth's orbit, we were in microgravity, more or less a free-fall orbit around the Earth. This is where shuttles did their work.

"Once in orbit, we would take time to check our systems once again. If we detected problems caused by the launch, we'd abort the mission.

"This almost happened to Apollo 12. Just thirty-six seconds after liftoff, the spacecraft was struck by lightning and took a power hit. Astronaut Alan Bean saved the day. After the lightning strike, he was asked to flick an obscure switch to bring everything back on line. He almost subconsciously performed the task because he had been trained so well.

"The astronauts of Apollo 12 used the first orbit of the Earth to check all the systems and made sure there wasn't any damage. When everything checked out okay, the crew was given the go ahead by Mission Control to go to the Moon. Apollo 12's Pete Conrad told the people back on Earth, 'We didn't train for anything else.'

"Follow me," Knox said. They walked across the cavern to the Command and Service Module. "Again, as in the other stages, Apollo reflects life as you make your way to your goal. As with the first stage, the second stage is used and left behind. You keep the passion, the drive, and the edge, but you're modifying them as you go along, dropping excess weight and concentrating on the goal.

"We have twelve minutes before the meeting. Here, let's get in the Command Module for a second. Take off your shoes."

Hunter took off his shoes and climbed the ladder to the Command Module. As he climbed, Hunter's eyes caught the scaffolding he and Knox had climbed the day before. Hunter could see the plank, and at one end, the two boxes containing the two diamonds worth several million dollars. Was he ready to walk across? He still wasn't sure.

When Hunter got to the top of the ladder of the Command Module, a technician greeted him on the platform showing how to get through the hatch. Hunter carefully pulled himself into the spacecraft as instructed and moved into the right-hand seat. Once he was in place, his back was pointed to the ground and his feet were above him. Hunter thought it was somewhat uncomfortable, looking straight up through the windows and at the glass panel displays.

A few seconds later, Knox got into the spacecraft. Getting into his seat, he said, "It may seem cramped and uncomfortable now, but remember, in the microgravity of space, the astronauts could float around and use more room. There was no up or down." Knox began flipping virtual switches, adjusting knobs displayed on the glass. He was almost like a grand pianist as he played the screens. "There will come a point, Hunter, as you make your way to your goal, that you'll find yourself in an unusual position," he said.

"Like this?" Hunter asked, feeling the blood rush to his head. He then thought about the bombs in his bloodstream. "Knox, what about the microscopic—"

"Our science is good, but not that good, at least not yet." Knox smiled. "We only injected you with water."

As Hunter let out a breath, Knox continued. "The unusual position is that you've left your past. And because of what you've done so far, your life looks different than it did. You've changed your circumstances, but changing your circumstances is not the same thing as arriving at, or even going to your goal. You're not where you were, but you're not where you want to be either. Sometimes this is hard to see, because from orbit everything looks different, and sometimes that can be overwhelming."

Knox flipped a switch in the glowing maze of lights and dials. It was eerily quiet except for several cooling fans. Then a central screen lit up to display the following: LAUNCH VECHILE EMERGENCY DETECTION, FLIGHT ATTITUDE, MISSION SEQUENCE AND NAVIGATION, VELOCITY CHANGE MONITOR, ENTRY MONITOR, PROPELLENT GAUGING, ENVIRONMENTAL CONTROL, COMMUNICATIONS CONTROL, POWER DISTRIBUTION, CAUTION AND WARNING, MISSION DISPLAY AND SIMULATION.

Knox touched the part of the screen that read: MISSION DISPLAY AND SIMULATION.

"Here, put these on." Knox gave Hunter a pair of glasses. They looked like the kind of glasses used in virtual reality games. Hunter put them on.

In the glasses, Hunter saw a 3-D display of stars. The Earth and Moon appeared. Between the Earth and Moon were different colored lines with numbers and dates. Hunter heard Knox say, "Every time I've gone into space, Hunter, the first thing I do is look back at the beauty of the Earth. It's hard to believe it's the same planet I just left. From space, it's a blue and white jewel with no boundaries. And this jewel is set on the black velvet of space. The computer image lines you see are the various timelines of leaving the planet."

Hunter looked at the image and saw the overwhelming picture of the Earth: a magnificent swirl of tan, blue, and white. Hunter felt the freedom and peace of mind of flying over the planet. Suddenly the lines and dates disappeared, leaving just the Earth and the Moon. A single line appeared with the words: MISSION OF APOLLO 8. The Earth came back into view. Knox continued, "The astronauts on board Apollo 8, the first spacecraft to travel around the Moon, were amazed when they looked back to see the entire Earth. It was small and fragile, like a Christmas tree ornament. A 'grand oasis in the great vastness of space.' The astronauts saw the entire planet floating and spinning quietly in eternal blackness, no strings attached. In a matter of seconds, humanity's view of the Earth had forever shifted."

As Knox talked, the Earth slowly rotated to reveal an amazing sunrise. From up here there seemed to be no worries, no violence, no death. Then the virtual simulation took Hunter to the Moon. It was stark, but wonderful. Hunter noticed the crisp clarity of the features, and the colorless splendor of the lunar surface. He noticed the shadows, the rich texture of the landscape. The incredible desolation was overwhelming. He heard Knox's voice again, "On Christmas Eve, December 24, 1968, the Apollo 8 astronauts orbit the Moon. How do you describe something no human had ever seen before? All they could do was go back to the beginning. So astronauts Frank Borman, Jim Lovell, and Bill Anders took turns reading from Genesis."

From the backside of the Moon, Hunter saw an Earthrise. Just as spectacular as the sunrise he'd only seen moments before. The

Earth, now far away. The hopes and dreams and lives of so many people on just a tiny ball in space. It was small from out here and yet everything Hunter knew was there. Everything.

Knox continued, "They read, 'In the beginning, God created the heaven and the Earth. And the Earth was without form and void, and darkness was upon the face of the deep. And the spirit of God moved upon the face of the waters. And God said: Let there be light and God saw the light: That it was good.' The crew finished by saying, 'Good night, good luck, a Merry Christmas, and God bless all of you, all of you on the good Earth.'"

As a full earth hovers on the screen, Knox continued, "'All of you on the good Earth.' From space, there are no boundaries. There's only unlimited visibility of one blue and white planet bathed in gentle light from a nearby star. One peaceful spinning world of life. Even with all our troubles on Earth, move out a hundred miles into space, and all our troubles are gone. In the words of Jules Verne, 'Man's reign ceases.' There's just peace. Heaven."

Hunter watched the Earth spinning quietly and beautifully. Hunter heard Knox say, "I sometimes wonder what would happen if all of humanity could see the world like this. How would it change us? How would it change our evolution? And how have these images already changed us?

"Getting what you really want is about your view and your perspective. Do you understand, Hunter?"

"Yes," Hunter said, looking at the Earth.

"How?" Knox asked.

Hunter looked at the Earth. He wanted to get this answer right. Taking another second to consider, he said, "True goal achievement comes when you can shift your perspective to see things in a way you've never seen them before. And when you shift, you begin to move to what you really want, because you realize it's possible. The boundaries we place on ourselves are the ones we build in our minds."

The image of the Earth disappeared. In its place appeared the words: VIRTUAL LAUNCH TO ORBIT SIMULATION. Those words faded, and then Hunter saw the 3-D image of a fully stacked Saturn V on the launch pad.

"Watch and feel this," Knox said. With an ear-shattering rumble, the Saturn V climbed into the sky. "As you pick up speed and leave to your goal, you begin to see across your life, you begin to see what you've done. Your true abilities are not blurred anymore. The past, present, and future become clearly defined. That's because when you leave the ground, you see the planet. When you leave your past for the future, you see the brighter possibilities."

The Saturn V dropped its first stage, and ignited its second stage. A few moments later, the Saturn V dropped its second stage, and the third stage kicked in. Hunter heard Knox say, "Something amazing happens as you build up speed and see across your life. You begin to see your life for what it really is: a grand oasis in the great vastness of time."

On cue, the third stage shut down. Now the image showed the Command and Service Module and the third stage in orbit around the Earth. Knox said, "Once in orbit, the past is behind you. That will make it easier to move on. After all, gravity gets weaker with distance. It's a law of nature. The greater distance you put between the past and the present, the easier it is to realize your future, right now."

The virtual reality simulation was incredible. Hunter felt like he was really seeing the Apollo spacecraft in orbit. It was massive and captivating. "Knox, this is incredible."

"Hunter, that's why there's a trap here. You can come up with the plan and the systems to do what you want to do, achieve an amazing liftoff, even attain orbit, but it's possible to become stuck."

"What do you mean, 'stuck'?"

"Being in orbit is not a bad situation; a lot of people never even get this far. But for the first time in the flight plan, once you're in orbit, you're not accelerating, you're in free fall. There are a lot of people who get stuck around their pasts, even though they still have a vision for their future. That can lead to frustration, hostility, or worse. Remember, it may be a great view from up here, and you may have renewed understanding once in orbit, but you're not where you what to be yet. You've changed your circumstances, but changing your circumstances is not the same thing as arriving at your goal."

Knox was right. Hunter thought of the times he had started on something, achieved a bit, but never quite finished what he set out to do. Knox continued, "We orbited the Earth one and a half times and went through an exhaustive system checkout. But that was it. We had to follow the timeline. We couldn't wait. After we checked the details of our flight plan, we performed the translunar injection burn by using the third stage. We committed ourselves to the Moon."

The Earth, Moon, and the lines and dates appeared back in the image. The third stage ignited for a second time. Knox said, "During this time, the third stage burned for five minutes and twenty seconds, pushing our spacecraft to a speed of twenty-five thousand miles per hour, or 35,570 feet per second. After that, the engine shut down and we were truly on our way. It would take three days to coast to the Moon.

"It's important to note that getting out of orbit and on a path to your goal is the summation of everything you've done so far. So, once you're ready, don't get distracted. Take the next step to send you to your goal.

"Think about it this way: In orbit, you're traveling seventeen thousand five hundred miles an hour; to leave orbit and break free, all you have to do is achieve a speed of twenty-five thousand miles an hour. You've got plenty of fuel left.

"Here's where you really find the edge. If you have intense passion and vision, you'll create the circumstances and opportunities to take you to where you want to go."

Now the image displayed the third stage attached to the Command and Service Module. The Earth was gone, replaced by a sea of stars. Hunter heard Knox say, "When we were on our way to the Moon, we had a critical task to perform. We separated the Command and Service Module away from the exhausted third stage, turned around, and docked with the Lunar Module."

The Command and Service Module pulled away from the third stage. A covering broke away from the third stage to reveal the Lunar Module. Knox continued, "The Lunar Module and the third stage are traveling at the same speed as the Command and Service Module, so we fire rockets on our spacecraft to move a little faster than the third stage. As we do, we turn our ship around. We then go back and dock with the Lunar Module and pull it free from the third stage. Apollo is now down to its vital parts: the Command Module, the Service Module, and the Lunar Module. The launch is over; staging is over. We have only the things necessary to achieve our goal."

As Knox talked, the image displayed the Command and Service Module maneuvering with the Lunar Module. "Once you're on your way, concentrate on the goal and don't become distracted. In space, it's easy to see why it's critical to do this. The Earth's gravity is always working on the spacecraft. As we made our way to the Moon, we were constantly slowing down. In fact, just four hours away from Earth our speed had dropped from 35,570 feet per second, to 17,014 feet per second. Other gravities are always trying to deter you from your goal, but with enough passion at liftoff, you'll get to your goal before gravity pulls you back.

"The next step for Apollo was to go into a passive thermal roll. The crew did this because of the temperature extremes in space. Basically, as the spaceship rolls, the sun heats all sides evenly."

The spacecraft began to roll.

"What's the comparison, Knox?" Hunter asked, knowing there was a reason Knox was pointing this out.

Knox said, "We talked about it a little at the house. The fact is you must balance the stress you'll face in life by constantly rotating perspective. A negative perspective for too long may allow damaging heat to build up. Likewise, if you get too excited about something, you may be hit by something else you didn't see. You've got to see the bad and good from different angles."

The images disappeared and the screen display read: END VIRTUAL LAUNCH SEQUENCE: PART 1. PLEASE REMOVE GLASSES NOW.

Hunter took off his virtual glasses and rubbed his eyes.

"Okay, Hunter, let's go," Knox said, hitting a series of five switches to shut down the spacecraft. "This virtual system is pretty nice. Kathy designed it. We use it for training." Knox got out of the Command Module first. Hunter took a few moments extra to study the interior. It was richly appointed, with streamlined, modern equipment. With one final glance, Hunter climbed out of the spacecraft.

As they walked away, Knox said, "While it's important to keep an eye on your perspective, it's also important that you constantly watch your course. If you veer away from your flight plan, you've got to make fine adjustments as soon as you can to get back on track. In the space business we call it the mid-course correction.

"Do me a favor, Hunter. Think about your golf swing."

"Okay," Hunter said.

"Now, if your swing is off, what happens to the golf ball?"

"Well, in my case, probably a slice."

"A slice is caused by something that may only be slightly off at the beginning. To avoid a path that will take you off target, always stay focused on the goal. It must be a part of your daily life; it must be ingrained into your soul.

"Here's another way to look at it." Knox walked up to a big board on one side of the cavern and pulled out a pen. He drew a circle on one side of the board. Then he drew a smaller circle at the other side. Between the circles, he drew a line that went directly from the large circle to the smaller circle, and then another line from the large circle to another point away from the smaller circle.

Knox said, "Okay, Hunter. Notice something about the line that leaves the large circle and veers away from the smaller circle. Compare that to the line that's on course. Notice a tiny change at the beginning continues to grow. The farther off course, the more of a correction you have to make to get back. The sooner you make adjustments to get back on course, the smaller the adjustment needed. That's why you need to keep track of your progress on the way to your goal every day, and be ready to quickly make corrections."

"How will I know if I'm off course?" Hunter asked.

"You've got to simulate success everyday, so you know what success looks like. Keep track and ask the question, 'Are you hitting your milestones?'

"Consider Apollo: we only had a limited amount of fuel, so if we veered hopelessly away from the Moon, we would have to abort and go home. Keeping navigation and guidance in check was the key. We watched our course at all times and made small adjustments when we had to.

"Now that you've come this far, it's important to notice something. Once you're on your way, your perspective continues to change. You adjust to the new surroundings. You see things like you've never seen them before. When you notice these changes in your life, you'll know you're leaving the past. Compare the changes to the flight plan and make sure they're what you want.

"We've got just a few more minutes. Let's go to my office," Knox said as he started toward the administration building.

As Hunter and Knox walked, Knox continued to talk. "As you journey to your goal, it's important to consider some of the things you'll face. We live in an age where there seems to be a lack of commitment in human capital. Before you complain, remember, you've got to invest in yourself first. Your goals are critical and solely determined by you. Besides," Knox said, opening a door, "you're the only person who can pull them off.

"You also live in an age where a lot of people become depressed and lost. Lost because they've forgotten the most important thing about life: that it's based on the evolution of personal ideas and goals.

"When you realize what you can do for yourself and the people around you, it's a powerful force for good."

"Knox, are you saying a massive ego is the key?"

"No," Knox said. "That's not it. I'm talking about saying, 'This is what I'm thankful for. But I want more for my fellow man and myself. Here's what I'm willing to do to make it happen.' If you want a visual example, just look around you. Look at what we've created in this cavern."

"Isn't that self-centered?" Hunter asked.

"No. I'm talking about positive motives to push the edge of humanity. To push the edge for everybody. To push evolution. That's the key."

Hunter and Knox took the elevator to the third floor of the administration building. They stepped out of the elevator and made their way into an impressive room. Knox's office.

His desk was black marble. There were golf clubs, a mini-putting area, at least four computers, a kitchen, a model of the cavern, and models of various airplanes, rockets, and a model of a strange-looking ship.

Knox's office overlooked the longest view of the cavern, and his office windows went from the floor to the ceiling. The most amazing thing was a 3-D hologram of the Earth and the Moon, which floated above Knox's desk. The Earth slowly rotated. It looked like the virtual reality display Hunter had experienced in the Command Module.

Knox noticed Hunter's mouth was open in amazement. "What you saw in the spacecraft was only a tiny version of this hologram," Knox said. "There's one like it in the conference room as well of course. It's displayed in real time. This hologram can be accessed from anywhere inside the cavern."

Knox pointed at the dated lines displayed in the hologram. "Those lines represent our opportunities to get back to the Moon," he said.

"It's all about opportunities, Hunter. Have a seat." Knox gestured to a seat and continued talking. "There are learning puzzles and solutions at every juncture. Keep working, keep learning, keep an excellent attitude. Every second counts. You're going to your goal and that's a powerful force. You've come a long way. Now with the will, hunger, and drive, you can continue to leave the gravity of the past to enter the gravity of your future.

"Keep your goal in mind, don't lose track of it, don't be distracted, keep visualizing what you want, see yourself getting it. Keep taking the steps to—"

Knox stopped as a security officer ran into the room. "Knox, your men are ready to meet, and they say four planes are on the way to the island to try and stop us."

Without missing a beat, Knox looked at Hunter and said, "Success is still my only option."

12

Descent into Darkness

Oscar was holding his head, suffering from a massive headache. Robert McCaully helped Phil Styles walk into the tent. Oscar looked up. "Knox's men knocked us out."

"He did the same thing to Phil on the beach," McCaully said as he helped Phil to a stretcher.

"Yeah, if that dart he shot at me had hit any harder, well I don't want to think about it." Phil groaned in intense pain. He held his leg with both hands as he sat at the edge of the stretcher. Whatever Knox had knocked him out with had done its job very well.

Oscar was trying to figure out exactly what happened. He'd been looking at a monitor one minute, and then awoke about an hour later with a major headache.

Oscar rubbed his temples and looked at Phil. "What about Hunter?"

Phil shrugged. "He was with Knox. I asked him to back away two times. He didn't move."

"Do you think he joined Knox?" Oscar asked.

Phil didn't answer directly, but he gave Oscar a slight nod. McCaully, who was reaching for a phone, didn't notice the gesture.

Oscar picked up a piece of paper. "Well, it doesn't matter much now anyway. All we have to do is use this chart and find out a way to enter the cavern."

"Four C-130s are coming in," McCaully said, hanging up the phone. "Whatever happened is behind us. This whole mess will be over soon."

***

Back in the cavern conference room, Knox was making the final pitch. He explained the blueprints had been taken from the house.

Because of that, the cavern would have to be shut down and destroyed. The launch would take place in about an hour. They would only get one shot. "Good luck to all of you," he said as he finished.

Kathy sat beside her father and glared at Hunter.

"All of you are now wearing security breach identifiers," Knox said. Hunter looked at the one he'd been given. It was a glass display on a band. "If the alarm goes off on your identifier, that means the security of the cavern has been compromised. At that point, watch out for the safety of your team and proceed to the dock to board the submarine."

Submarine, so that's how he did it, Hunter thought.

"What if it's a false alarm?" someone asked.

Knox glanced at his watch and said, "No matter what, proceed to the sub. We'll regroup there. Any other questions?"

The room was silent.

"That's it then," Knox said. The men and women making up Knox's inner circle got up to leave. They were ready to stand by him. Hunter knew they'd complete the mission. They really would get back to the Moon. No army or country would be able to stop them.

Knox turned to his daughter. "Okay, Kathy, you know what you've got to do. Begin downloading the information from the computer onto the server in the sub."

"Okay," Kathy said.

"Hunter, you and I will activate the timer and security system. Kathy, we'll see you—"

Knox was interrupted by the ring of a special phone built into his position at the table. He picked up the receiver. "This is Knox." He listened to the voice on the other end and then said, "Okay, we'll go to plan C then." He hung up.

"Kathy, you and Hunter will have to activate the timer and security system. That was Lynn on the phone. Because we're still in the progress of getting ready for launch, I'll have to come up with a different flight plan."

Kathy glared at Hunter again and Knox felt the escalating tension. "I could try to find someone else to do the activation," Knox offered to his daughter.

"Dad, I'll do it. But can I trust him?" she asked, looking at Hunter.

"I trust him," Knox said.

"I'd like to have a backup just in case," Kathy said, pulling out a small pistol and pointing it at Hunter. "We can't continue unless the cavern is collapsed and destroyed."

"Okay," Knox said. "I'll meet you at *Tranquility*." Knox left the room, followed by the men and women responsible for the computer equipment.

Kathy pointed the gun squarely at Hunter. "Let's go."

A short time later, Kathy and Hunter arrived at the elevator airlock. Kathy opened the door and activated a control panel. They both walked in and the door closed automatically.

A computer voice said, "Begin pressurization sequence. Airlock will be pressurized in five minutes."

Hunter was silent. He looked at Kathy and then looked at the gun. "Do you really think you'll be able to pull off the launch?"

"Yes, with complete confidence."

"I understand your dad's motivation. But what about your motivation?" Hunter asked.

"Just look at it this way, Hunter. Some people get this far and wonder how they've done it. They think everything's going so well and they think, 'Maybe this is too much, too fast. I'd better slow down.' Or maybe they think, 'Today shouldn't be such a great day. Maybe I should save a good day for when I really need it.' After thinking that way, they begin to suspect their whole flight plan is flawed. They begin to think their 'luck' is about to run out. They begin to panic on the way to their goal. They don't know how much longer they can maintain the vision, and they're afraid to become too attached because they think it will shatter. That's a self-fulfilling prophecy. That's what makes my dad's team different. The people working on this project are already there."

She didn't say anything else as she waited for the airlock to do its work.

"Airlock pressurization complete," the computer said. Kathy moved away from Hunter to open a storage chest in the airlock. She reached inside to grab a backpack.

They left the airlock to enter another dimly lit cave. Hunter saw two adjacent tunnels and neither one looked very friendly.

Kathy looked at each one, and then back at Hunter. "Let's go," she said as she gestured with the gun for Hunter to walk into the tunnel to the left.

"Kathy, what you said back there in the airlock, about luck running out. I've always believed in that," Hunter said, trying to break the tension.

"Hunter, luck is mental," Kathy said as they started into the tunnel. "My father and I share a vision. Like I said, we're already there."

"Yes, but aren't you a bit nervous, all the same—"

She interrupted, "On Apollo 13, a catastrophic failure forced the crew to circle the Moon instead of land there. They couldn't do anything about it, all they could do was get home safely, and that's exactly what they did.

"The crew of the next mission couldn't sit there and think, 'Things are going too well. What if a catastrophic failure occurs somewhere during this mission like the last one?' No, the crew simply had to learn the lesson of Apollo 13 and continue. That's the key: learn all you can, and keep on going. Every step you take to your goal is a step in the right direction, no matter what happens."

They continued down the passageway, lit by a small track of lights embedded in the floor.

Kathy went on talking, slightly out of breath. "Fear of failure is the reason most people don't achieve what they really want. So fear of failure must be replaced with a vision of success."

Eventually, they made their way into a large cave. On one wall was a box. Kathy pulled out a key from the backpack to unlock the box. Without saying a word, she opened the box, pulled out a keyboard, and began typing. She did it all with one hand while she kept the gun pointed at Hunter. Kathy stopped for a second, waiting for the computer to accept the command.

Then for an instant, the floor shook. Hunter looked at the ceiling. "If I didn't know any better, I'd say that was a plane landing."

"We're underneath the Cayman Brac Airport."

The floor shook again. This time Kathy stopped typing and looked at Hunter. "There's another one," Kathy said. "Wait a minute, that's too heavy to be commercial. It must be a transport."

***

At the Cayman Brac Airport, a large transport plane landed and taxied to the main terminal. Oscar's troops were assembling for the invasion of the cavern.

* * *

"It looks like your friends are pulling out all the stops," Kathy said. "They're bringing in reinforcements. We're going to have even less time than we thought." She keyed in another sequence. Hunter looked at her. She was wearing hiking shorts and a tight, tan, short-sleeved shirt. Her long hair was pulled back to reveal her soft face. Her fingers moved quickly across the keyboard. *Another time, another place...*

She turned to catch his stare, bringing Hunter back to reality.

He asked, "So, this system protects the cavern?"

"This timer is connected to the security system," Kathy said, looking at the computer. "The system will cause the cavern to collapse at the first sign of outside trouble. They may have a map, but by the time they get in, there won't be anything left of our operation. It will be buried and crushed by several tons of rock. It will also be under a few hundred feet of sea water."

"What about all the equipment?"

"It can be replaced," she said as she flipped the keyboard back in the box and shut the cover. "Let's get out of here."

The room shook again. "That's three transports."

"How do you plan to launch?" Hunter asked as they started walking back out of the tunnel. Kathy still had the gun pointed at him.

"Dad's been planning for this, like he always says: 'Don't take success for granted; reinvest success to guarantee more success. Have a great week, but also do what it takes to have a better week. Count your blessings, but say your prayers.'"

"I...I don't understand," Hunter said. "How can losing most of what you've worked for be a success?"

"That's because we've planned for success no matter what. Sure we may lose part of our work, but we won't lose the plan," she said confidently.

They made their way out of the tunnel, and back to the central cave. She pulled another display glass from the backpack she was carrying.

She typed on the glass: CONTROL. TIMER SET. DID THREE TRANSPORTS LAND? KATHY.

A few seconds later a response appeared on the screen. It was somewhat jumbled:

KATHY. GOOD W&RK. YES, THREE TRANSPORTS LANDED AT *IRPORT. NOT SURE HOW MA@Y PEOPLE INVOLVED. TIME CRITIC+L FACTOR. TRANSF&RRED MOST OF THE INFORMATION TO THE SUB.. BE CAREFUL GET(ING TO SECURITY SYSTEM. REMEMBER@#&DERS IN THE TUNNEL. OCKET BEI"G FUELED. CONTROL.

She looked at the screen. "We're having some display issues. Must be the connection, every aspect of our operation is working overtime." She put down the glass and they walked to the tunnel on the right.

Hunter took a long look at the tunnel. From his perspective, it looked like the gateway to hell itself.

"This is the tunnel to the main security system," Kathy said. "It will be a tough climb. And there are some other things as well," Kathy said as she looked inside.

"Other things? Like what?" Hunter asked.

"It would probably be better if you just found out for yourself. Let's move it and don't touch the walls." Kathy gestured with the gun again. Hunter walked into the tunnel.

As they entered, Hunter noticed that the track lights on the floor weren't as bright this time. The climb was steep. The damp air made the floor slippery. As Hunter led the way, he felt a shiver down his spine. Something wasn't right. Pretty soon the tunnel opened to a larger path. At that point, Hunter noticed the walls were white in color. And the walls seemed to pulsate...

"What's the point in having to activate the timer and security system?" Hunter asked.

"It may seem redundant, but it's safe. To activate the second system you'd have to be pretty desperate. Look for yourself," she said, reaching into her backpack. She pulled out a strange looking flashlight. She turned it on and put the beam on one of the walls.

Hunter caught his breath.

Spiders, thousands of them, all over the walls. And they were big, at least three inches long. Add legs and they were enormous. They were milky white in color and furry. Some moved up and down very slowly. It gave the illusion the wall was pulsating. Hunter was speechless. Kathy, on the other hand, had seen them before. She said, "Blind Cayman Brac cave spiders. We were the first to discover them, or rather a worker was. That's how we found out they were very poisonous, but they are blind. Just don't touch the wall."

"Don't worry," Hunter whispered as he moved to the middle of the tunnel. "What the hell do they eat?" he asked as he looked up and saw more of them on the ceiling. They seemed to avoid the floor.

"We think this part of the tunnel floods and fish get trapped. Spiders do the rest," she said as she pointed the flashlight at the floor. Small fish skeletons covered certain areas. "We were planning to send our biologist up here, but there won't be enough time now. Let's go," Kathy said, once again waving the gun.

As Kathy took a step, she slipped and fell on the ground, dropping the gun. Hunter recovered the gun in a flash and pointed it at Kathy's face. "Now you know how it feels."

"Kill me. You're as good as dead anyway," Kathy said.

"Bullshit," Hunter responded, throwing the gun down the cavern. Kathy just looked at him.

"What do you want?" she asked, looking at her watch.

"I want to help you and your dad. I think that's pretty obvious now. I've learned a hell of a lot in the past twenty-four hours. I'm here to help you finish."

Kathy tried to get up, but fell back down and rolled dangerously close to the wall.

The spiders in that section froze. Several stuck their front legs in the air to find the source of the disturbance. Hunter pulled her away from the wall.

"Kathy, give me the light," he said. Hunter put the beam of light on her ankle. It looked twisted maybe even broken. "You'd better call for help," Hunter said as he reached for the backpack.

"The display doesn't work this far back in the tunnel," Kathy said. "We're on our own."

"What do we do?" Hunter asked as he watched several of the spiders move up the wall.

"You're going to have to activate the security system. I broke this foot a year ago while coming down Everest with my dad. Even with the ZR5 it's been operated on four times," she said.

Hunter looked ahead into the dark tunnel, "How long will it take?"

"This one doesn't need to be programmed. It's just a simple matter of flipping a switch. Here's the key." She gave Hunter a key from her pocket.

"It's another hundred yards up. Be careful," she said. Hunter looked at where he had to go and hesitated.

Kathy looked at Hunter. "If that security system isn't activated, launch will be impossible and they'll find the cavern. End of story."

Hunter hesitated again.

Kathy smiled. "Hunter, it's like my dad always says, 'Live right now, and you don't miss out on anything, there's nothing to wait for, and you don't make any mistakes.'" Kathy reached into her backpack and pulled out what looked like a band of rubber. "Put this on. I'll be able to keep in contact with you for as long as possible."

Hunter put on the band. "Testing, one, two," Kathy said.

"It sounds clear," Hunter said as he moved on through the tunnel, under the spiders.

Hunter looked back and gave her a thumbs up. As he started walking forward again, four spiders fell on the floor in front of him and scrambled back to the wall. Hunter took a deep breath.

Hunter heard Kathy's voice and looked at the band. He wasn't sure how he was hearing it, but her voice was loud and clear—like she was right there. "Amazing bit of technology. These bands use the air to transmit sound to another band. As long as you're in the same air space, you can hear, it's almost like what they used to call Blue Tooth, but more sophisticated. So where did my dad leave off on the voyage to the Moon?"

Hunter smiled. She was beginning to relax. "We had left the Earth in that incredible simulator you built back in the cavern," Hunter said.

Hunter heard Kathy say, "Then let's continue, shall we? I'll try to be as dramatic as my father, but no promises."

She took a deep breath and started by saying, "As the astronauts left the Earth and traveled to the Moon at twenty-four thousand miles per hour, the Apollo astronauts traveled faster than man had ever gone before, but they couldn't feel it. There's no sense of motion in deep space, and there are no waypoints.

"For us, it's the same. Sometimes in the long haul, when you're really out there, when you're really moving fast towards your goal, it may seem like you're moving slowly. But just keep taking the steps, because one day things will click into place. Have trust in yourself to make it happen. Have trust in yourself to build the momentum."

Hunter had no waypoints to look at as he made his way. He tried not to think about the spiders above his head. Kathy continued, "As you make your way, look for feedback from your flight plan and ask key questions. The questions will help you stay on course. You've invested a lot of time and energy in this, you don't want to lose what you've invested, so finish and find the payoff. Concentrate on the fundamentals and consistently look at the results. If you see any potential problems, be ready to steer back on course. It's what we call a mid-course correction burn to stay on the flight plan and on the timeline."

Hunter was starting to see the logic in all this. Even though they had to destroy this cavern, it was a necessary course adjustment. They weren't starting over as much as they were just finding a way that worked.

The tunnel began to widen. There were fewer spiders. Finally Hunter reached a point in the tunnel where there weren't any more spiders. He looked back. There must be something that attracts them to just that part. Hunter turned back around and saw a small light ahead.

The light got brighter. Hunter saw another box at the end of this tunnel. The path narrowed, and he saw deep black on both sides of the floor. Hunter grabbed the flashlight out of his pocket and turned it on. The floor dropped off on each side. He couldn't see the bottom. The box was on a wall about fifty feet ahead of him. All that was separating him was this walkway over some kind of pit.

Hunter picked up a rock and tossed it over the side. He never heard it hit. He took another look across the pit at the box, the box that would open a pathway for Knox's rocket.

"I'm over some kind of pit," Hunter said.

"Yeah, you'll see the box on the other side. The pit is extremely deep, so watch your step."

"Not very comforting, Kathy."

"Hunter, don't think about that. Don't you see how close you are to the goal now?" Kathy continued talking. "Let the reasons for it become the gravity to pull you in."

Hunter thought quickly. The gravity of the goal. What is it really? The goal is what you create in your mind first. Physical action is what it takes to get you there.

Kathy's voice was crystal clear. "The gravity of the past and the gravity of your comfort zone are always working against you until you enter the gravity of the goal. That's what people really mean when they say, 'You don't realize the gravity of the situation.'

"Earth's gravity extends into space several tens of thousands of miles. Escape velocity is the true speed it takes to leave the influence of the Earth's gravity: twenty-six thousand miles per hour. What kind of effect did the Earth's gravity have? Consider this: Apollo slowed to 2,990 feet per second just before leaving the Earth's sphere of influence and entering the gravity of the Moon.

"The gravity of the past is just as strong. You've got to break away from it," Kathy said.

Hunter thought about what he had learned in the past seventy-two hours. If he made it to the box, he'd help Knox get to his goal. Hunter's old life was over and old fears were beginning to fall away once and for all.

Kathy said, "You've got to make sure you're moving at a pace that will allow you to complete your goal in a reasonable amount of time. You've got to stick to your timeline and take the steps to stay ahead when possible. If you give in now and push back the goal, you may not have enough passion left to finish, you may have to do a restart, you may not get all you wanted, or you could veer severely off course. Hang in there and follow through."

Hunter started across the walkway as Kathy kept talking. "What pushes you ahead are the vision and the edge for what you really want. Something wonderful happens to your vision on the way to your future. Your vision of the past continues to shrink in size and becomes a shiny ball of the best of what you've done.

"For the astronauts in space, Earth becomes the most beautiful thing outside the spacecraft. When you go after your goal, the most beautiful thing you see is your life. You need to look back and see that beauty as you venture out. The beauty that's in you."

Hunter was now a fourth of the way across the walkway.

"As you go for your goal," Kathy continued, "you look out ahead and there's the future, growing bigger and brighter every minute. It's strange, mysterious, and wonderful all at the same time. The future is just begging to be explored. With every second, you know you'll get there, you know you'll make it to your goal because you're making it happen right now!"

Halfway there, Hunter centered his focus on the box ahead.

With pain in her voice from the injury, Kathy continued, "As you look for those payoffs and continue to make investments and move forward, be careful of distractions, other false gravities moving through. Continue to focus on the goal you really want. Look at your flight plan and know the sheer force you've got to put behind it."

Hunter took a misstep and almost fell. "Shit," he said to himself

As Hunter continued to walk across, he hit a pebble with his shoe, and this time he really did fall. As he stumbled off the side of the walkway, he reached for a cable and snagged it. Hunter held on, suspended by the cable.

***

Back in the main cavern, Greg watched on a monitor as the first troops set up a perimeter around the entrance to the beach tunnel to the cavern.

Knox entered the room, "What's up?"

"This is the first of them," Greg said, pointing to the monitor. "Twenty-five by my count."

Knox looked at the men on the monitor. "Activate countermeasures, sound the alarm, and evacuate the cavern. Alert all the breach identifiers."

Greg turned to Knox, "What about Kathy and Hunter?"

"They should be on their way back by now," Knox said.

***

Hunter hung on with every ounce of energy he had left. He closed his eyes and realized that Kathy was still talking to him. He listened to her soothing voice. "The gravity of the past is always reduced as you travel to the future. That means you need less power after you've escaped the past. Mental fine-tuning becomes most important at this stage." As Hunter listened to the words, the cable he was holding on to started to give. It was the very same cable attached to the cavern collapse mechanism. He was on the verge of pulling everything down with him.

Hunter saw this and realized how tightly he was holding on, and when he did, he relaxed. Suddenly, just by relaxing, it became easier to hold on. He pulled his feet up and found he could get some leverage off the ridge just below him. He slowly started to pull himself up as he listened to Kathy. "Then one day it happens," she said. "The things you've done to reach your goal outweigh the longings for the past and you enter the gravity of the goal. The target is coming up, and the journey is almost complete. In fact, you're speeding up again and you're not even providing thrust. You're being pulled in by the gravity of what you want, because now you know you can do what you need to do."

Hunter pulled himself back onto the ridge just as the cable was about to snap.

Once he was standing on his feet again, Hunter paused for a second. He had come so close to falling off the edge. But it didn't matter. He also knew it wouldn't happen again. Hunter looked at the box on the wall. He put the key in and confidently flipped the switch.

Nothing happened. His heart sank.

Hunter held his breath and flipped the switch again. He heard a low buzzing sound and then the computer screen lit up and read: WARNING: PHYSICAL COLLAPSE WILL BE FORCED IN THIRTY MINUTES.

Hunter looked at his watch. It had taken him five minutes just to get to where he was now. Did he have enough time?

"Kathy, we're set. Thirty minutes until collapse," Hunter said.

"Thank you, Hunter," he heard Kathy say.

Hunter hurried across the walkway. This time he didn't even think about the danger. He just wanted to get back to Kathy.

Hunter reached the other side and started down the tunnel. At one point, he almost put his hand on a wall but at the last instant he saw the spiders, and even though Hunter was petrified of spiders, it just didn't seem to matter.

In what seemed like just a few seconds later, Hunter reached Kathy.

"Thanks for the coaching," Hunter said, out of breath. "By my estimates, we have about twenty-five minutes left.

"Right," Kathy said. "Let's go." Hunter helped her up.

"Here, hang on to my back," he said as he reached out a hand. With Kathy holding on, Hunter went back down the tunnel. They were moving at a pretty good pace but Hunter could tell Kathy was in pain. He had to distract her. "Kathy, what would Knox say at a time like this?"

"Probably that you're close," Kathy said. "Now you need to perform two specific systems checks: the edge and communication."

"Why's that?" Hunter asked.

"It's important to think about where you are and anticipate what's to come. This is the thinking stage of goal achievement. Passion was what you used to start. Concentrate on the fine edge it will take to achieve your goal. Focus and finish."

Hunter was focused. The tunnel had changed him. He could feel it. He felt free, like a massive burden had been lifted from his shoulders. He carefully watched his step as he made his way down the tunnel.

***

About eleven hundred feet above their heads, in the skies over Cayman Brac, the final transport was circling the airport, getting ready to land.

***

"Let's rest for just a second," Hunter said, letting Kathy relax.

Kathy looked at Hunter. "Communication is also critical. If it's true that only you can help yourself, you don't need outside influences making the job any harder. Find only the positive influences that will push you on.

"No matter what happens, you're going to run into the 'people factor.' It goes something like this: some people won't pay any attention to you and just do their own thing; some people will help you out; some people will want to watch you fail. It's sad, but true.

"Mission Control watched over the astronauts every second during the mission, ready to help them at a moment's notice.

"Like Apollo, you've got to focus on the people trying to make you better. It's easy to see who they are. These people will be the ones who criticize you, but only to help push you. They know about your goals, and they care about you reaching them. Not only do they supply support, but they're also eager to point out the good things about life in general. These are the people you need to bring into your flight plan, the ones who bring you up. Usually they're making their way to their own goals as well."

Hunter looked at Kathy. *She is beautiful. I want her in my life. This time it would be right. The pain over Angie is disappearing into my past.*

***

At the airport, the transport was now on final approach. It was the heaviest of all the flights, with the most equipment.

***

Back in the tunnel, Hunter was falling in love. Kathy noticed the expression on his face. Even in pain, she continued to talk. "Make sure the people you know provide you with a source of drive to help you reach your goal," Kathy said. "Let me say that again: There are plenty of people out there, plenty of potential allies, so spend time with the people who empower you. And make sure you give the energy back."

She looked at him longingly. He thought, *Does she feel the same way?*

He wanted to kiss Kathy, but he also saw all the spiders at the edge of his vision. He knew it wasn't the time. "Let's take a few more steps out of here," he said, once again lifting her up.

***

The pilot of the transport made a few final adjustments to compensate for the Cayman Island breeze. The wheels of the transport hit the ground in a screech of rubber.

***

At the same moment, Hunter and Kathy cleared the tunnel. They felt the vibration and watched as hundreds of spiders were knocked on the floor.

"Shit," Hunter said, looking back.

Hunter helped Kathy over to the airlock. She punched a button and the door opened. They went inside, and the door closed and locked.

Leaning against the wall, Kathy activated the system. "Pressurization in five minutes," the computer said.

"Kathy, what happens now?" Hunter asked, watching the time on the airlock clock.

She looked at Hunter and said, "We're in new territory now. The most important thing is to get as many assets out of here as we can, especially before they get here."

***

At that moment, about a half mile away, twenty-five heavily armed men and women walked down the tunnel entrance. With a copy of a cavern map in hand, the assault on Knox's fortress was underway. But it would take time.

As the troops walked carefully down the tunnel, a man tripped an electronic switch hidden in the ground. Seconds later a gut-wrenching prehistoric roar was heard.

Everyone stopped in their tracks and looked down the tunnel, weapons raised.

Suddenly, a full-grown dinosaur appeared in the center of the tunnel. Some soldiers ran and some fired their weapons. One by one all of them began to run, except for one woman. She took careful aim and fired at what looked like a massive T-Rex. The dinosaur continued to growl. She pulled the trigger and fired off a round into the beast. The bullets seemed to go right through the creature.

When the she realized it was a hologram, she shouted, "Wait! Wait! It's not real." She fired again in a circle and suddenly the beast turned into a patch of static.

"It's a dammed hologram!" the woman yelled, slightly amused. Still, there was no way she would continue down the tunnel by herself. She turned around to try and find the other soldiers.

***

The alarm on Hunter's indicator went off. "The cavern security has been breached," Hunter reported.

Kathy didn't seem concerned. She just said, "Hunter, did you ever wonder what the real key to life is? What it's really all about? Here's my guess: I think it's to add value on a daily basis to your life and the lives of others. You do that, and this really becomes a better place."

By this point, Hunter was not really listening. He looked at the clock and realized if he'd only crossed the walkway sooner, they would have more time.

Kathy looked at Hunter. "And there's still one more step to this: make sure you don't interfere with your own flight plan.

"A lot of people become self-centered in a negative way, saying, 'My life is hell.' Or, 'Why should other people have all the good stuff?' Or, 'I wish I'd done this or that or that.' If it's true, you should only spend time with the people who empower you. You've got to empower yourself. You spend every waking hour with yourself. Don't bring yourself down. Provide yourself with encouragement and criticism in a non-personal way. Give yourself everything you'd expect to give and be given from other people. Know your worth, because it's determined by you. It all starts with the power inside you.

"Get help from people, encouragement, but don't rely on others directly for fulfillment. That's up to you."

Hunter watched Kathy's lips as she finished. She was beautiful. She was smart. She was dedicated to something amazing. She was amazing. He looked deeply into her eyes. Into her soul. He began leaning towards her.

Kathy must have been feeling the same way. "I believe you are a good man, Hunter." She leaned forward to receive his kiss.

The passion was interrupted by a loud hiss. The sign read and the computer said, "Emergency release."

The door opened to the cavern where Knox was waiting.

—STAGE THREE—

13

Launch Commit

"No time for airlocks, they've already tried to enter the cave," Knox said. "In fact, soldiers in the main tunnel just ran into the first hologram."

Knox looked at Kathy's ankle. "What happened?" he asked. "The spiders?"

"No, she fell," Hunter said.

Hunter and Knox helped Kathy through the airlock. "Let's get to the sub," Knox said.

Kathy and Hunter looked at each other, knowing the spark between them was growing into a flame.

As Hunter walked back into the cavern, his breath was taken away by what he saw. The Saturn V was now fully stacked. Enormous flexible tubes fed propellant to all three stages. The rocket now looked like it was alive. Steaming vapors made the thing breathe. It was eerie, yet incredible all the same.

"She's almost fueled, with all the power of a atomic bomb. If anything goes wrong, we're all history," Knox said.

They made their way across the cavern floor. The rocket groaned and hissed, but otherwise it was now strangely quiet. The administration building was empty. The equipment in the cavern deserted. Except for several lights on the Saturn V, the cavern was dark.

As they reached a spiral staircase going down, Hunter looked back at the scaffolding he'd climbed with Knox the day before. He could see the plank, but the boxes with the diamonds were gone. He'd missed his chance. Although that upset him, he was truly focused on the beauty of the Saturn V.

They went down the steps to another part of the cavern and arrived at another airlock.

"No time." Knox hit a release button and with a hiss, the door opened. They walked through the airlock and came out to a large underground lake. The scene was brilliantly illuminated with lights. There was a large submarine by the dock. Hunter estimated it was three hundred feet long. He remembered the model of it in Knox's office. There was a huge hatch on its main deck. Hunter quickly realized that's how Knox had been able to get the equipment into the cavern.

"So this is how you got supplies in without being detected?" Hunter asked.

"Yes, most of them anyway. We moved everything in piece by piece and did the construction inside the cavern. But we must hurry, we've only got fifteen minutes," Knox said.

***

Oscar was running the operation from a fortified position on the beach in front of the cliffs at Cayman Brac. Fifty soldiers stood ready this time to go into the tunnel of the main cavern. Oscar turned to McCaully. "We also need to be at the top of the cavern as well."

"Why's that?"

"I think he's going to collapse the cavern to launch a rocket."

"What rocket?" McCaully was stunned.

"I guess it's time I told you everything. We have reason to believe that within this cavern," Oscar paused, "Commander Knox Long has built a fully functional Saturn V rocket."

McCaully said nothing.

"I'm deadly serious," Oscar said. "I also think we've made a serious mistake. I think we've pushed Knox to an early launch."

Irritated for being left in the dark, McCaully picked up a radio. "Get me my communications team immediately," he shouted into the microphone.

***

Hunter boarded the submarine and saw its name painted on the side: *Tranquility*.

He followed Knox down a passageway inside the submarine.

A few seconds later, they entered a large room with a window facing the clear water of the underground lake. Hunter could see underneath the surface of the water through the glass.

In the command center of the submarine, several people worked at computers.

Knox said, "Hunter, you're in the control room of the *Tranquility*. We'll conduct the launch from here. Relax and have a seat."

"Who's going to fly it?" Hunter asked.

"No one. The rocket is remotely controlled. We'll be able to test our new engines, and the exhaust from the rocket will destroy everything in the cavern. We'll also be able to make a very important point to the entire world."

Knox took his position behind a control wheel. He activated the submarine's navigation system. "Secure all hatches," Knox said into a microphone.

A voice came back on. "All hatches secured. Ready for departure."

Knox touched the computer screen several times and the sub began moving forward. Through the window, Hunter could see a tunnel in front of them, lit by underwater lights.

"Standby to submerge. Set a course for the Cayman Trench," Knox said.

One of the workers turned to Knox. "Knox, I'm reading a problem in power supply to the Saturn V remote control."

Greg came running into the room. "Several of my men encountered heavy resistance outside the cavern, they made it past the other T-Rex. I think they're trying to jam your remote."

Another worker said, "They have jammed it. Correction, they've disabled it. At this point, we can't launch."

"All engines stop. Surface the *Tranquility*," Knox said calmly. Knox turned to Greg. "Is the cavern still secure?"

"Yes," Greg said. "But the collapse takes place in twelve minutes. They just got through the second level of security. At best we have about twenty minutes until they're in the cavern."

"Vicki, stop the countdown."

A woman turned and said, "Countdown holding at T minus twelve minutes."

"Reset the countdown for twenty-five minutes."

"Countdown is now at T minus twenty-five minutes and holding," she said.

Knox looked at a man working by three monitors. "Fred, can we wait about thirty minutes and still hit our launch window?"

"It will be close, Knox, but I think we can," Fred said.

"You've got to be sure."

The man tapped his keyboard and looked at his computer screen. "Yes, we can. By about twenty-five seconds."

"Close enough," Knox said. "We'll launch in thirty minutes. Vicki, the current hold will expire in five minutes."

"Remember, Knox,' Greg said, "the cavern will still collapse in eleven minutes. That leaves us exposed at the top for nineteen minutes until liftoff. The vehicle could be compromised."

"I want the instant acceleration vehicles used to set up a perimeter. That should scare them from opening fire," Knox said.

"No problem, Knox, the XIAs are ready," Greg said. "But what about the Saturn V? Without the remote, somebody's going to have to ride that thing out of here."

"Harris was the most qualified," one man said. "But it will take time before the ZR5 heals his arm."

Knox looked around. "Everyone's got a job to do. There are only three people who can go."

Knox looked at Hunter. Hunter felt a shiver run down his back.

Hunter looked back at Knox. "I'll help you in whatever way I can."

"Thank you, Hunter," Knox said. "Call sick bay. Tell them Kathy needs to be ready for flight in ten minutes."

"Who's the third person?" Greg asked.

"Greg, you know this sub. You helped me build it. I want you here."

"But, Knox—"

"I'll go. Besides, I'm the only one with flight experience."

"But—" Greg started to say.

"Greg, I need you here. You'll complete the mission from our other location if anything happens to me."

"Knox, the hold expires in two minutes," Vicki said.

"Proceed," Knox said. He picked up a microphone to communicate over the submarine's paging system.

"Attention. This is Knox. I'll keep this simple. First, excellent job evacuating the cavern. The flight plan has been slightly adjusted, but nothing has changed. You know what you have to do. I'm flying the rocket out of the cavern. I'll be taking Hunter Algier and Kathy with me. I'll see you when we splashdown on the other side of the world. Then we'll head to our other base and continue our mission. I assure you, we will get to the Moon."

Greg looked at Knox and shook his hand. Then Knox looked at Hunter. "Hunter, follow me."

Hunter and Knox walked down the hall of the sub. "We've only got ten minutes until we've got to get to the spacecraft, but there are still a few things we've got to talk about," Knox said. "We're going into dangerous territory, so I want you to know everything in case anything happens.

"There's got to be a question you've been wanting to ask," Knox said. "Now is the time."

"Why did you want to go back to the Moon? You told me NASA couldn't find a reason to go back. What's your reason?"

"Follow me."

They went down steps and down a long passageway. As they walked, Knox said, "This is where it all started, on board the *Tranquility*. I built her many years ago. One of my hobbies is metal detection. Remote sensing. I created a program and a system to detect all kinds of things. Then I called a few of my former classmates at MIT. They were frustrated with their jobs. We pooled our resources and developed a special device to detect precious metals."

The passageway ended at a single door. It didn't have a doorknob, only a computer number pad.

"Once we had the sensing device, we developed a plan," Knox said as he entered a series of numbers on the keypad. With a hiss, the door opened. Knox turned on the light and stepped inside. Hunter followed him.

Even after everything else Hunter had seen in the past few days, this room amazed him. It was full of neatly stacked bars of gold, precious stones, and other treasures. The bright lights made everything glisten and sparkle.

Incredible, Hunter thought.

Knox continued. "We used *Tranquility* and the device I invented to find the forgotten treasures of the ocean. That's how I financed most everything you've seen. All my other companies were basically just a front. Once we complete the voyage to the Moon, we plan to donate most of this to the world's museums."

Once again, Hunter was speechless. Finally, after a long pause, Hunter asked, "How much is all this worth?"

"Enough for everything I need, and then some," Knox said. "When it comes to wealth, this is the most valuable room in the world."

Precious stones were neatly laid out in containers on a table in the center of the room. "That explains the diamonds," Hunter said.

"Right. Actually, I got the idea from *20,000 Leagues Under the Sea*. Captain Nemo used treasure for ballast. I use the treasure for ballast as well as financing. It's a great idea," Knox said as he looked over his collection. "The sea is full of riches. Even with everything here, I've still only tapped the surface. Space is the same way.

"So, why did I want to go back to the Moon?" Knox asked rhetorically. "I wanted to go back and use my remote sensing equipment to—"

At that instant, Hunter felt a shudder through the floor. Everything shook. The feeling seemed to last for about ten seconds. Then a loudspeaker went off: "T minus twenty minutes and counting."

"Was that an Earthquake?" Hunter asked.

"The roof of the cavern has collapsed. That means the roof is open and we're ready to fly. We'll finish this discussion later," Knox said as he started for the door.

***

The soldiers watched in shock as the ground in front of them disappeared.

"Damn, get ready to open fire!" One man shouted.

But before the man could take another breath, four XIA rockets were launched from the cavern. Maintaining straight and level flight over the roof of the cavern, the rockets began moving in a carefully orchestrated circle.

"Hold your fire!" one of the men yelled. "Those are the rockets we were warned about. If we hit one, we'll be dead."

***

McCaully put down the phone and looked at Oscar. "We found the XIAs. Knox is using them to set up a perimeter around the cavern. They're moving extremely fast. There's no way—"

"For God's sake, tell them to hold their fire!" Oscar yelled.

***

"XIA rockets activated," the submarine's loudspeaker bellowed.

"That gives us a few more minutes," Knox said.

They went up some steps and into a room packed with equipment. Kathy was there, already outfitted in an orange pressure suit. Several people continued to help her get ready.

There were about six other suits hanging by a pole.

"Are you feeling up to this?" Knox asked his daughter.

"Wouldn't miss it," Kathy smiled. "The foot doesn't even hurt anymore." Kathy looked at Hunter. "Good to see you. Are you ready?"

"For the flight of the century? I'm nervous as hell," Hunter said.

"Let's get you in a PGA," Knox said as he started to undress.

"PGA?"

"Pressure garment assembly. These orange suits."

Hunter started to undress.

"T minus fifteen minutes and counting."

"Knox," Hunter said as he was swiftly helped into a suit. "Isn't it a bit late to be getting inside at this point? I remember during the Apollo program astronauts had to sit on the launch pad for hours getting things ready."

"Not here. The interior of the ship is automated at this point. And due to some new technology I'm using, it will be fully pressurized on take off." The people helping Knox were making the final adjustments to his suit. Hunter was almost ready as well.

"We've tried to plan everything, Hunter," Kathy said as she smiled at him. Moments later they were each given a helmet.

"Let's get to the Saturn V," Knox said through the communications system in his helmet. At that point, Hunter couldn't hear much else except for his own breathing. He felt like he was walking in a dream.

***

The assault on the main tunnel to the cavern continued. More soldiers walked down the tunnel with great care, avoiding any traps that could trip another holographic dinosaur or something worse.

It didn't take long for one of the soldiers to set off another motion detector. Instantly, the tunnel in front of the men turned into an inferno.

"Is it real?" a woman asked.

"Let's find out." A man reached into his pocket, pulled out a piece of cloth, and threw it down the tunnel. It burned instantly.

Another soldier ran up from behind them. "Sir, I just talked to Bravo Company. The cavern has collapsed. We can go in through the roof."

"Let's go!"

***

Kathy, Knox, and Hunter were escorted off the submarine, with assistants carrying the oxygen support suitcases now connected to their pressure suits. They all walked across the dock and entered an elevator.

Once the three were safely in the elevator, the assistants gave Knox a final salute and walked away, leaving the oxygen cases behind. The elevator door slid close.

"Well, Kathy and Hunter, this is it," Knox said as he punched a button. The three were quiet as the elevator took them to the top floor of the cavern.

"T minus ten minutes and counting," the speaker in the elevator said as the door slid open to bright light.

It took Hunter a moment to adjust his vision. When he did, he looked out to see a long scaffolding from the elevator to the top of the gleaming silver Command Module in the sunlight. *At least this walkway has rails*, Hunter thought.

Looking up, Hunter could see that the cavern had collapsed. The ship was exposed. Two workers were making last minute checks around the hatch.

As Hunter walked out of the elevator, his heart stopped. The Saturn V was now totally exposed to daylight. It had been protected from the cavern collapse by a massive shield now being pulled away. Hunter looked down and saw the equipment and buildings had been buried under a pile of rocks.

A worker on the scaffolding walked up to them on the walkway. "Welcome to the *Resolution*," Pete said. "Let's get you inside and on your way."

Meanwhile, at the top of the cavern, the XIA rockets still circled at a violent speed. "You're sure they're nuclear powered?" one of the men asked as he watched the strange machines.

"Yes, they were taken from an Air Force base in Nevada. We've been told not to shoot."

"Well, it doesn't matter anyway," the soldier said. "We're about out of time."

The soldier lifted a gun and shot one of the rockets.

"No!" the other soldier screamed, but it was too late. Like a stack of dominoes all of the rockets collided and fell.

Lt. Shaw was helping Kathy into the Command Module when the first bullets hit.

She sat on the right. Shaw looked at Knox. "You've got to hurry, Knox."

A flurry of gunfire hit the scaffolding.

The soldiers around the cavern continued to fire. One solider took aim at a man on the scaffolding by the rocket.

A bullet hit Shaw and he fell to the ground. Knox ran to him.

"Go, Knox," Shaw said. "It's time to go. If you don't, all this was meaningless."

"It's time, Knox," Pete reiterated.

Knox left Shaw and started for the rocket, aided by Pete. Hunter helped them both as best as he could through the spacesuit.

More bullets hit the scaffolding as Knox worked his way into the left seat. Hunter was to get in last, but he couldn't. The suit was too heavy. Suddenly, he felt Pete and Shaw's hands push him in the rest of the way.

***

As Hunter got situated and strapped in, Knox and Kathy each faced a computer and started typing in commands.

"Knox, everything checks out," Kathy said.

"I'm still waiting for the fuel pumps to come on line," Knox said. "Okay, there they are… Kathy check the sound suppression system in the cavern and the ventilation, make sure the baffles are in place to dampen the shockwave.

"Okay," Kathy said. "Everything checks out. We're ready."

"T minus five minutes and counting."

***

Outside the command module, Pete helped Shaw and they gave the Command Module a final look over, pulling all the "Remove before Flight" tags.

As they removed the last one, Pete said, "Let's get to the boat."

With that they walked and ducked their way to the elevator.

***

The *Tranquillity* was already making its way to sea. Greg Mitchell watched a display showing the army amassed at the top of the cavern. With no one to shoot at, they were just looking at the rocket, several had started to quickly walk away.

"Come on, just a few more minutes," he whispered to himself

***

"Hunter, how are you feeling?" Knox asked.

"I'm ready."

"Let me tell you two quick things," Knox stated, adjusting a virtual control. "First, I could be nervous, I know the three of our lives could be over in a matter of minutes, but I've weighed the risks. I know I'm better off out here with something at risk on the verge of achieving a dream.

"So, don't get nervous. Connect yourself to the things that make your mental imaging more powerful. Connect to the things that push you, so you're not stuck. Because when you're stuck, you're just stuck. You've just got to have the courage to push through. The courage to achieve your dreams.

"I believe we're all born with a certain number of dreams. If we disband them all, and have no others, maybe that's when the spirit and soul really pass on," Knox said. "One other thing. The other day when we were talking about the edge, I offered you six million dollars in diamonds."

Knox punched a button.

A monitor in front of them lit up. It was a recording of Hunter and Knox on the scaffolding, looking across at the diamonds.

"I had my people record this using a security camera," Knox said. "If you hadn't been afraid, the walk would have been easy for you. The plank was secure." Hunter looked at the picture and thought about what had been going through his mind at that moment.

"Now watch this," Knox said.

Knox hit another button. The monitor went to black, and up came another image. At the bottom of the television screen were the words: SECURITY CAM 4. The image was grainy, but Hunter could make out what looked like a narrow walkway. Suddenly someone started to walk across. It was Hunter in the tunnel after Kathy had fallen.

"The walkway you did go across was more narrow than the plank. The drop off the side was about a thousand feet. In fact, when we were building the cavern, three people died in this area. Two fell off the walkway; one was killed by the spiders."

Knox hit the stop button and said, "The difference? In the tunnel you were thinking about the goal, while carefully considering the obstacles you had to navigate. In the cavern, you were thinking about the obstacles, and not the goal."

When Hunter realized what Knox meant, he said, "So, in the tunnel, success was my only option. I had the edge."

Knox nodded. "That's right. Now you understand what it means to be pulled in by the gravity of your goal. By the way, the diamonds are waiting for you on board the *Tranquility*. You've earned them."

"T minus one minute and counting."

The speaker crackled. "Knox, this is Greg. I wanted to say good luck to you, but I know you'd rather make it happen yourself. By the way, we're standing by at the launch location just offshore. All telemetry looks good. We'll see you tomorrow on the other side of the world."

"Thanks, Greg," Knox said as the speaker came on for the final count…

"T minus ten, sound suppression system on, nine, main engine start, eight, seven, six, five, four, three, two, one, launch commit."

14

At Heaven's Door

At the last moment before liftoff, Knox punched a button on the control panel inside the Command Module. The central television monitor showed the blast from the main engines.

On the beach, Oscar felt the rumble and knew exactly what it meant. "Everybody into the water!" he shouted as he ran for the surf.

The men surrounding the edge of the cavern felt the rumble, and then the heat. Unlike the men on the beach, they had nowhere to run.

The four instant acceleration rockets at the base of the cavern floor came only inches away from melting in the heat, which would have caused a nuclear disaster. General Greg Mitchell had seen the potential for this problem, so he'd taken extra time to secure the core of each engine.

Because of the pressure suit and helmet, Hunter could hear very little during liftoff, but he could feel the motion. The whole cabin shook.

Hunter closed his eyes. Knox had told him that the first twelve seconds of liftoff were the most dangerous. At least the end would come quickly, engulfed in fire.

As Hunter held his breath, he heard: "*Resolution*, we have liftoff. You've cleared the cavern. Godspeed." It was Greg on the radio.

"*Tranquility*, this is the *Resolution*, roll program is in," Knox said.

The big, lumbering Saturn V began its graceful arc over the ocean. The men in the water watched in awe as the orange flame seemed to magically lift the skyscraper.

Oscar's heart felt the launch and whispered, "Knox, you did it. You son of a bitch."

"Roll's complete," Knox added seconds later.

Hunter opened his eyes and looked at the monitor in front of him again, his vision blurred by the vibration. As he concentrated on the image, he could see it was a shot of where they'd been. They were now over the island, moving rapidly away from what appeared to be a crater.

The violent shaking continued.

Hunter looked over at Knox. Commander Knox Long had a smile on his face, but Hunter noticed a tear as well. Hunter felt the same joy. He realized the complete emotional release the launch represented. *You just let go*, Hunter thought. *You let go and apply the force of passion.* Hunter looked over at Kathy. Tears of joy were streaming down her face as well.

The worst is over. We are on our way. Sometimes leaving or letting go is the hardest part, Hunter thought. *And once you let go, there's a complete release of tension.*

Hunter was speechless because there was simply nothing to say. The force of Knox's passion, plan, and action were sending them into space.

"The shaking should calm itself in just about a minute," Knox announced.

"All computers on line; all stages pressurized," Kathy said. "Stage one is performing beautifully. The g-force will reach a maximum of four point five."

Hunter looked at the monitor. Nothing but blue ocean. They were now somewhere over the Atlantic.

"*Resolution*, this is *Tranquility*," the loudspeaker said. "Welcome to the big time, Knox. You've just activated launch detection systems around the world. Cuba is now on full military alert.

Our source in the White House says the president is talking to the New Soviet Union. People on Cayman Brac are not happy. Do your best to get the hell out of here."

"Doing our best," Knox said.

"The ride is getting smoother," Kathy said.

"That's right," Knox agreed. "We'll lose around two million pounds each minute. As we get lighter, our relative speed will increase. The increased speed and lack of friction from the higher atmosphere will help smooth out the ride."

"*Resolution,* all systems normal," Greg reported, over the radio. "You're three minutes in and traveling six thousand miles an hour. All systems operational. You're go for staging."

"Okay, folks, we're about forty-three miles high, about seventy miles from the island. Here we are coming up on staging," Knox said as he made a few more adjustments.

Staging. Hunter had several uncomfortable feelings at once. *Boom*! It was like they'd stopped. He was slammed forward. A queasy feeling hit his stomach and he took a quick breath. *Boom*! Hunter was pushed back in his seat again by the g-force. In a sudden flash, the windows of the *Resolution* were uncovered. Hunter looked and saw some debris from the spacecraft outside. Hunter could also see the Atlantic and the horizon.

Watching staging from the ground, Oscar could only shake his head. He still couldn't believe it. A soldier gave him a phone. Most likely it would be the president trying to find out what went wrong. Oscar took the phone and hung up without saying anything.

"Staging complete. Escape tower away," Knox said.

"Stage two coming up to power," Kathy said, punching the keypad by the computer screen. "Burn time six minutes."

"*Resolution*, this is *Tranquility*. Knox, you've got a lot of people back here angry as hell. Several U.S. Navy vessels are now heading to Cayman Brac. My crew says the launch destroyed all evidence in the cavern. Pete and Shaw escaped on the boat; we'll be picking them up in just a few minutes. All they'll ever be able to find is just one massive— Oh, what's this? CNN, FOX News, and all the networks have broken in with special reports."

Hunter was missing one of the biggest stories of the year, by being a part of it.

"*Tranquility*, this is *Resolution.* Greg, give my apologies to the Cayman Islands. Offer them seventy million dollars in gold for any rebuilding. Although I'm sure they'll make it up in tourism."

"Roger, *Resolution.* We're having our shadow ship by the Panama Canal wait for us. We're out of here and making way for the rendezvous point at high speed. Congratulations. It looks like you really did it, Knox."

"Thanks, Greg." The radio went to static and Knox touched his monitor.

"We're coming up on third stage ignition," Kathy said.

"Let's do it," Knox replied as he watched his panel carefully.

The third stage was much smoother.

Knox looked at the instruments. "Third and final stage on line. We're traveling at fifteen thousand miles an hour, almost home. Once we get to orbit, Hunter, that's where your job really begins."

Hunter looked away from the window and at Knox. "My job?"

"You'll find out soon enough." Knox said with a smile.

Two and a half minutes later, Hunter noticed he felt completely different.

"Shutdown, right on the money!" Knox said.

"Time to check the orbit," Kathy said. Using a small joystick, she began to twist and turn the spacecraft.

"I'll run primary diagnostics," Knox replied. Hunter had the best view in the spacecraft for all this. He could watch both Knox and Kathy work, and look outside.

"We're in orbit," Kathy said. "Velocity 18,112 miles an hour. Altitude one hundred miles. Everything normal." She unbuckled her seatbelt and floated over to a window.

She floated.

We are weightless.

It was a strange kind of feeling. Hunter thought the best way to describe it was going down a road and hitting a bump and your stomach drops out for a second. But in space, it stays that way.

Hunter unbuckled and floated over to a window.

Agent Hunter Algier looked outside at the breathtaking view of the Earth. His stomach, however, didn't seem to care. In a matter of seconds, he felt ill.

"Knox, I'm going to be sick," he said.

Kathy quickly reached over to a wall and opened a panel. She pulled out a funnel attached to a hose. Meantime, Knox reached into a pocket of his space suit and pulled out a small spray device.

"Hunter, don't throw up in your helmet," Kathy said. "It could be very dangerous. You could choke. You moved your head too fast. Stay still, close your eyes, and relax."

Hunter closed his eyes and felt Kathy's touch at the base of his helmet. He felt a sudden release of pressure in his suit and a second later he felt a slight breeze on his face as she removed his helmet.

"Okay, Hunter, open your eyes," Kathy said.

Hunter opened his eyes, and that's when he first noticed a droplet of blood floating in the capsule.

"I need you to spray this in your mouth," Knox said. Hunter took the bottle and squirted the contents into his mouth. It had a sweet and sour taste, kind of like a kiwi with ginger.

"That stuff is pretty amazing," Knox said. "It alleviates any form of stomach upset with no side effects. Once the FDA approves it, it will do wonders for chemotherapy patients. While you're waiting for it to work, why don't you come back and buckle in. I need you in top form."

Hunter watched as Knox and Kathy took off their helmets and then their spacesuits. Knox's right arm was covered in blood.

Kathy saw the injury first. "Dad!"

"It's nothing."

Kathy pulled up Knox's sleeve. A bullet had ripped through his suit and torn a hole in his arm. Knox's uniform had caught most of the blood. Kathy quickly stored the spacesuits in a compartment so the blood wouldn't float all over the cabin. She could see her father's face was turning pale.

"Please get the ZR5," Knox said.

Kathy floated behind her to a cabinet marked "Medical." She opened the door to find it empty.

She looked back at her father. "The techs thought the rocket would be launched remotely. We don't have it."

Kathy did the best she could treating the injury. But without proper equipment, it was only temporary.

"It's only going to be a twenty-four-hour flight. Don't worry," Knox said as he touched his daughter's face.

Knox smiled, "Let's finish this."

He then paged though several screens on his computer to make sure all the systems were functioning. "We're in orbit; orbit is good. Hunter, it's time for your final lesson."

Secure in his seat, Hunter looked at Knox.

"Reaching for your goal is like flying over the Earth. It puts the small stuff into perspective, so you see the big picture.

"Once you've seen this perspective, it's very hard for people to push you back down. In fact, some of the things you thought were challenging in the past you'll simply shrug off. In other words, what you're trying to do on the way to your goal is climb a set of steps that allows you to put everything in perspective. You climb those steps with your attitude, your passion, your drive, your energy. The aspects that make you see the whole picture, even when things are rough.

"You see, the gravity of the goal is pulling me in now. I'm moving faster and faster. I just need to be careful of how I make the final adjustments. I don't want to become rigid and inflexible, except to know that success is my only option."

The medication Hunter had taken was starting to take effect. He felt energized and was no longer aware of his stomach.

"I have a question," Hunter said.

"Ask."

"Why me, Knox? Why didn't you get someone else to share the ride?"

"Hunter, I needed someone whose life could be changed by a flight. You fit the bill."

Hunter nodded and said "But you knew we were on to you, and yet you took time to talk in Pinehurst. Wasn't that a bit risky?"

"I had no idea we would be ambushed in Pinehurst."

"But why take time out?"

"Late in the game, I realized I needed someone to give me advice on how to get the word out. I have something very important to tell the world. Unfortunately, you were an agent. But you can still help me.

"There's something else I've got to show you." Knox reached into a panel and pulled out the virtual glasses. "How's your stomach?"

"Much better," Hunter said.

"Kathy, this should only take a few minutes. Bring me back out if something comes up."

"Sure, Dad."

Hunter put on the glasses. In a matter of moments, Hunter was in Knox's virtual world again, represented by a sea of stars and the Moon. He heard Knox: "When we approached the Moon, we had to perform several critical maneuvers.

"The first was lunar orbit insertion. The spacecraft had to slow down enough to achieve lunar orbit. In order to do this, we started the service propulsion engine on the spacecraft when we reached the backside of the Moon. We'd perform this maneuver out of radio contact with the Earth. If we burned our engine for too long, we would slow down too much and smash into the Moon. If we burned the engine too quickly, we would simply swing around the Moon and head back to Earth.

"The engine on the Service Module would be used for a six-minute burn. It was time for intense concentration. The maneuver had to be perfect and precise, and it was. In every case, it worked, it slowed us down and we dropped into orbit.

"Once we achieved orbit, it was time for the final checkout. There's an old saying, 'If you take a trip of a hundred miles, consider the first ninety only halfway.'"

In the virtual image, Hunter could make out a tiny white dot underneath him. It was the Command and Service Module and the Lunar Module. Underneath the 3-D image were the words: HOLOGRAPHIC LANDING SIMULATION.

Hunter heard Knox again. "It's dangerous to be so close, yet so far. You must make the final adjustments carefully. If not, you'll simply pass your goal and return to the past, or slam into your goal without any control.

"At this point, it's very easy to get caught up in the heat of the moment and do something or say something now that you'll regret after reaching your goal. You've got to maintain the edge all the way to the end."

The image zoomed in on the spacecraft over the Moon. "It's so easy to get distracted. It's so easy to let the gravity of other things affect you. It's almost like it's human nature to back away from success when you're nearly there. If you get this feeling, isolate those thoughts before they contaminate your flight plan. If you think you're about to do something that will impact other things in a negative way, think about the integrity of the mission so far. Mentally go back to stage one and replay what you've done. Look at how far you've come and the positive aspects of what you've achieved to this point.

"And, Hunter, here's another very important consideration. On the way to success, you may reach a new level of comfort.

That's because your body adjusts to every benchmark you set. At this stage, you may think living near the goal is not that bad of a situation. You may try to adjust, thinking, 'Why keep up the risk when I've already accomplished so much?' Here's why: One day the date of competition of your real goal will come to pass, and if you're not there, you'll feel severe dissatisfaction. Deep down you'll know what you could have had.

"Here's an example, Hunter. Think of your goal and think of your flight plan. Think of everything you need to do to achieve your flight plan. Now let's say somebody comes along, takes all your information, and your work, and achieves your goal. Should you be angry or jealous? No, that person is the person you could have been. That's right. You either go to the Moon, or somebody else will. Use or lose the talents you're given, and if you lose them, they'll be given to someone else.

"So make sure you continue to focus on the final goal or your mind will adjust to something that's not quite what you want. That may be fine for now, but believe me, you'll become frustrated in the future if you don't get everything you've set out for. Follow through on the mission.

"Following through is a constant theme. This hasn't changed during the entire trip. It just becomes more critical the closer you get.

"For me, the goal is to accomplish this mission and get back to the Moon. The reason, passion, and vision come from my heart."

The virtual simulation continued to show the spacecraft over the surface of the Moon. The image was crystal clear. Hunter wished they were going to the Moon this trip. Knox continued talking.

"Carefully make the move that puts you in orbit around your goal. Once you've done that, make a final systems check and concentrate on landing."

In the simulation, the Lunar Module pulled away from the Command and Service Module. "Orbiting the Moon puts us in new territory. We used one way of thinking to get us to where we are now. Now we need something else to take us the rest of the way. Apollo had the Lunar Module."

Hunter looked at the image. The Lunar Module was moving away from the Command and Service Module, on its way to the surface of the Moon. "For Apollo 11 it was called Eagle. Eagle was a marvelous ship that was very strange looking."

The virtual picture enlarged and focused on the Lunar Module. The LEM looked like a crab or spider with four legs. Knox continued, "The LEM was a craft that could only operate in space. It didn't have to be aerodynamic. It simply needed the systems to take two men to the surface of the Moon, keep them alive during their visit, let them walk around, and then take them back to lunar orbit. The Lunar Module I've built has all that and more. Form is determined entirely by function.

"You'll need your own ship of reasoning for traveling the last bit of distance to your goal. It should be planned specifically for taking you the rest of the way.

"So if you're feeling stuck for some reason, now is the time to look at the flight plan and think about the reason to complete the mission. After everything else, it all comes down to your landing craft. It must be in top form. You've worked hard to get here.

"It's just like the short game in golf: you can blast a ball down a fairway, but you must make the short putts to win."

The LEM or Lunar Module was getting closer to the surface of the Moon as Knox talked.

"Another thing to remember. As you enrich your life, you automatically enrich the lives of others. Everyone's been given a gift. If you use your gift and give back, you'll always be heading in the right direction.

"Landing or arriving at your goal takes the most care and precision. At this point, it's still all too easy to blow everything because you're so close. So concentrate on finishing.

"The crew of Apollo 11 almost had to abort the landing. The computer system was confused because it was getting too much information. The computer was confused, but not the men who trained for the mission. They knew exactly what landing on the Moon was like. They'd been there through thousands of simulations. They knew they could land."

The LEM was close to the surface; now it seemed to drift a bit.

"In the final moments before the first landing, there was another problem. Large boulders covered the original landing area. Neil Armstrong had to take control of the Lunar Module from the computer and with less than twenty seconds of fuel left, Armstrong adjusted the course and set the craft down on Tranquility Base.

"In the end, it all came down to a man's individual will and brainpower. That's what put us on the Moon. Technology was only part of it.

"True wisdom is realizing the things you don't know. When we first went to the Moon, we were afraid of bacteria, or some kind of other life form on the surface of the Moon. We were afraid we'd bring it back with us and these bugs would contaminate the Earth. Maybe wipe out all life. The astronauts from the first three missions to the Moon had to be quarantined when they got back. We were also nervous that the Lunar Module would sink into the lunar dust. We were even afraid that the lunar soil would explode once we landed on it because it had been exposed for so long to the sun. We thought the lunar rocks would explode when they came in contact with oxygen. But through hard work and dedication, we learned these theories were wrong. That's the beauty of achievement: you begin to realize what's right and what's wrong.

"That's why you can't let the things you don't know delay you. That's why you can't wait forever to achieve your goal. Plan carefully, prepare for challenges, but then go for it. You'll discover what you need to know along the way.

"Look at where NASA is today. They have brilliant ideas, brilliant people, and brilliant goals. But after all this time, they still have a hard time selling the 'why.' That's what it comes down to for us all. For anyone. Hunter, once you find the 'why,' you'll have a great life as well.

"So," Knox said, "here's the bottom line. If you're not already after your goal, if you haven't already started, get up and do it now. Go after what you really want. Don't wait. Go. It's time. You've got to move it, find the momentum, and come up with the flight plan."

The LEM was now very close. Hunter could see the engine give tiny blasts as the spacecraft prepared to touchdown.

"Hunter, I need to know what you're thinking," Knox said.

Hunter considered his words for a second, and then said, "Knox, you've given me new vision. I've read self-development books in the past filled with quotes. It's easy to find quotes to push you, and they're great to think about. But positive affirmations alone won't do it. If you try to use them in an atmosphere you're used to, with feelings you're used to, it's like trying to land a terrestrial aircraft on the Moon. It's about having the form and function for the right flight plan.

"In my job, it's easy to get caught up in all the stuff that goes on; it's easy to lose my foundation. Everything can change in a matter of seconds.

"Knox, through the history of Project Apollo, you've taught me a lot. You've taught me that you can have the best equipment in the world, but unless it's organized in a very specific way, with clear thinking, you'll never get to your goal. You've taught me action is critical and with action the past is forgiven and forgotten. The basic principles you learn must become an intrinsic part of your flight plan to your personal goal. It's knowing that you'll find a way, or you'll make a way. Success is the only option. And you've got to do it for yourself and with the ones you love.

"With the fundamentals, I'll refocus on the bigger picture, to make sure I know where I'm really headed. My attitude will be based on my goal. My goal will be based on a reason I really care about. With that as a foundation, I'll be able to maintain more consistency. The good days will out number the bad days.

"Eventually, I'll find out how to have only good days," Hunter said confidently. "Every step I take will be a step in the right direction, no matter what the challenge."

Knox said, "Hunter, that's exactly what I wanted you to see. Welcome to the future. Welcome to your goal."

Hunter hadn't noticed but the virtual Lunar Module had landed on the Moon. There was a sign under the image: END VIRTUAL LANDING SEQUENCE.

The glasses went dark.

Hunter took off the glasses and looked over at Knox. He glanced out the window back to the Earth then he smiled at Kathy.

Knox looked at Hunter. "As I've always told Kathy, commitment to a flight plan takes discipline and drive. It can't be achieved overnight. But seeing the vision is a step in the right direction. From now on, you'll see your life from a new perspective daily that will change the old perspectives. Before you know it, you'll have another new vision, something else you never realized. A true flight plan offers constant renewal."

Knox stared out the window back at the Earth. "One more thing, Hunter. In life there are two parts of goal achievement to watch out for. Fear of success and fear of failure. Fear of success may be something like: 'Well, if I get everything I've always wanted, won't there be some other price I haven't learned about?' 'Will I be the same?' 'Won't God or some form of cosmic Karma be angry if I achieve too much?'

"Fear of failure is much less complex. Some people ask: 'Why even bother? I've tried before and I never got what I wanted.'

"Why bother? Because success is the only option. And because each step taken in the direction of your dream or goal is a success. End of story. You're successful as long as you take steps to your goal. There are no failures.

"Now, let's go back to the first part of that—fear of success. What's the price of success? Taking the steps to get it. Just remember, no matter how successful you are, you'll have more success for every new step you take. Success builds on itself.

"Will you be the same? You'll be the same person but with a successful outlook. It's up to you to decide if that will change you.

"Will God be angry? God won't be angry if you continue to build on what he's given you.

"What is there to be afraid of? Nothing."

Hunter thought about the mistakes he'd made in the past.

"Don't think about the past, Hunter," Knox said, like he was reading Hunter's mind. "Make sure you're at peace with yourself. At peace with yourself before you go out into the world in the morning, and before you go to bed each night. Make peace with your family.

"What really matters in your life are the people you love, your goals, and your real challenges in the present.

"Make sure you have a positive attitude that will carry you through the day, and make sure it's contagious. Spread your optimism. Think about how to enrich everything in your life right now, because that's really the way to a long life. Realize what was amazing about yesterday, what's amazing about right now, and what will be amazing about tomorrow. Realize everything has been a success, and everything will be a success. It's that simple."

Knox paused for a second to think, and then said, "I've told you everything I wanted to tell you. You now know the true story behind Project Apollo. Now it's up to you. When we get back, you'll have a lot to answer for. You're a smart man, and you'll do what's in your heart. Without question."

The *Resolution* continued its flight around the surface of the Earth.

15

The Message

It took Knox about fifteen minutes to go over his plan. As he did, one thing became clear to Hunter: the chaos that ruled the universe was about to be felt around the world, in an instant.

"*Resolution*, this is *Tranquility*," the speaker crackled.

"Go ahead *Tranquility*, good to hear from you," Knox said.

"Knox," it was Greg, "just wanted to let you know we're making our way. Should be able to meet you at the rendezvous point on time. We're using the new hydrodynamic engine. Making seventy knots and increasing speed. It's a good thing we were able to adapt the stealth technology to the submarine. We came close to a few Virginia class submarines on their way to the Caymans. We left them in our wake. Scared the hell out of a few whales, though."

"Safe journey, Greg." Although the bleeding had stopped, Knox did not look the same. For the first time, Hunter thought he looked frail. But there was still that sparkle in his eyes.

"Our sources continue to monitor what's going on in the White House," Greg said. "The president and his staff met with the joint chiefs. They're in contact with the ambush team on Cayman Brac. But apparently they're still trying to determine if anyone is on board the spacecraft."

"They'll find out soon enough," Knox said, without hesitation.

"Right. Well, Knox, this is what you wanted. We'll be in touch. *Tranquility* out."

"Thanks, Greg. This is *Resolution* out." Knox clicked off the radio.

"Okay, Hunter," Knox said, giving Hunter a headset attached to a keypad. "Just dial direct. Country code, area code, and then the number."

"What time is it?" Hunter asked.
"About 12:35 Eastern Standard Time."

***

Oscar's phone rang. It would be the president once again, looking for answers. It was time to face up to his commander in chief.

"Morrow here," he said.

"Hello, boss." It was Hunter.

Oscar was speechless for a moment, motioning for McCaully to pick up another line. "Hello, Hunter. Where are you?"

"I'm on board the *Resolution*. Knox's little surprise."

Oscar paused, thinking deeply of the ramifications. "Where is the spacecraft now?"

Hunter looked out the window, and then at a computer by the window keeping a record of the *Resolution*'s location. "The Horn of Africa."

"Describe it," Oscar said, looking at McCaully.

"It's tan," Hunter replied. "I see small clouds a hundred miles below. In fact, it looks like somebody dumped out a bag of cotton balls. The water is blue. It's spectacular."

McCaully looked at a computer screen and then nodded to Oscar. "That's exactly where they are."

"Okay, Hunter," Oscar said. "What do you want? What does Knox want?"

"They want television access."

"Why should we give it to them?"

"Because if you don't, Knox has other plans. He still has stealth capability and he still has one more instant acceleration rocket left at another location. A rocket designed with one mission in mind.

"Knox has tested it, in fact his men flew it by the White House about an hour ago."

"Hunter," Oscar said as he let out a sigh. "I can't believe you've turned to his side."

"Oscar, believe me, I've looked at this from all sides. I truly think Knox has a few points people should hear."

"Why couldn't he have just approached us personally?"

"He tried," Hunter said.

"He should have tried harder."

"Why?" Hunter asked. "Why should space be shut off from any man?"

"Hunter, it's not that simple," Oscar said.

Hunter looked at Knox. It was obvious he wanted him to keep the conversation short.

"No, Oscar. It's that simple," Hunter said. "Give us the time or the instant acceleration rocket launches with a personalized target of Knox's choice: nothing civilian, just military."

Hunter heard the line go silent for a few moments and then, "The United States never has and never will, negotiate with terrorists." Oscar was calling Knox's threat.

"Understood, Oscar. We don't need permission. We'll broadcast at five p.m. That was the original deadline."

Oscar took a deep sigh. "Hunter, are you sure you want to do this?"

"Sorry, Oscar," Hunter said. "I've got to move on."

"Sure, Hunter, one more thing. Was it worth it?"

"More than you'll ever know, Oscar. I've been given a new vision." Hunter ended the call.

Now they had to wait.

"What's ironic," Knox said as he made an adjustment to the controls, "is they can track us—we are a sitting target."

"What about the stealth?" Hunter asked as he floated over to a window.

"We didn't have time to test it in space. They're tracking us now," Knox said. "That's for sure."

Hunter glanced out the window of the *Resolution*. In a short time he'd seen the Grand Canyon, the Sahara Desert, and the coast of Europe. Each orbit took them on a slightly different track. Hunter thought he could see a purpose to it all. A purpose he could have never seen on the ground.

Knox and Kathy worked in different locations in the spacecraft checking various pieces of equipment. Knox made a few adjustments and then said, "I think I'm going to kick back for a few minutes, to get ready. I've been waiting for this for a long time. I want to be ready." Knox floated to the back of the cabin and strapped himself in a sleeping bag. A few minutes later he was asleep.

Hunter looked at Kathy. "Is he going to be all right? "

"He's lost a lot of blood, but he's tough and we won't be up here for that long."

"He's a good man, Kathy." Hunter looked back at the Earth. They were passing over the tan landmass surrounding the Nile River. Hunter said, "He changed the course of my life in a week."

"Maybe," Kathy said. "But maybe you knew it all along. Maybe it was tucked away in your subconscious. He just helped you with your vision and perspective. The rest is up to you."

Hunter looked at her. Knox's daughter was another wonderful creation. "Kathy, I hardly know you, but I know I'll miss you when all this is over. Being with you in the tunnel helped change my perspective. When I crossed that walkway, getting back to you was all that mattered. I've been alone for a long time, Kathy. You and Knox have shown me that is no way to live. I can't punish myself for mistakes that were made so many years ago. I've got to move to the future now. I've got to live the rest of my life." Hunter looked away from Kathy and back at the Earth.

"When I found out who you were, Hunter, you almost broke my heart. I wanted to kill you, I really did. But you're also a good man. A good man who lost his way. You're right. It's time for you to stop beating yourself up." Kathy floated over to Hunter.

"I know, Kathy. Maybe now I finally can."

"The Earth is incredible from up here," she said.

"So are you, Kathy."

In the Earth's blue light reflected through the spacecraft window, Kathy and Hunter kissed deeply and passionately, with the universe as their only witness.

***

Back on Cayman Brac, Oscar was alerting everyone about the upcoming broadcast, including his counterparts overseas. It was tense and he wasn't happy. "I don't care where he is, just get him!" Oscar shouted into the phone. "I only have ten minutes."

***

"We're still about ten minutes away from the broadcast," Knox said, fresh from a nap. Even though the spacecraft was on the dark side of the Earth, Hunter and Kathy continued their window vigil. "Those flashes you see underneath us are lightning storms," Knox said, looking over Hunter's shoulder.

Hunter looked out the window at the spectacular sight: trails of lightning that seemed to go on forever.

"What happens when all this is over?" Hunter asked Knox, knowing they'd be back on Earth in a matter of hours.

"It's just the beginning. When people see my transmission, they'll be left with a decision they've never had to face before. I'm about to introduce them to evolution face to face, and a very short list of options: stay or go.

"Hunter, now it's time for you to also start thinking about the next step. The next step is simple. Just honestly ask yourself what you want.

"You need a reason from within," Knox said. "Beyond the job and the people around you. A reason that brushes your soul and keeps it spotless, giving you the ability to live your dreams.

"Remember: another day will come after the day you achieve your highest goal. So be ready to set new goals. Your body and mind will always be hungry for more. And that hunger must be fulfilled.

"If you procrastinate, your past will be filled with unused yesterdays leading to an unfulfilled future. If you act and do whatever it takes to achieve what you really want right now, your present will be filled with the promise of today and tomorrow."

"About four minutes till the broadcast," Kathy said.

Knox nodded. "Aim for what's next by acting on what you have right now. That's really what goal attainment is all about, knowing what it takes to get what you want, and using everything you have right now to get it.

"Physics teaches us that an object at rest tends to stay at rest, but an object in motion tends to stay in motion. It's time to put your life and dreams into motion and keep them in motion.

"The future can be as bright as you want it to be. You hold the power. It's time to stop dwelling on past mistakes. Take the lessons and move on. Don't get caught missing the future.

"Remember, the foundation for everything else begins with you and your family. When you're not happy or the family breaks apart, the building blocks for society wobble on a weak foundation. Some people will say they came from a 'dysfunctional' family. If that's the case, just look back at the people who may have done you wrong and forgive them. Move on. They can't hurt you now. You make your own decisions. They made the mistake of not ending the pattern and that's a mistake you don't want to make again. Don't use them as an excuse. Break the pattern.

"Release yourself from the past by knowing all that really matters is the present and the future."

Kathy looked at her watch and said, "Dad, you may want to comb your hair."

She gave her father a comb as he was about to finish. "Sometimes people can be blinded by misery because negative thoughts have the larger voice. Even if these people develop the perfect flight plan, they won't enjoy success because they're always worried about the 'bad thing' that can happen next. To avoid that, concentrate on how you've achieved success and build on that.

"It's easy to believe in the 'eighteen-wheeler theory.' The feeling that once you get to the next level, forces of the universe will look down upon you and you'll face a setback or be hit by a large truck out of nowhere. Studying Project Apollo brings a new definition of hubris: it's when you let the extraordinary become routine. Savor the extraordinary and push for it hard every day. Help others do the same, but never let it become routine.

"Use your gifts and push yourself and everyone you know higher. Enjoy the successes of life as they come, and begin building on those successes right away. Don't confuse the next challenge with hubris. The challenges are there to push you to stress you to survive."

A control panel started to beep.

Kathy said. "Okay, here we go."

Knox, as always, had to say one final thing, "Look for the challenges that will make you grow. Growth spreads. When you grow, you improve yourself. When you improve yourself, you improve the lives of others around you by setting examples.

"Project Apollo is humanity's best example. We put everything together and our footprints are on the Moon. They will always be there, and we'll leave more footprints one day soon."

The panel beeped again. Hunter would introduce Knox.

Hunter found his mark in front of the camera. The red light was just ten seconds away from coming on. His remarks would be translated into most every language by technology on board the *Resolution*.

It started with a test pattern, then a shot from a live camera outside the spacecraft.

At precisely 1700 the red light came on, and Hunter started talking.

"Hello, my name is Hunter Algier. This evening I'm coming to you from the civilian spacecraft *Resolution*, approximately one hundred miles above the Earth. The view, as you can see, is spectacular."

Kathy switched the camera to Hunter. "It is with great honor that I present to you the man who made today's first manned independent orbital spaceflight possible, Commander Knox Long."

Hunter moved out of the frame and Knox moved in.

"Thank you, Hunter." Knox took a deep breath. He looked better than he had even an hour ago. "People of the world, the new frontier is open and it's time to hit the road. The human mind needs new direction. It needs to grow and it needs to stretch. Out here we can do it. Space is the next step.

"The only type of recession we face is a recession of ideas. The global economy and governments around the world need to think anew.

"It's time to take the higher view and think about where we are heading as a civilization. It's time to stop the fighting over politics and beliefs in the East and in the West.

"Stopping humanity's tendency to fight would be a bold step. Perhaps bolder than creating a civilian spacecraft. But we can change. We can become something more than we are now. It's time for a mental evolution that will allow us to physically evolve as a species.

"People of the world, you must take your future into your own hands. It's time to stop blaming others. It's time to start relying on yourself. You must push for your goals.

"This is the *Resolution*, and it's only the first step. Soon, I'm taking a crew back to the Moon. For all intents and purposes, I will claim a great deal of the Moon as my own. Through the use of a remote sensing device, I've found a great deal of wealth there. For now the wealth belongs to my organization. But I'll be willing to share it with the people who can reach the Moon. I challenge you to do so.

"There are so many new horizons to explore, each one of us must choose a different way. But it's time to get started. We must take the next step.

"That's all for this evening. On my final orbit tomorrow, I'll have another announcement. This is the *Resolution*, signing off."

Knox's words were somewhat surprising, even to Hunter. An American hero was now claiming "a great deal" of the Moon as his own. He'd found wealth there as well.

For a moment, Knox seemed grim and almost afraid, but it passed quickly.

He floated over to a window to look back at the Earth. "Kathy and Hunter, the world will never be the same. Now Apollo's promise is fulfilled."

16

Evolution's Horizon

Oscar turned off the television monitor and picked up a ringing phone. It was the president.

"Oscar, how in the hell could you let that happen?"

"Sir, we tried."

"Tried? You have twenty-four hours to bring them in, or I want your letter of resignation." The line clicked.

Oscar's world had most certainly changed.

***

"Now I'm the most hated man on Earth," Knox said. "Or, as the case may be, in space."

"Knox, can you do this?" Hunter asked.

"I've already done a great deal."

"But don't forget about international law," Hunter said. "You can't claim the Moon."

"Just because the United States walked there first? Check your facts. History waits for no one. America and the world had its chance. You expect me to wait? For what?"

"Share your technology!" Hunter pleaded. "Share what you've learned. We can explore it together as one world."

"You're mistaken, Hunter. I want to share what I've learned. But it must be from a new perspective. Otherwise I'll watch what I've done be dismantled in some bureaucratic scrap heap or get caught up in years of negotiations or some congressional oversight committee. No thank you. Those who want to join me can. But the age of waiting is over. It's time for this next step in human evolution."

"Knox, they'll stop you at all costs," Hunter warned.

"That's right. I've just staked my claim on something no one else can have right now. So, what's the easiest thing to do? Kill me. Kill my daughter. Kill all the people who made this possible. There are only three places I'll be safe. Here, on board the *Resolution*, on board *Tranquility*, or on the Moon. Even the second base will be destroyed in a matter of time."

The radio beeped. "*Resolution*, this is *Tranquility*."

Kathy reached for the microphone and said, "Go ahead, *Tranquility*."

"Kathy, tell Knox he's done it again. A lot of people are really stirred up. Your flight is all anybody wants to talk about. The networks continue their coverage. You're spreading across the Internet and even *Wired Magazine* says it will dedicate its entire website to you and space, with the headline: 'The New Frontier Is Open.'"

Knox looked at Hunter and took the microphone from Kathy. "Greg, thanks. We're going to start to close down for the night. We'll review everything in a few hours."

"We'll gather information down here as well, Knox," Greg said. "We'll talk to you in the morning, and see you at around 1315 at the rendezvous point."

"See you then. This is *Resolution*, good night."

Knox put the microphone down. "It's time to get some sleep."

Kathy punched some buttons. "I'm putting the *Resolution* in the hands of the computer for the night."

Knox pulled blinds over the portholes and then offered Hunter a sleeping pill.

"No," Hunter said. "I don't feel like sleeping right now."

"I understand," Knox said. He opened a porthole cover slightly so Hunter could look out. Then Knox reached into a cabinet and pulled out a piece of glass and floated it over to Hunter. "Here," he said. "Here are some final notes I've made. You may want to review them. It's kind of a summary of everything we've talked about and more."

"Thanks," Hunter said. Then Knox went to the back of the spacecraft by Kathy to get ready to sleep.

Hunter touched the front of the glass and a message from Knox appeared on the screen:

If human footprints are on the Moon, anything is possible. All you have to do is discover the path used to get to the Moon, and apply that path to your own goals.

The Path:
* Written reason for the goal.
* Passion for the reason.
* Written statement of the goal.
* Written flight plan to the goal with timeline.
* Mental vision and mental achievement of the flight plan and goal.
* Physical action on the flight plan.
* Physical achievement of the goal.

To make something happen you must visualize it in your mind first. That's the hard part, but that's how we got to the Moon. We visualized it, and followed the vision.

It's never too late to go after what you really want. Everyone is given a lifetime of opportunities. You don't need the time you've spent back—you just need to make a commitment to your goal right now.

Find the reason that will push you until you get what you're looking for.

You were probably told growing up, "Don't waste your life daydreaming." I'm here to tell you, you'll waste your life if you don't daydream.

The people on top of the world daydreamed about how to get there, and then acted on those dreams.

Daydreams, combined with action, put us on the Moon. When it comes to daydreams, you have the control to make them come true!

Remember the edge!

You get the edge by realizing that success is your only option. Having the edge is weighing the options, and setting sail while everyone else stays on shore. With the edge you continue to take the steps until you complete your mission.

Walter Cunningham (Apollo 7) described an astronaut as: somebody who's intelligent without being a genius; knowledgeable without being inflexible; a person who shows a high degree of skill without overtraining; a person who has some fear, but not in a cowardly manner; a person who shows bravery without being a fool: a person who is self-confident without having a giant ego; a person who is physically fit without being muscle bound; a person who has a preference for acting instead of watching; a person who is frank, but not loudmouthed; a person who enjoys life, but is not overly indulgent; someone is humorous, but not so much so; someone who is ready to act, but not in a panic stricken way.

Remember you choose to achieve your goal, not because it's easy, but because it's hard. In the words of John F. Kennedy, "Because that goal will serve to organize and measure the best of your energies and skills."

We live in an age where we can get the positive things we want, for ourselves and for the others we care about. All it takes is a reason to do so. Sometimes finding the right reason is the hardest part.

It should be an age of giving thanks.
It should be an age of new discoveries.
It should be an age of exploration.
Here's to the time we get to live.
Here's to your goal.
Here's to finding unlimited visibility in your life.
There are no boundaries.

After Hunter read the message, he looked out the window. This computer said they were over the Pacific Ocean. Hunter could see Hawaii as they approached the terminator between day and night.

As they crossed the terminator into blackness, Hunter looked at the lights of the United States. Major cities were brightly lit. The people in those cities were talking about this flight and what it would mean. Beyond exhaustion, Hunter closed his eyes and considered the meaning of evolution.

Saturday, October 26

Hunter awoke to the sound of the radio beeping.

"*Resolution*, this is *Tranquility*." It was General Mitchell. "We're six hours away from rendezvous. In a moment you may want to begin reviewing the top Internet sites." Exhausted, Hunter had slept the entire night.

Hunter floated over to the computer on the wall. Knox and Kathy were already waiting there. "Good morning, Hunter," Knox said. "How'd you sleep?"

"Pretty good, except my stomach is acting up again."

"Here," Kathy said. She took out the small spray bottle again and gave him a squirt. Hunter knew he'd start feeling better soon.

"How's the arm, Knox?" Hunter asked.

"Better," Knox said. "Time to check out the Internet to see what the world thinks."

Hunter floated over to a porthole again to look at the Earth. This time he saw wavy lines on the ground. He looked at the computer. It read: Amazon Basin, Brazil.

"That should do it," Knox said, making a final adjustment to another computer. The first page was from the *New York Times* site:

Surprise Astronaut Sends Earth A Message: The Moon is Mine!

(Washington)—Astronaut Knox Long sent countries into a frenzy yesterday as he took a manned rocket into space and claimed "a great deal of the Moon" as his.

"The new frontier is open," Long said in a televised speech to the world. He plans a second speech sometime today.

According to U.S. authorities, Knox used international relaying stations to pirate broadcasts worldwide.

The transmission, in the past twenty-four hours, has become the most watched piece of content ever produced. At least six of the world's top video sharing sites online crashed due to heavy traffic.

The launch shocked the White House and the president cancelled all appearances to look at the situation.

The *Resolution*, as Long calls his spacecraft, lifted off from the island of Cayman Brac in the Caribbean. Island officials say a full-scale investigation is underway to find out how the project went undetected. Sources say the launch left a large crater in the island. Cayman Brac, until now, was known for its sport diving.

"The human mind needs new direction," Long said, from his perch high above the world. "It needs to grow and it needs to stretch. Here we can do it."

NASA and the U.S. Air Force refuse to give details on the *Resolution*'s orbit. The FBI is investigating Long's background, and trying to come up with a list of laws and treaties that have been broken by the flight.

"Certainly someone must pay for the hole in Cayman Brac," said one investigator.

Knox laughed, "The Caymans will be well compensated."

The second page was from the Los Angeles Times:

Former Astronaut Stakes Moon Claim From Space

(Los Angeles)—People around the world were caught off guard yesterday as a manned rocket took at least two people into space.

"It's time to hit the road," said former NASA astronaut Commander Knox Long. Long becomes the first private civilian orbital astronaut in history not affiliated with any government.

Long says he has the ability to go to the Moon and he's claiming "a great deal of it" as his own.

White House sources say the president is considering his options. A spokesperson said, "This challenge from space is perplexing, because at least for now, Commander Long is operating on his own level. We'd like to meet with him, but we can't get up there. In the meantime, we are eager to hear what he says today."

"I'll bet you are," Knox said.

The article continued:

Space analysts say the unprecedented launch raises questions about lunar territory, and if someone can truly stake a claim on their own.

They read other headlines in the news and Knox pointed out the New Soviet Union had talked to the U.S. government more in the past twelve hours than the two countries had spoken in the past five years. There was a temporary cease-fire in the Pacific War. One editorial said, "Instead of looking to kill one another, many people are just looking up."

"I think Greg is pulling a few comments from the Internet," Kathy said as she opened an email. "Okay, here they are."

The comments were various:

"It's about time we went back out there."

"I just have a simple question for Mr. Long: how can I join you?"

"I'm glad he did it. It's time for people to go. "

"I think Knox Long should reveal what he knows about UFOs."

"It just goes to show the bureaucracy in government. A private man goes into orbit, supported by nobody except himself. The president should take notice."

"He's a dead man. What government is going to let a private citizen claim the Moon as his own? He should go there now, because he's not going to be welcome back here. "

"All this guy is saying is that anything's possible. We just need to reach. "

After they all had a chance to read the comments, Knox cleared the screen.

"Okay, it's time to get ready for the next broadcast," Knox said. "It's 0900. Hunter, tell them we're going to go again at 1200."

***

Oscar had just finished packing the base camp at Cayman Brac when the phone rang. They'd spent all night examining what was left of the cavern. But it was no use; the flames from Knox's rocket had destroyed nearly everything inside.

He picked up the phone. "Oscar here."

"Hello, Oscar," Hunter said.

"Nice speech, Hunter. Tell Knox to enjoy his first and only flight."

Hunter ignored the comment. "He'll have more comments at noon."

Oscar took a deep breath. "What do you want me to say?"

But Hunter had already ended the call.

***

Hunter passed the morning hours by looking back at the Earth. Time flew by quickly watching the beauty of the Earth from space.

Kathy would introduce Knox this time. The camera light went on at twelve o'clock sharp.

"Good morning from the *Resolution*," Kathy said. "My name is Kathy Long. I've worked with my father on this project for the past five years. In time, he will be able to answer your questions. But for now, the conversation will have to be one way. Dad?"

"Thank you, Kathy. People of the Earth, you've had time to think about my offer yesterday.

"I've set up two production facilities. They are yours. But I must make a request: I will land on the Earth later today and finish business so I can go back to the Moon. In the meantime, I want to be left alone. Hunter Algier will do all my speaking for me. If he's harmed in any way, I will not make my production facilities available to you."

Knox continued, "Many of you are still probably having a hard time figuring out why I'm doing this. Perhaps Neil Armstrong said it best: 'I believed, I think we all believed, that a successful lunar landing could inspire men and women around the world to believe that impossible goals were possible, that the hope for solutions to humanity's problems was not a joke.'

"This is not a joke, either," Knox said. "If there are any more attacks on my staff by anyone, I will barricade myself on the Moon and share its resources with no one.

"I don't want it to be that way. Remember, the frontier is open for everyone.

"Next time I speak to the world, I will be on my way to the Moon. Expect more information at that time," Knox said, and the red light went off on the camera.

"Okay, Kathy, let's get back to *Tranquility*."

"Right, Dad," Kathy said as she pushed buttons on her control panel.

"Hunter, the de-orbit burn has to be exact or the *Resolution* will burn up on reentry. You may want to go ahead and strap yourself in."

While Hunter strapped in, Knox floated through the cabin making sure everything was secure.

Greg's voice came across the radio, "*Resolution*, this is *Tranquility*. We are on location for splashdown. Here's a quick weather update. The sky's cloudy, the base is at two thousand feet, scattered. Winds are out of the northeast at ten knots. The waves are three feet. Temperature is eighty degrees. Not great, but looks pretty good. You are go for the de-orbit burn."

"Roger, Greg," Knox said.

"The computer has found the nominal entry range." Kathy said, "We've also acquired *Tranquility*'s signal. It's well inside the target zone for splashdown. The computer says once we're down they should be able to get us on board within three minutes."

"Greg," Kathy added, looking at her dad, "have ten ccs of ZR5 standing by on splashdown. Dad was injured during liftoff."

"Roger, Kathy."

"Okay, Greg," Knox said. "That's pretty much everything. We're going to finish preparing. We'll see you on the other side of the blackout." Knox paused and then said, "Thank the crew for me. *Resolution* out."

"Hunter, we'll splashdown in the middle of the Southern Pacific. But because we'll leave a five-mile trail of fire behind us as we re-enter the Earth's atmosphere, they'll be able to find us. We'll have three minutes to get everything on board the *Tranquility*.

"I must ask a favor of you, and it will probably be more frightening than what you've dealt with so far."

"What is it, Knox?"

"After we splashdown, I need you to wait at sea on the surface. I'm certain you will be taken into custody by the U.S. military. They'll take you back to the States. They won't hurt you because of the attention we've already gotten. But they will interrogate you and make your life miserable. I'll be able to help you escape within forty-eight hours after they take you in. That's just enough time to throw them off."

Hunter thought about it and looked at Knox, then Kathy. "Okay, Knox. I'll do everything I can."

"I know you will, Hunter. Kathy, begin the de-orbit burn."

It seemed like they'd been in space for just a few hours, but it had already been more than twenty-four.

Before Hunter put on his pressure suit and helmet, he looked out the porthole one last time and thought, *If you see the Earth from up here, you can never be the same. It's something everyone needs to feel. Maybe soon more people will.*

"The control jets are looking good for entry," Kathy said as she put on her helmet.

"Get ready to separate the Service Module," Knox said. He hadn't put on his spacesuit because of the blood.

"Computer separation confirmed," Kathy replied.

At four hundred thousand feet they began to hit the Earth's atmosphere. An orange glow filtered through the windows and the craft began to shake. Slowly, Hunter could feel the effects of gravity again.

The craft continued to rumble and no one said anything for a while. The radio was silent. The windows gave off an orange glow.

"Activate drogues," Knox said.

"Drogues," Kathy said. A light lit up: PARACHUTES DEPLOYED.

The spacecraft floated down gently on three red-and-white parachutes.

Then Knox spoke quickly. "Okay, here's the deal. As soon as we touch down, the *Tranquility* will steer underneath us. They'll open the capsule containment hatch and pull the spacecraft in. Then they'll open the hatch of the *Resolution* and let you out, Hunter. They'll put you in a raft. The *Tranquility* will submerge. We'll be gone in a heartbeat."

"One minute till landing," Kathy said.

"*Resolution*, this is *Tranquility*," the speaker crackled. "We have your parachutes on the periscope. We've got to make this quick. At least five supersonic aircraft are following you down. You're a sitting duck until you hit the water."

"*Tranquility*, this is *Resolution*. Greg, we'll be ready to move. Have the *Tranquility* set for invisible running and have the raft ready. Hunter will stay behind."

"Roger, Knox. *Tranquility* out."

"When we hit the water it will be a little rough. But just relax," Knox said. "The command capsule is designed for the impact."

"Fifteen seconds," Kathy said.

Hunter held his breath.

"Breathe normally," Knox said. "Hunter, remember what I told you. You'll probably be taken to Washington. I'll set up shop at the second base and have you out within forty-eight hours. Hang on."

"Five, four, three, two, one...splashdown," Kathy said as Hunter was slammed in the back by the force of the spacecraft hitting the water. In an instant, it was over.

"Welcome home," Knox said. "Kathy, quickly please."

Kathy reached over to a special panel marked "Security." "Here, Hunter, please roll up your sleeve."

Hunter pulled off the pressure glove and rolled up his sleeve.

"*Resolution*, welcome home, this is *Tranquility*. We'll be underneath you in another thirty seconds. Divers are already in the water."

"Hurry, Greg,' Knox said.

Kathy took out a large hypodermic needle.

"What's that for?" Hunter asked.

"Tracking, we keep these everywhere at all times."

She stuck the needle in Hunter's arm. It was very painful.

"Shit," Hunter said.

"It's for a good cause," Kathy said.

A metal clank came through the bulkhead.

"Hunter, get ready. You'd better unbuckle."

Hunter pulled off the strap and looked behind him. He could see workers through the window in wet suits already around the hatch. Kathy pulled off her helmet quickly and kissed the clear window of Hunter's helmet. "You are a good man," she said. "Your past is over. Now the future begins."

"We'll see you within the next forty-eight hours," Knox said as he reached out his hand. "Do whatever it takes."

"What do I say to the media?" Hunter asked, shaking Knox's hand.

As the door opened, Knox answered, "Chances are you won't be dealing with them at all."

"What do you mean—" Hunter never had time to finish. He was pulled out of the capsule and onto the half-submerged deck of the *Tranquility*. Divers were adjusting the capsule over a large hatch. Greg walked up to him.

"We've come a long way in a short time, Agent Algier. Thanks for your help." The two men shook hands.

"Stand by to dive," Greg said to his crew on deck.

"Hunter, it's time," said a man as he pointed to a large raft with an outboard motor and covering.

A second later, the *Resolution* began to sink. Hunter realized the spacecraft was actually being pulled inside the *Tranquility* through a hatch.

As Hunter sat down in the raft, he saw the top of the *Resolution* go down into the submarine. The hatch closed and in another second, the submarine was gone.

Hunter was somewhere in the Pacific Ocean, on a raft, all alone. But it wouldn't last. He could already see at least one helicopter in the distance. Four minutes after the *Tranquility* submerged, Hunter was taken into custody.

***

October 27

Washington, D.C., National Security Agency Holding Cell: 1907 hours

A day later, Hunter sat in a solid white room alone.

Suddenly his arm started tingling where Kathy had put the hypodermic. He rolled up his sleeve and looked closely at the tiny dot the needle had left. As he looked closer, he could see a thin wire about two inches long underneath the surface of his skin. Knox would be able to find him as long as the wire was in place, and his captors hadn't found the implant yet.

The recessed door to the room opened. Three people came in. Oscar Morrow, Robert McCaully, and Phil Styles. Oscar and Phil, his boss and best friend. Now he was a refugee with no friends.

"Hunter, the president wants to see you," Oscar said.

"I've already told you everything, Oscar," Hunter said looking at the men.

"The president feels differently. Go ahead and cuff him, Phil," McCaully said.

In an instant, Phil turned around and knocked Robert McCaully on the back of his head with a gun. McCaully fell to the ground.

Oscar pulled out his gun and pointed it at Phil, who did exactly the same. A standoff. "Phil, good work," Oscar said, pulling down the gun.

Hunter's jaw dropped. Seconds later a man entered the room. A man with a broken arm. "Come with me, Hunter." It was Harris. Apache feather. Harris walked up to McCaully and kicked him in the side. "That's for breaking my arm, you son of a bitch."

Hunter looked at Oscar. "Why didn't you tell me?" Hunter asked. "Was it a set up from the start?"

"I had doubts about everything from the very start," Oscar said. "I know you knew that." Hunter shook his head.

"It was my idea to let Knox run," Oscar continued. "At first I wanted to see how far he could take it. After the rocket took off, and Knox sent his message to the world, I was taken in by his mission. Besides, you were one of my best agents. I knew you wouldn't have turned your back on everything on a whim."

"Oscar, I—" Hunter started to say.

"Another time, Hunter. A helicopter is on the top floor. You and Harris better hurry. In thirty seconds I've got to sound the alarm."

McCaully was not totally knocked out. He opened one eye and silently reached for his gun, pointing it at Oscar. Out of the corner of his eye, Phil caught the move and shot McCaully.

As McCaully cringed with pain, he squeezed off a shot, hitting Phil in the chest and knocking him to the ground.

Hunter ran to him but realized Phil was wearing a bulletproof vest. He opened his eyes. "Damn, that hurts," Phil said, rubbing his chest. He looked at Hunter. "Remember, stay aware. I won't be there to protect you. Follow your hunches."

"Hunter, you've got to go," Oscar said as he helped Phil back to his feet. "Harris will take you."

Harris was already running out the door. "Thank—" Hunter started to say.

"Save it, and get the hell out of here," Oscar whispered.

Hunter looked at the body of McCaully on the floor and ran through the door and into the hall.

Harris was waiting for him by an elevator.

As they waited, Harris said, "Thanks for saving me back at the house."

"We're even," Hunter said.

"Not yet."

As the elevator doors opened, an alarm sounded.

"I see what you mean," Hunter said as they got into the elevator. Harris held up a small device to the elevator button marked H.

"We have about twenty seconds left before they realize what's happening and kill the power to the building," Harris said.

Hunter looked at the elevator display. They were still two floors away, and the elevator was moving slowly.

The lights began to flicker and the elevator stopped. "Shit," Harris said. "Less time than I thought."

They were one floor away from the helipad.

Harris reached for the door. "Hunter, my arm hasn't fully healed. You're going to have to try to open these doors."

Hunter reached for the doors and tried to pull them apart. They moved a little bit. He tried again and moved the doors a little bit more. Now they could see outside lights, and hear the sound of a helicopter.

The light gave Hunter new incentive, and he put everything into it. The doors opened. Only half a floor to go.

Hunter helped Harris out of the elevator and they made their way to the helicopter. From inside, Kathy opened the door of the aircraft. "Good to see you, but you almost missed this flight. Let's go," Kathy said.

"Let's go," Harris repeated as he climbed in. Hunter got in the back seat. Knox was there waiting.

"Told you I'd get you back, Hunter," Knox said. "Are you ready?" Hunter looked at Knox and Harris not sure of what to say.

"Are you sure you're in?" Knox asked. "I could set you up on a permanent vacation with a very large bank account, living a life of luxury."

Hunter took a long look at Kathy igniting the growing passion between them.

"Life is not about luxury, Knox," Hunter replied, still looking at Kathy. "It's about living. I'm with you. Besides, I've got a few more questions."

Commander Knox Long looked at Hunter. "Hunter, before you ask your questions, it's time we talked about evolution." Knox then turned to his daughter in the co-pilot's seat. "Kathy, activate the stealth mode. The timeline moves on and so do we."

If a person looked into the skies of Washington, D.C., that day, they would have watched a blue-and-white helicopter lift off from a modern looking building and then disappear.

A short time later, the Moon mockingly rose into the skies above Washington, D.C.

Thanks to Commander Knox Long, Project Apollo had now reached full maturity, and its version of evolution was about to be unleashed on the world.

***

Acknowledgements

Over the course of writing a book, you meet a lot of influential people, and since this book took a little longer than anticipated, I've got a lot of people to thank.

Great appreciation goes to my parents, for being my best friends, and to Kersten Ahrens, for being the friend of a lifetime; Jim Abernethy, for the impossible adventures; Diane and Ian Murphy, for teaching me how to aggressively think on my feet; Tim and Jennifer Bailey, my adopted space parents; Al Reitz and Susan Poulton, who understand why space is so critical; Peter Diamandis and Robert K. Weiss, for teaching me how to make the impossible possible; Michael Cassutt, for being my accomplice on one of the first air and rocket shows; Josh Robinson, for being a friend at a critical part of my life; Jim Spencer, for supporting all my craziness over the years, even though we passionately disagreed on how things should be done (the police were once called to his house because I was playing a recording of a Saturn V launch over and over again); Tom Dolan, for career recommendations and for simply listening; Ann Chruch for always being supportive; and to Guy Harvey, for teaching me about the spirit of mastery—and for taking me into environments usually reserved only for scientists. John Craton and Arron Chappel, thanks for your support as well. Darrell Cain, you will be missed by all of us; I think you would have liked this book.

Thanks to the friends I've made at the Kennedy Space Center during the Space Shuttle program (Maggie) and to the scientists working on saving sharks and saving the ocean (Mahmood and Brad). Sincere thanks also to Alan Bean and the other moonwalkers I've been fortunate enough to meet-and to those I've met who are no longer with us: Neil Armstrong and Alan Shepard.

Thanks to my work associates at WRIC, WLKY (Liz, Vicki, Laura, Alison, Dawn, Robert, Michael, and Steve), WCNC (especially Danny Diehl, who said to make this a novel so many years ago), WYFF (Michael, Andy, Mike, Jay, Tim, Carol), Microsoft, MSNBC, AOL, Time-Warner, The X PRIZE Foundation, World Space Expo (Bryan and Frank), The University of Missouri-Columbia, Guy Harvey Inc. (Steve Stock), the Stevens Center for Innovation at USC (Ian and Erin), Robert Cantrell, Julia, Z, Jennifer Nolan, past and present crew members of the Shear Water, and the large team at Status Productions (Dan). Thanks also to Cayman Brac for serving as the launch pad and, Bryson, thanks for the laughs.

I also want to thank my two brothers, Norm and Jon. The three of us turned out extremely different and followed our own paths—which, after all, is what life is about. Thanks for always being there.

Thanks to the veterans I've had the pleasure of meeting in my career. Your service and sacrifice allow us to do things like go to the Moon.

I've also got to thank Al Rheinhart for his film *For All Mankind*. This documentary had a profound impact on my life and sparked my lifelong love of Project Apollo. My life was forever and fundamentally altered when I heard John F. Kennedy say at the start of the film: "We choose to go to the moon in this decade and do the other things, not because they are easy but because they are hard…." Those words started this book and led to the life I've had so far. So it was, is, and always will be…

George C. Schellenger

Tiger Beach, Bahamas

About the Author:

George C. Schellenger was born in Miami, in 1962, at the start of Project Apollo. He has a Masters in Journalism from the University of Missouri and is a two-time Emmy Award winning television producer. He's worked for Microsoft, America Online, Time Warner and the X PRIZE Foundation. He's produced air and rocket shows in New Mexico and at the Kennedy Space Center. When he's not focused on space, he's dedicated to innovation and ocean conservation. He is director of the award-winning film *This is Your Ocean: Sharks,* which seeks to shatter the public's perception of sharks. He spends as much time as he can swimming with sharks in the Bahamas.